NO TIME TO DIE

A LEGAL THRILLER
FEATURING MICHAEL COLLINS

J.D. Trafford

Publisher's Note: This is a work of fiction. Names, characters, places, and incidents are a product of the author's imagination. Locales and public names are sometimes used for atmospheric purposes. Any resemblance to actual people, living or dead, or to businesses, companies, events, institutions, or locales is completely coincidental.

Book Layout ©2013 BookDesignTemplates.com

Ordering Information:
Quantity sales. Special discounts are available on quantity purchases by corporations, associations, and others. For details, contact the "Special Sales Department" at JDTrafford01@gmail.com.

No Time To Die/ J.D. Trafford. -- 1st ed.
ISBN-13: 978-1484169827
Book cover design by Scarlett Rugers Design www.ScarlettRugers.com

Other Books By J.D. Trafford:

No Time To Run

No Time To Die

No Time To Hide

To my family (up and down the line).

—J.D.

CHAPTER ONE

The big man hated the trailers. His employer owned these six as well as another two dozen scattered throughout Collier County. Located on the edge of the fields, the trailers were always dirty. They were always crowded, and they smelled raw.

He knocked on the cheap metal door. It rattled, but there were no other sounds.

"Time for work." He knocked on the door, again, but louder this time. "You're 300 in the hole, and causing problems for the boss."

No response.

The big man looked behind him. A driver waited, his pickup truck full of workers. The workers needed to be in the fields and picking by seven. He checked his watch.

"Go." The big man directed the truck to leave.

After the truck disappeared – dust clouding behind it – the big man noticed an aluminum baseball bat on the ground, underneath a couple of wild shrubs.

A random aluminum bat would be better than his own nightstick or his gun. *Less traceable*, he thought.

The big man pulled a pair of thin, disposable rubber gloves out of his pocket. He slipped them on, and then knelt beside the shrubs. He pushed aside a few rusting Tecate beer cans and an empty fast-food container and picked up the bat.

He walked back to the door, got out his master key, and opened the door.

Inside, there was only one person still in the trailer, although there were a dozen other empty mattresses on the crowded floor.

He walked across the room.

The big man stood over a lump inside a thin sleeping bag. He nudged it with the toe of his boot.

No movement.

"Get up." He nudged harder.

A little groan.

"I'm sick." The voice coming from the sleeping bag was soft.

"You owe us too much money to be sick."

"Can't work today." The lump in the sleeping bag didn't move.

"We been over this."

"No work today." The lump still didn't move.

"I'm telling you to work." The big man adjusted his grip on the bat. "You gotta work or you gotta go."

The big man took a step back. He thought for a moment, but the call had already been made. It was a simple cost-benefit analysis. There were lots of workers who wanted to find wealth in America. Sick days and paid vacations weren't part of the deal. And this one, well, this one was a pain in the ass. He was giving the other migrants ideas. Ideas were never good.

It was time to solve a problem.

He raised the bat over his head and brought it down hard. The lump coiled and tried to roll, but the bat came down again.

The lump in the sleeping bag tried to get up.

Then once more, the bat came down. This time it came down square, cracking the skull. Everything stopped. Then he hit it again, just to be sure.

The big man stepped back. He was breathing hard. A bead of sweat rolled down from beneath his hat as his heart rate kept going. He couldn't seem to catch his breath, even though it had all taken less than a minute.

The trailer's air was too thick.

The big man took another couple steps back. He leaned over and put his head between his knees, a breath in and an exhale, then another, and then another. His heart rate slowed, and he finally calmed down.

He needed to finish the job.

The big man stood up. He looked around the tiny trailer.

His employer charged workers $250 per month to live there. He looked at the floor strewn with mattresses, dirty clothes and garbage. He looked at the plastic bucket in the corner that served as the unit's only toilet, which his employer charged each worker $10 per month to use. Then he looked at the lifeless lump in the sleeping bag.

Some blood began to seep out. It pooled on the floor.

There would be more questions about this one. He supposedly had a lawyer. Lawyers were never good. The big man hated lawyers even more than he hated the trailers.

"What a mess."

CHAPTER TWO

Kermit Guillardo was too close when he spoke. "You gotta go, *mi amigo.*" His ratty beard tickled Michael's cheek.

Michael felt it. He turned and opened his eyes. He brought Kermit's face into focus, but didn't want to. It was an involuntary act.

Michael's preference would have been for the world to remain dark and blurred.

His mouth was dry, and his body ached. The night before came back to him in pieces. It was an evening of tequila and dancing with the other misfits who resided at the Sunset Resort & Hostel, a series of rundown huts about a mile down the road from the mega-resorts of Playa del Carmen and Cancun. Michael could complain, but he wouldn't. The pain was self-inflicted.

He looked at Kermit, just a few inches away from him. Michael cycled through his memories.

No matter how hard he tried, those memories did not explain the present.

"What are you doing in my bed?" Michael moved away. "And I hope you have some clothes on."

Kermit's eyes got wide, and then narrowed.

"I love ya', but I ain't lovin' ya, man." Kermit nodded, agreeing with himself. "The airplane shoots to the sky in just a few ticks of the clock, *mi amigo*."

Kermit sat up, pulled the sheet off of Michael, and sprung out of the bed.

"You gotta pack." Kermit clapped his hands a few times. The sound rang in Michael's head. "A whole bunch of kiddos and their momma are depending on us to find their daddy."

Michael didn't respond. A dozen tiny screws inched their way into the deeper portions of his brain. It was a feeling that was all too familiar.

"What are you talking about?"

"You promised." Kermit put his hands on his hips. "We were all there and heard you promise."

"When?"

"Last night." Kermit's head bobbled back and forth; his graying dreadlocks dangled on either side. "A promise is a promise, especially when we're talking about our little Pace." Pace was a local boy who was also the star of Michael's soccer team. He hung around the resort so much that Michael had started giving him odd jobs and paying him a little money.

"I don't know anything about that." Michael put his feet on the floor, and then stood. Easy does it.

He walked over to his dresser, opened a sticky drawer, and removed some clothes.

Michael put on a pair of shorts and a fresh shirt. He slid the drawer shut.

"Why would I get on a plane to find Pace's dad?"

"For two reasons." Kermit tapped his foot, getting agitated. "*Numero uno* is that you promised –"

"And a promise is a promise," Michael said. "I heard that before."

"And, *numero dos*," Kermit continued, "is that you've been driving everybody around here crazy for the past few months. You need to get outta here."

"I really don't know what you're talking about." Michael walked into the tiny bathroom in Hut No.7. He turned on the faucet. Pipes rattled, and then water sputtered out of the faucet and into the sink.

Michael cupped his hands beneath it, and then he splashed a handful of cold water on his face.

"You know exactly what I'm talking about." Kermit wandered around the bedroom, looking. "Here, use this." Kermit found a duffel bag and picked it up. He threw it onto the bed, and then walked back toward the bathroom doorway. "Andie dumped your ass and took off, and ever since then you've mostly been a surly, self-absorbed pinhead." Kermit clicked his head to the side, evaluating his last statement. "And I mean that in the nicest sort of way."

Michael brushed his teeth as Kermit continued.

"I get dumped all the time and you don't see me being all surly-whirly." Kermit's latest dalliance with Lowell Moore's ex-wife, Valerie, ended when she had found somebody with more money and a nicer car. Nobody was surprised, especially after Kermit lost most of his money in a Nigerian lottery scheme.

Kermit had found his "numeric equilibrium" based upon the teachings of Dr. Moo Yung Song. His knowledge was gleaned from a back-page advertisement in an in-flight magazine as well as a random assortment of psychotropic and recreational drugs. But even Kermit's cosmic balance was no match for the Nigerian scammers.

"If you want her back," Kermit paused for drama, "which I know you do," Kermit paused for even more drama, "then you have to fight for her."

Michael looked at the reflection in the mirror. He saw Kermit standing behind him. Kermit was striking an exaggerated boxer's pose while he spoke.

Michael did want Andie back. Kermit and the rest of the gang at the Sunset Resort, however, didn't know the full story.

Everybody knew that he had asked Andie Larone to marry him. That was true. Kermit and the others also knew that she had said no. But, they didn't know that she had initially said yes.

It was only after Michael had told her everything about his past that she packed up and left. She blamed him for what had happened in New York, and hated the fact that he now owned her cash-strapped resort. Andie had been about to lose the resort when Michael had set up a shell company to buy half the Sunset from her. It had seemed like a good idea at the time, but Andie didn't agree.

Michael rinsed his toothbrush under the faucet and he ran his finger across the bristles to get it clean.

"I don't even know what I said, where I agreed to go, or what I told people that I'd do." Michael put the toothbrush down on the side of the sink, splashed another handful of water on his face, and then wiped his face dry with a towel.

Out of habit, Michael touched the small scar on his cheek. He looked at it in the mirror. The scar was something that he never got used to seeing; a daily reminder that he was still on the run.

Michael turned away from the sink, and then squeezed past Kermit to get back into Hut No. 7's main room. He saw the duffel bag that Kermit had thrown on the bed.

"What's this?"

"It's your bag, dude."

Michael kept walking toward his dresser to get his paperback and sunglasses for the beach, but Kermit took a quick step behind him. He extended his long arm and grabbed Michael's shoulder.

"I toy with you not, bro." Kermit let go of Michael's shoulder and lowered his voice. He pointed at the duffel bag. "You need to pack up and go help Pace's dad. I can explain on the way."

"Where? On the way where?" Michael asked.

"To Florida, of course." Kermit smiled.

Michael began to protest yet again, when there was quick knock at the door. Michael turned.

"Who's there?"

"It's Pace."

Michael looked at Kermit. He was trapped.

"Come on in," he said.

The front door opened, and Pace stepped inside Hut No. 7.

"Senor Collins, I wanted to come and say thank you before you left."

"Well, there's no need, I'm sorry but I'm —"

Kermit cut Michael off.

"There's no need for thanks, little buddy, because it makes Senor Collins here sort of embarrassed. He knows that you're grateful."

Pace smiled and nodded his head, as if this made sense.

Michael raised his hand, halting the conversation.

"No, it's not necessary because ..." He looked at Pace. Then he looked at Kermit. Kermit's eyes were wide, pleading.

Michael turned away from Kermit and looked back at Pace. He started again, but stopped himself. Michael took a deep breath, and then resigned himself to keeping a drunken promise that he didn't remember making.

"Thanks aren't necessary," Michael said. "It's just a quick trip, only a few days." Michael looked over at Kermit, who beamed. "We'll figure out what's going on and then let you and your mom know."

CHAPTER THREE

Kermit decided that he would drive Michael from the Sunset Resort to the Cancun airport.

"We gotta make good time, and that's only possible in this classic piece of Detroit's mechanized glory." Kermit ran his hand along the dashboard of his El Camino. Then he punched the gas. The triple-carb, V8 engine roared, and the El Camino shot onto Highway 307.

The sudden motion jerked Michael's head back. He tried to keep himself from getting sick as the half-car, half-truck barreled north.

Kermit weaved from one side of the road to the other, avoiding the frequent potholes. The Mexican economy had been battered by a combination of bad weather, violent turf battles among the country's various drug-runners, and a global recession. None of it was good for the tourism industry. And when tourists stopped spending their money in Mexico, a major source of revenue went away. Infrastructure was the first to be cut.

"You think you can slow down?" Michael grabbed the side of his seat as Kermit cut left, and then back to the right.

"Not possible, *mi amigo*." Kermit shook his head. "We've got a schedule." Kermit smiled, and then he fiddled with the radio.

He found a classic rock station, bobbed his head to a few Led Zeppelin power chords, and then began to tell Michael more about Tommy Estrada, the man they were going to Florida to find.

"You were awesome last night," Kermit said. "You gave this big speech about justice and truth, and I was, like, blown away by your passion for helping Pace and his family. Everybody in the bar was going crazy."

Michael shook his head.

"I was drunk."

Kermit reached out and squeezed Michael's shoulder.

"I know," he laughed. "Drunken bravado is, like, the best kind of bravado."

Kermit jerked the wheel, dodging a dead animal of some sort. The El Camino groaned.

"Pace says that his dad was a crew leader, like, out in the fields." The Zeppelin song finished, and so Kermit stopped talking and fiddled with the dial again. He found a station playing some alternative Mexican music by a band from Tijuana. It was a fusion of classic mariachi and punk ska.

Kermit listened for a minute, making sure it was acceptable, and then he continued.

"Name of the company is Jolly Boy." Kermit avoided another pothole. "They've got a lot of farms up there. They hire a lot of illegals to pick the crops."

Michael listened, but didn't say much as Kermit continued relaying what Pace had told him. Between bumps, swerves, and waves of nausea, Michael simultaneously tried to comprehend what Kermit was telling him and not to pass out.

According to Kermit, Tommy Estrada had been staying at a furnished townhome paid for by Jolly Boy. The townhome was part of a larger complex. It wasn't a mansion, but Pace told Kermit that the housing complex had a pool and a gym.

Pace and his dad had talked every week, but about a month-and-a-half ago, the phone calls stopped. Before the calls ended, Pace's dad told him that he was a little sick, but his dad hadn't gone into too much detail.

"We got an address for his dad, but not a whole lot else to go on. We gotta be, like, super-sleuths, yo." Kermit honked the El Camino's horn, and then pressed the gas pedal down even further as he turned the radio up louder. "Watch out world, the boys are back in town. A little adventure."

Kermit looked at Michael and laughed, but Michael didn't laugh. Michael just shut his eyes and said a few prayers.

From Cancun it was a two-hour plane ride to the Southwest Florida International Airport in Fort Myers. At each step along the way, Michael had paid with his credit card. He felt uncomfortable every time his card had been swiped.

It wasn't because he didn't have the money. Michael had plenty of money. Last time he checked, his balance was still close to $500 million.

Spending money made him feel uncomfortable for other reasons.

His actions were leaving an electronic trail. He knew that the trail would eventually be found and the money would lead to him. It was only a matter of time.

Bank secrecy wasn't what it used to be. When the secrecy broke down and his banks started responding to the government's subpoenas, he would be revealed as a thief. It didn't matter that he stole the money from a crook. As a matter of policy, the government didn't like attorneys taking client funds and moving to Mexico – even if that client was a horrible human being.

As the plane descended and the seat belt lights turned on, Michael's concern grew. Everything that morning had happened fast. Living at the Sunset, it was easy to forget the reality of what he left behind in the United States. Although the initial grand jury had decided not to indict him, questions still remained. The money was still missing. Some FBI agents believed that Lowell Moore and his assistant, Patty Bernice, had simply laundered it through Michael's old law firm and the money was gone, but Agent Frank Vatch hadn't given up.

Vatch had never believed Michael's story. Vatch looked at Michael's background and current lifestyle, and he knew that somehow Michael had gotten a piece of his old client's hidden assets. He didn't believe that Michael had simply walked away from one of New York's largest and most prestigious law firms for a life of shorts, T-shirts, and sandals.

With his partner dead, Vatch was still obsessed. It didn't matter that Michael had nearly died along with Vatch's partner, or that nearly everyone else involved in the matter was dead or in prison. Vatch wanted Michael to go down, too. He was certain that Michael had taken millions, but still needed the proof.

###

Michael was tentative. He took small steps when he got off the plane; slowly he walked into the terminal. He looked around, scanning every face. He half-expected Vatch to emerge with a pair of handcuffs, but nothing happened.

Michael and Kermit walked down the airport terminal, and then passed through customs. It was easy for them. They had U.S. passports and they weren't Latino. Michael looked across the room and saw a Mexican family that had been pulled aside. They were being questioned. Two agents examined their documents. They were agents from Immigration and Customs Enforcement, otherwise known as ICE.

A few years ago, they had been called INS agents. "INS" stood for Immigration and Naturalization Service. Then the politicians in Washington, D.C., had decided that sounded too friendly. The purpose of the agency wasn't to help people immigrate and naturalize. That era was gone. The purpose of the agency was to keep people out, and so ICE was born.

After getting their passports scanned and stamped, Michael and Kermit took a shuttle that ran around the airport's rental car loop. They got off at the first stop, Michael filled out some paperwork, and then they got in line.

It wasn't too busy. Before long, they were called to the counter.

"Let's get a nice ride, man, nothing sub-compacted. I need air, man. I need lots of air." Kermit pointed to the picture of a Mustang convertible as they approached the agent. "I needs me some room for the legs to stretch and the cool wind to blow through my beautiful hair."

Michael looked at the agent.

"I'll take the SUV."

Michael slid the paperwork across the counter, and Kermit shook his head in disapproval.

"SUVs are bad karma, yo, real bad karma. They're the ride of the devil." Kermit made his fingers into little devil horns.

The clerk took the paper that Michael had filled out.

"Is he also going to be driving?" She nodded toward Kermit, looking concerned.

"I'm afraid so," Michael said, "so we'd better buy some of that insurance, too."

###

Michael and Kermit passed the last cookie-cutter housing development after just 30 minutes on Highway 82 toward the town of Jesser, Florida.

The transition from suburbs to farmland wasn't gradual. There was an abrupt line. On one side of the line were hundreds of new brown and tan houses. On the other side of the line was nothing but fields. The ground turned from plush green grass to sandy brown dirt.

As they drove, the fields encircled them.

The fields were still. There was no breeze to push. The air just stopped, hazing over the crops.

Kermit looked down at the map and a wrinkled piece of paper with Tommy Estrada's address written on it.

"Turn this boat due north at that intersection." Kermit pointed.

"Got it." Michael turned on his left blinker, leaving the highway. They started down a long gravel road. The road's small rocks popped and cracked beneath the SUV's tires. Every few seconds there would be high-pitched clink as a rock hit the metal undercarriage and ricocheted off to the side.

"What's the address again?" Michael turned to Kermit and glanced down at the map in Kermit's lap. "I don't see anything but fields."

"Shouldn't be far." Kermit looked at the wrinkled piece of paper. "3587 Greenway," he said.

The rental SUV continued, and then, just on the other side of a small hill, there were a half-dozen rusted trailers.

"We have to be close." Michael slowed, looking at the trailers as they drove past. "What's the address on those?"

"I missed it," Kermit said. "Turn around."

Michael slowed the SUV down even further and then pulled a U-turn. They drove back to the shambled trailers, and then stopped. "You see an address?"

"Nope, but this can't be it." Kermit shook his head. "No pool, man."

"Not exactly townhomes, either." Michael put the SUV in park. He turned the key. The engine stopped, and then he unlocked and opened the door.

He got out, looking around.

A little further into the turn-off there were six rusted poles with faded plastic mailboxes wired to the top.

Michael walked over to the mailboxes with Kermit trailing behind. He lifted the lid on the top box, and Michael looked.

Inside the mailbox there were a few letters. Michael pulled out one of the letters. The address was 3587 Greenway.

"This is the place." Michael put the letter back into the mailbox. "Wonder what else Pace's dad didn't tell his son." Michael started walking toward one of the trailers.

Kermit continued to follow behind. He was happy to let Michael take the lead.

They got to the door of the first trailer. Michael knocked, waiting for an answer.

Silence.

Michael shrugged his shoulders, and then he started to turn. "Well I guess that's a dead-end for now. We could check the others or we could wait and see if anybody –"

Michael stopped.

He saw the gun pointed at Kermit's head, and Michael put his hands in the air.

CHAPTER FOUR

Inside the interrogation room at the Collier County Sheriff's Department, the walls were all white and plain, except one. One wall had a large mirror. It was unclear if anybody was watching from the other side of the mirror, but Michael stared. He wondered about Agent Vatch. Michael wondered whether Vatch already knew that he was back in the United States and whether he was behind that mirror.

The Sheriff's Deputy pounded his fist on the table to get Michael's attention. Both Michael and Kermit jumped.

"Listen up." The deputy glared. "I'm not messing around with you two."

The Sheriff's Deputy looked like he had been a big high school football player. Not big enough, however, to make it any further than the varsity team. Now as a grown man, he still had that chip on his shoulder. He was the team captain. Kermit and Michael were the dorks in charge of the pep band.

"I ran your identification, Mr. Michael Collins." The deputy pulled out a chair and sat across the table from him. His badge said his name was T. MAUS.

"No record that I could see." The deputy crooked his head to the side, looking at Kermit. "But you, on the other hand, have a more colorful history."

Kermit blinked.

"These fluorescent lights make my eyes hurt." Kermit closed his eyes and then leaned his head against the wall. "Is there, like, a dimmer, man?"

"Wake up." The deputy slammed his hand on the table, again.

"Dude, chill." Kermit opened his eyes.

"Are we under arrest?" Michael made sure his voice was slow and overly calm. It was a way of sounding polite, without actually being polite. It also concealed a growing panic.

"Are you a lawyer?" The deputy's eyebrows arched, disliking Michael even more.

Michael decided not to answer Maus' question, but Kermit had other ideas.

"He *is* a lawyer." Kermit pointed at Michael. "This fact should not be doubted, my kind sir." Kermit was now awake, reaching the top of his emotional roller-coaster. In a few minutes, he'd be crashing again.

Kermit continued, "Smart as a whip, too, provided he's not three sheets to the wind. Alcohol tends to dull the sharper edges of his mind. But I want to make this clear: do not mess with the legal eagle sitting to my right."

Deputy Maus shook his head. He'd had enough. He raised his hand in surrender.

"Listen, we're not charging you with trespass today. I talked to the owners and they said to give you a warning —"

"But," said Kermit.

"But we catch you out there again, then there's gonna be some consequences." Deputy Maus stood. "You're free to go, and I hope you get as far away from here as possible."

Michael and Kermit stood and Deputy Maus led them into the hallway. Michael allowed himself to relax a little as they got closer to the exit. He wanted to get out and to the airport as soon as possible, but then there was the promise.

There was a time when Michael wouldn't have cared about the promise. He believed the world was against him, and he didn't owe anything to anybody. But he was starting to soften. There were people he relied on, and there were people who relied on him.

Just find Pace's dad and get out, Michael thought. *Try and be a good person for once in your life.*

###

"You want to tell me where my client is?" Her voice was loud. The other people waiting in the front room of the jail stopped talking.

"He's in detention, now." The clerk looked at her computer screen, reading the green lettering generated by an ancient software program developed by the government in the early 1980s. "Says they've got an ICE hold on him." The clerk checked the screen, again, and then looked back at the woman through the bulletproof glass.

The clerk had a pleading face. It wasn't that she wanted the matter resolved. It wasn't as if the clerk even wanted to help the woman. The clerk simply wanted the woman to leave so that she could finish her shift in relative peace and go home.

"I'm his attorney and I have a right to speak with him, regardless of who is holding him." She pointed at the door next to the window that led to the holding area. "You need to buzz me in and let me talk to my client."

The clerk looked at the door and shook her head.

"Talk to the local ICE agent. I've got nothing to do with it."

"That's where you're wrong. You do have something to do with it," the woman said. "He's in your jail."

"Talk to the local ICE agent." The clerk looked beyond the woman at the other people waiting in line. "Next."

"Damn it." She turned and began to walk away just as the door to the holding area opened.

She and Kermit collided.

"Whoa, princess." Kermit stepped back and smiled. "We haven't even had dinner, yet."

She looked at Kermit. The collision made her even madder.

"Who the hell are you?"

"Kermit Guillardo, my miss." Kermit bowed to her, and then gracefully waved his long arm toward Michael. "This is my co-conspirator, Mr. Michael Collins."

"Well, I'm not your princess, and I'd appreciate it if you'd get out of my way."

Michael stepped in.

"I'm sorry." He glared at Kermit, and then looked back at her. "My friend's got some mental problems."

They all began to walk toward the door, although she was trying to get some space between them. Michael wasn't letting her get too far.

"You represent some of the workers here?" Michael matched her, stride for stride.

"I don't have time for you and I'm not going to give you my number, not even for business reasons." She kept walking.

"Well, I didn't ask for it, so that resolves that issue." Michael continued to follow her out of the police station and into the parking lot. "I have a friend. He's a worker." They walked down the front steps; Michael still chasing her. "Wondering if you know him or somebody who might? Tommy Estrada?"

Mention of the name stopped her.

She turned and looked at both Michael and Kermit. She looked carefully before responding.

CHAPTER FIVE

Her name was Jane Nance. Her "office" was on Main Street, and it was as neglected and sad as every other building on Main Street.

About 20 years ago, things had been different. Back then, Main Street was the center of activity and the pride of Jesser. Things changed when big agricultural companies started buying all of the farmland in Collier County. It was terrible farmland. It was sandy and devoid of nutrients, but that didn't matter. The agricultural companies had developed special seeds that would grow almost anywhere, and they pumped the dirt full of chemicals to guarantee a crop. Now, 60 percent of the tomatoes eaten in the United States were grown in Collier County.

Thousands of immigrant workers – some legal, most not – came to Jesser to work in the fields. Jesser's growth prompted Wal-Mart and Home Depot to open mega-stores along the highway. Other chains opened next to the big boxes, and soon people stopped coming downtown. Local shops began to close. The Chamber of Commerce called it "progress."

Michael and Kermit parked behind Jane and got out. The faded, hand painted sign above the door said, "Community Immigrant Legal Services, Inc."

Sitting next to the door was a homeless Mexican man, folded on top of himself. When Jane fished the key out of her purse, he heard the jingle. His eyes opened.

"Miss Nance," he said. "Got to talk to you."

Jane put the key in the door, unlocking it.

"I can't right now." She looked at Michael and Kermit, and then back at the homeless man. His name was Miguel, but everybody knew him as Miggy. "I've got to talk with these two men, but I'll make some time for you later."

"It's important." Miggy picked up his crutch and pulled himself up. "I seen more spirits."

"I know it's important." Jane nodded. She put her keys back in her purse, and then got out her wallet. She removed a crumpled five-dollar bill and gave it to Miggy. "Get yourself some dinner, and we'll talk later, okay?"

"Tonight?" Miggy asked.

"Not tonight." Jane shook her head, and then put her hand on his shoulder. "Soon."

Miggy nodded, disappointed, but happy about the money in his hand.

"Soon," he said, and then he hobbled away.

They watched Miggy until he got to the end of the block.

"He's one of our biggest clients," Jane said, smiling. Opening the door, Jane added, "A nice man, just struggles."

Jane went inside and Michael and Kermit followed.

It was just one large room with desks in each corner, and three folding tables strung together in the middle as a makeshift conference table. The tops of the tables were piled high with files and other documents.

Jane gestured toward them, while walking past.

"There's a method to our madness, but it's best to ignore it all. Pretend this is a paperless office." She continued toward a desk in the far corner.

The desk in the far corner was also piled high with files. On the wall above the files, Jane had stuck yellow sticky notes with various scribbles ranging from "to-do" lists to court dates to contact names.

"We have a couple of *pro bono* attorneys from Fort Myers who drive over once or twice a month to help out. Then there's an attorney from Miami who also shows up off and on. He's atoning for the sins of his corporate overlords."

Jane thought for a moment.

"We might also occasionally get a recent law grad that scraped together some foundation money to work here for a year." She sat down. "But mostly ... it's just me."

She gave a little smile and a small laugh, signs of resignation.

When she tilted her head, the light from the window hit her face in a soft light. Michael noticed how pretty she was; tired, but pretty.

Her skin was naturally light, but her cheeks were kissed by the sun. Her nose was delicate, and her features were sharp.

Kermit was watching, too. He noticed how Michael's demeanor changed, and Kermit kept it mellow. He wasn't going to ruin whatever was happening, especially if it meant Michael would stop yelling at him.

"So, we went out to the trailers on Green Haven. That's the address where Tommy's son said his dad was living." Michael grabbed one of the chairs from the conference table and rolled it closer to Jane. He sat down. "But we got arrested before we could figure out if he even lived there. It wasn't at all like what –"

"Tommy had told the family back home." Jane completed Michael's thought. She shook her head, knowingly. "Let me guess." She pointed one finger in the air. "A swimming pool." Then Jane pointed the second finger in the air, "and a weight room."

"Something like that," Michael said.

"Pretty typical. I don't quite understand it." Jane paused, thought, and then corrected herself. "Well, maybe that's not ac-curate. I do understand it, but I'm not sure who they think they're fooling. Everybody knows why they're coming and what they're doing. They're modern slaves. It's been going on for a long time, but perhaps pretending makes it easier, makes the sacrifices easier."

"Do you know where Tommy is?"

"No." Jane slid a stack of files closer to her from the side of the desk, and then picked up a folded newspaper article that had been underneath the files. "Read this and you'll understand why I wish I did."

Holding an actual piece of newspaper printed on real paper was a small shock. Michael had forgotten the feel. At the Sun-set he was isolated from the tabloids and 24/7 cable news shout-fests. Seeing the article, Michael remembered how loud everything was in the United States. So-called news reporting, to the extent there was any, had no subtlety.

The article was about four months old and took up half the page. Another quarter of the page featured a picture of Tommy Estrada. He held a large poster above his head along with a half-dozen other workers. The headline across the top of the page read: WORKERS RALLY FOR BETTER CONDITIONS.

Underneath, the article summarized an organizing campaign.

The article talked about unsafe conditions in the fields and unsanitary conditions where the workers were housed. There were also multiple quotes from Jane Nance, Supervising Attorney and Director of Community Immigrant Legal Services, Inc.

"We were supposed to have a meeting to negotiate with Jolly Boy this week. Tommy was our lead representative." Jane tensed. "I honestly don't know how we can do it without Tommy. Tommy was a leader. He was a little older than the others, and the workers looked up to him."

Michael nodded, although he had never really met Tommy. Most of his interactions were with Pace and sometimes Tommy's wife, Elana. But Michael knew that Pace was a leader. It was a skill he had probably inherited from his dad.

Michael handed the article back to Jane.

"His family thinks he might be sick, but they didn't know any details."

Jane nodded, considering whether to trust Michael and Kermit.

"He was dying," she said, eventually. Jane placed the newspaper article back on her desk. "He had cancer."

"The big C." Kermit looked up at the ceiling, drifting away in his own thoughts.

"I took him to a free clinic in Miami and got the diagnosis," Jane said. "We talked about whether he should go home, but Tommy said his family needed the money and he wanted to work." She looked away. "That's when he also decided to fight. He wanted to improve the conditions of the workers, and we were making some progress. Then he disappeared."

Jane looked at the picture of Tommy holding the sign.

"I was kind of hoping he had gone home, but now you're here looking for him." She shook her head.

"We'll figure out what to do." Michael knew he sounded silly as soon as he heard himself say it. He had no idea what to do. But before he could recover, a loud, rusted pickup truck stopped in front of the office.

There were three young white kids in the front, and another four in the open back of the truck. All of them were drinking. Music blasted from the truck's aftermarket speakers, and the driver revved the engine.

Kermit, Michael, and Jane turned, trying to figure out what they were yelling.

One of the boys in the back stood up. He had a short, military-style haircut, although he was way too young to be in the military.

He narrowed his eyes and pinched his lips together in concentration. Then his arm cocked back. He threw a paper bag at the office's large plate-glass window.

It hit with a thud.

The bag broke and a brown mass of feces ran down the window.

Kermit, Michael and Jane sat frozen. Before any of them could move, the truck sped away with the horn sounding, "Dixie," like the General Lee in the old "Dukes of Hazzard" television show.

"You've gotta be kidding me," Michael said.

"Welcome to the other Florida." Jane looked up at the faded and peeling paint on the ceiling. She closed her eyes, almost ready to cry. "If you're looking for retirees, South Beach and Disney World, you've got the wrong one. This part of Florida is still fighting the Civil War."

Kermit stood. He clapped his hands together.

"Time to find a bar, yo."

CHAPTER SIX

The bar was about a half-mile from downtown, but clearly a part of "old" Jesser. Jane said it was a safe place to talk.

As they drove, Jane narrated the local landmarks. The businesses and the people they saw quickly fell into one of three categories. Either they were friends, enemies or enablers.

Jane was most frustrated with the enablers. These were people who lived their lives ignorant of what was happening to the workers in the fields and who were comfortable taking money from anybody who had it.

"They just don't care. They just want a lot of stuff as cheaply as possible."

Jane stopped rambling about systems and hierarchy. She pointed at a squat, concrete building with a gravel parking lot.

"But these folks are friends," she said, directing Michael to turn.

Michael drove into the lot, parked, and they got out.

The cinderblock building was a bar. It had a few small windows, with lighted signs for Bud and Coors. Metal bars stretched over each; it was unclear whether they were keeping people out or keeping people in.

On the top of the building, there was a rusted neon sign with a flashing arrow designating the site as, 'The Box Bar.' Michael looked at the sign, then at the building.

"Aptly named."

They started walking toward the door, and Michael felt his stomach growl. The sun was setting and he realized that he hadn't really eaten anything all day.

"Does this place have food?"

"Sort of," Jane said. "Greasy food, beer, and free popcorn."

Michael nodded.

"Perfect."

As they walked inside the front door, a stream of light cut through the darkness, and then disappeared as soon as the door closed. The regulars had already found their places at the bar. They were settled in for the night and didn't really give them a second look.

"There's my little Janie!" A large Hispanic man with a ponytail emerged from the kitchen. "We've been missing you." He walked over to them and gave Jane a big hug. He stepped back. "Who are your friends?"

Michael extended his hand.

"I'm Michael Collins and this is Kermit Guillardo." The man pushed Michael's hand to the side. He wrapped his arms around Michael and lifted him into the air.

"I'm Tyco," he laughed. "Handshakes are for the suits." Tyco set Michael down, and stepped back. "Here at the Box, friends are family, and family don't shake hands like we got poles up our asses."

Kermit laughed.

"I like this big *hombre*." Kermit pushed past Michael, and then he wrapped Tyco in a giant bear hug. "Let us begin our brotherhood, *mi amigo*."

###

They sat around a table in the back and shared a basket of salty popcorn and a pitcher of beer. Before the waitress made it to the table to take their food order, Michael asked, "You mentioned negotiations?"

Jane just shook her head.

"Doomed and probably cancelled. I've got a message from their lawyer, but I don't want to return his call." She stopped tracing the edge of her glass with her finger, picked it up, and finished her beer. "I was counting on those, too. We're running out of money, haven't had a grant in two years, and I was hoping to show funders that we were actually doing some good."

Jane made eye contact with the waitress, and the waitress started waddling over to the table.

"Another round?" the waitress asked.

Jane nodded, and then the waitress poured the remaining beer in their glasses, evenly distributing what was left in the pitcher.

"Food?"

She took their orders, writing code on her pad of paper. Then she turned and waddled back to the bar to place their order.

Jane ate a few pieces of popcorn and then continued talking.

"With Tommy gone, rumors are starting to circulate," she said. "A lot of people think that Jolly Boy farms had him deported, and I had thought that maybe he just went home, sick. Now I don't know what happened to him."

"That doesn't sound like doom." Michael tried to be comforting. "You still have others for the negotiations." Michael thought about the newspaper article. "What about the other protesters in that picture?"

Jane shook her head.

"They're spooked. Some of them already left town. Some are preparing to leave town. If you get deported, come back and then get caught, you could go to federal prison. None of them want that."

Jane started to continue, stopped herself, and then she lowered her voice.

"Then there's the big rumor," Jane paused, "that Jolly Boy had Tommy killed."

The waitress kept bringing drinks until the mood loosened. Eventually Kermit revealed Michael's most well-known secret.

"Dude's a lawyer," he said. "Can you believe it?"

Jane looked at Michael, smiling.

"No." She shook her head. "I don't believe it."

Michael didn't say anything. What was there to say? It was too complicated to explain. Instead, he focused on drinking the remaining liquid in his bottle.

Kermit prattled on.

"Big time. The dude was big time. I seen him work his legal voodoo, pretty impressive." Kermit stuffed a handful of popcorn in his mouth. "My bro cleans up real good. He could sue those Jolly Boy bastards."

Jane started to laugh, and Michael raised his hand.

"Enough," he said. "I'm retired."

Kermit shook his head.

"My man's not retired."

"I'm retired," Michael insisted, raising his bottle and his voice. Michael placed his other hand over his heart, taking a new oath. "No more suits, neither lawsuits nor navy pin-stripe suits. This I do pledge." He was only in Jesser to find out what happened to Tommy Estrada, and that was it.

###

Conversation wound around to lighter topics. Eventually Tyco rang a bell at the corner of the bar and flashed the lights. The patrons groaned.

They settled their bills, and then Michael, Kermit and Jane stumbled out into the parking lot.

It was dark. The sky stretched above them. No tall buildings or bright lights were there to break the night apart.

Hundreds of stars dotted the sky, and crickets rubbed away in the background.

"You got a place to stay?" Jane put an arm around Michael.

"We'll find a hotel." Michael unlocked the rental SUV, and slid Jane into the backseat. "But we'll get you home first."

"You're not going to take advantage of me?"

"Not tonight." Michael shut the door and walked around to the other side.

Before Michael opened the driver's side door, Kermit stopped Michael.

"You know I'm no expert in the female species," he nodded toward Jane. "But I think she wants you to take advantage of her, bro."

"I said, 'not tonight.'" Michael smiled, although it was a sad smile. His thoughts went back home to Hut No. 7 and, of course, Andie Larone.

###

They got two rooms at the Stay-Rite Motel. In Jesser, it was the "fancy" motel, because it had an outdoor pool. The Stay-Rite was also considered to be "new," because it was built in 1978. The other motel had been built in 1959.

The motel had two levels with an outdoor staircase and walkway. The clerk wanted to give Michael and Kermit rooms on the second level, but Michael insisted on the first floor. Even tired and somewhat intoxicated, he was still thinking about an escape.

Michael handed his credit card to the clerk. She ran it through the machine, and then she handed it back to Michael along with the keys. No further words or pleasantries were exchanged. Everybody just wanted to go to bed.

Michael looked down at the numbers on the keys. He handed one key to Kermit as they walked out the door.

"Must be this way." Michael turned and followed the numbers. "You need your stuff out of the car?"

Kermit shook his head as they walked.

"I sleep all natural, baby, and that's what I intend to do."

A little further down the walkway, Michael pointed at a door.

"Well, this is you. See you in the morning."

"Bright and early, boss." Kermit stuck his key in the lock, opened the door, and disappeared inside.

Michael walked to the next door. He started to put his key in the lock, but hesitated as he turned it.

There was a window next to the door. He looked at the reflection.

He saw the parking lot and the street, and then a dark blue Ford Taurus. Michael continued to open the door, while still looking at the reflection. He watched the Taurus slow, just a bit, as it continued past the motel.

CHAPTER SEVEN

Michael and Kermit arrived at Jane's office the next morning with a large container of Joe-To-Go from Cosmic Coffee in Fort Myers and a box of Krispy-Kremes. Good coffee was essential and worth the drive.

Jane sat alone at her desk. All the lights were off.

Kermit raised the box of doughnuts above his head with one hand.

"Breakfast of champions," he said while Michael turned on the lights.

Kermit put the box of doughnuts and coffee down on one of the tables in the center of the room.

"Please turn the lights back off and stop talking." Jane swiveled around in her chair. She slouched low. "And please take a few steps back. You're making me sick." Jane wore jeans, no make-up, flat hair, and large sunglasses. "Your voice hurts my head."

"Just part of life." Michael unscrewed the top of the coffee container. "You actually get used to Kermit's sound and smell after awhile." He poured Jane a cup of coffee and handed it to her. "Now we have to find Tommy."

"Seriously?" Jane asked.

"Seriously," Michael said. "So what's the plan?"

They pulled off to the side of the road. Michael looked out across the field and saw about 50 heads bobbing up and down between the rows of tomato plants. He had no plan of his own, but this one hadn't sounded particularly good. In fact, it sounded a lot like he and Kermit would end up being visited by Deputy Maus again and spend the next few nights in jail.

"I'm not thinking that any of them are going to talk to us," Michael said.

"I know one who will talk to me." Jane unlocked the door and got out. She was three steps into the field before Michael and Kermit caught up to her. Jane still had her sunglasses on, but the coffee and sugar had kicked in. Her fight was back.

"I'm just not sure this is," Michael dodged a hole in the dirt, "particularly subtle."

Kermit had the same doubts as Michael.

"Are we going to end up back in lock-up? I'm not an animal that does well in a caged environment." Kermit took a step around a tomato plant. "Plus the jail's fluorescent lights mess with my brain, yo."

Jane stopped, turned, and her two followers almost collided into her.

Jane looked Kermit in the eye. Mischief washed across her face.

"I don't know if we're going to end up in jail or not, but at this point in my career, I don't really care. Do you two want to find Tommy or not?"

Subtlety may be many things, but it has never been defined as two white lawyers and a dreadlocked stoner standing in a field of migrant farm workers.

Jane's "friend" was immediately spooked by her presence.

"Trying to get me fired?" He looked around. Then he picked up his basket and started walking away, waiving them off. "Leave me."

"I need to talk to you about Tommy."

"He's gone." The man continued walking, but Jane kept after him. "You harass me. You keep calling me. You keep coming here. I got nothing for you."

"That's not true." Jane caught up to the man and grabbed his arm. The basket that he was holding shook. A few hard, green tomatoes fell to the ground. "I want to know where he is."

"Let go of my arm." The man pulled free, knelt, and picked the tomatoes up off the ground. He put them back in the basket. He started to walk away, again.

"I'm not in the mood, Roberto." Jane followed. "You owe me."

Michael and Kermit watched from a short distance. To the extent that someone had overlooked their presence before, everyone noticed them now. The workers around them stopped picking. They stood, stared, and listened.

Michael figured that they had about five minutes before Deputy Maus found them and hauled them back to jail.

"Roberto, don't walk away from me." Jane took three fast steps and caught his arm. With a deliberate swipe, she knocked his basket of tomatoes to the ground.

"What are you doing?" Roberto looked at two hours of work scattered in the dirt.

"I'm trying to help your cousin."

"Help?" Roberto shook his head. "You got him killed."

"He was dying anyway and you know it." Jane looked around. She didn't care who heard her. "These fields – the chemicals that you're breathing right now – the fields were killing him."

"You're crazy." Roberto knelt again to pick up the scattered tomatoes. This time Jane knelt next to him.

"Listen, Roberto, I know everything about you." Her voice was soft, but sharp. She had Roberto's attention. "I know *everything*. You know what that means? Do you really understand what that means for you?" She held up a finger. "One phone call and you're going to prison. Just one."

"You can't do that," Roberto said. "It's confidential."

"It's actually called attorney-client privilege." Jane jabbed Roberto's chest with her finger. "And I'm at the end. I've got no other options." She got even closer to Roberto, quietly pleading. "Give me a name. Give me something to go on. Anything."

CHAPTER EIGHT

They waited until dusk to meet again. Jane had work at the office, and Michael and Kermit needed to call Pace and his family. It wasn't an easy phone call and there wasn't much to say. Tommy was still missing.

The only lead they had gotten was from Tommy's cousin, Roberto. But calling it a "lead" was a stretch. Michael didn't want to unnecessarily raise their hopes.

He had also thought about telling the family about the protest and about Tommy's cancer, but Michael held the information back. That's what lawyers did.

A lawyer should never give a client bad news without having something else to offer. Michael had been trained to tell people bad news, and then paid to tell them how it was going to be fixed. If he hadn't known how to fix it at the time, he waited until he did know. If he couldn't fix it, then he'd spend his time thinking about how to blame the problem on somebody else. *That's what lawyers did*, Michael thought. They held information back. It was usually better that way.

The bottom line was that making the family wait a few hours or a day to get the full picture wasn't going to hurt them or hurt Tommy.

Michael and Kermit pulled in front of Jane's office on Main Street. He parked the rental SUV. Michael got out, leaving Kermit inside with the engine running. He waved at Jane.

Jane was in the back of the office at her desk. She saw Michael wave through the front window, put her file away and came out the door.

As she locked the office, Michael looked at the large front window.

"Nice and shiny." The contents of the paper bag thrown from the pickup truck had been cleaned off. Its remnants were gone. "Kermit and I could've done that for you ... or maybe just Kermit."

"Very gentlemanly." Jane laughed.

Michael opened the door of the SUV.

"That's me, a complete gentleman," he said. "Been washing windows all afternoon?"

"Not all afternoon. Got most of the poop off with one spray, and then worked on some green card applications." She shrugged. "I'm still a lawyer, sort of."

"Me too." Michael shut the door. "But not really."

As he walked around the front of the SUV, Michael ran his hand through his hair. As he did it, Michael looked down the street. Behind them, just around the corner, he saw the front of a blue Taurus. It was parked with two people sitting inside. He was being watched.

###

The trailer complex sat about two miles off of Gopher Ridge. It was a bigger cluster than the one where Tommy had lived. This one had about 20 trailers. They were all white and beaten. Rust crept up their metal seams. Every window screen was either torn or missing, and garbage bags filled the spaces between each unit.

Michael parked the SUV, and the three ventured into the complex. As they walked, Michael noticed a few people in the trailers sneaking peeks through the windows.

"Any ideas about where to start?" Michael didn't want to knock on a door again. The last time he had done that he and Kermit had been arrested.

"Where there's smoke; there's fire, *mi amigo.*" Kermit pointed to a small stream of smoke tracing up into the air a short distance behind the trailers. "Looks like the party is back there."

They walked past the trailers and a handful of dented garbage cans and dumpsters, and into a clearing.

There were about 20 men sitting around a bonfire. Foil packets filled with food lined the edge of the fire, reflecting the orange flames and absorbing the heat. In the middle of the fire, there was a metal coffee pot. When Michael saw the coffee pot, he couldn't help himself from smiling.

He remembered an infamous case he had read in law school. The Fifth Circuit Court of Appeals had held that immigration agents were justified in checking the papers of men sitting around a fire with a metal coffee pot in the middle. The court opined, "The agent's investigation and detention of the men was reasonable under the Constitution, because only illegal immigrants brew coffee in metal coffee pots in the middle of an outdoor fire."

Michael, Kermit, and Jane continued to walk up to the group of men, and then stopped. The men looked up. A few whispered, "*immigracion,*" but none ran.

Jane stepped forward.

"I'm from the Community Immigrant Legal Services in town. I think I know some of you. I'm looking for my client, Tommy Estrada. He's missing." They sat in silence, staring at her. Nobody said a word, and then Jane repeated herself in Spanish.

Again, no response.

"Somebody knows where he is. I need your help. We were trying to make your life better, but now he's gone. I know some of you were in a van. You were going to the fields on the morning he disappeared. You stopped and waited for Tommy, but he didn't come. I want to know what you saw."

A young man with a thick black moustache and a barrel chest stood up.

"You are only making things worse." A few of the men nodded in agreement. "Tommy was making trouble, and whenever there is too much trouble, they just deport us and bring in new people."

"They can't do that. They need you to work the fields," Jane said.

"Jolly Boy struck a deal," another man said, standing. "They come get us, deporting us in waves – not all at once – that way the companies keep going. Fields still get picked."

Jane looked back at Michael for help. She knew they were right. In fact, the politicians in Florida were incredibly proud of their solution for "orderly" deportation. Everybody wins, except the field workers.

Michael put his hand on Jane's shoulder, and then took a few steps closer to the men.

"I think they killed Tommy." His stomach lurched, unsure whether he should continue. He was just supposed to follow Jane and keep his mouth shut.

Michael looked at the men, and then he looked at Jane. Neither knew what actually happened to Tommy, but she didn't stop him. So he kept going, hoping somebody would come forward with more information.

"They took him and they killed him. Nobody wants to say it, but it's obvious. He had a family that I care a lot about. I'd like to hold these people responsible. If you care, call Jane. Go to Jane. If you don't care, say nothing. It's your decision. But know that you're probably going to disappear next."

As they turned and started to walk away, Kermit smiled.

"You're always Mr. Happy." He put his hand on Michael's shoulder. "That's what I like about you."

Michael laughed, his mind already drifting to the blue Taurus and Agent Frank Vatch. He wasn't planning on saying anything, but he needed to make something happen and get out of Jesser. Whoever was in the blue Taurus wasn't going to wait forever.

CHAPTER NINE

Morning came early. It was a hot day in Jesser. The temperature already hovered around 92 with no breeze, baking the dirt. Standing in the middle of a field, a person could hear a soft crackle as the earth dried out, moisture evaporating.

The farmer sat atop a shiny green John Deere tractor with a 23-row applicator attachment, meaning it could fertilize 23 rows at one time. The cab was new and soft. A 7-Eleven Big Gulp of Mountain Dew rested in the cup holder. Jerry Jeff Walker's "Trashy Woman" played loudly on the stereo.

He rumbled across the vast field of soybeans. The sky was clear blue with no obstructions.

It was a good day to be a farmer, he thought. Nobody looking over his shoulder. Nobody telling him what to do.

His wife could deal with the screaming kids and the credit card bills.

He was working. And, more importantly, he was working *his* way – six hours to drive tractor, listen to music, and maybe smoke some weed.

In total, he farmed about 3,000 acres. He owned 1,000 and rented the rest of the acreage from neighbors and absentee landlords who were looking for a tax write-off and a government subsidy.

The farmer drove the land in loops. At the eastern property line, he cranked the wheel and circled back. At the western property line, he cranked the wheel and did it again. The whole thing had a simplicity and rhythm.

After a few hours, it was time to switch music. He turned the tractor, and then slowed it down to a stop.

He put on AC/DC's "Back in Black," and then opened the glove compartment and found his bag of weed. There were a few joints already rolled. He took one out of the bag, put it in his mouth and lit up. He took a big drag and let it settle over him. Then, with new tunes and a new state of mind, he was ready to go.

He put the tractor into gear, moving slowly at first. He was about a quarter-way down the row, about to accelerate, when he saw it.

There were two pale tree branches ahead, one large and one thin. He wondered how pieces of wood that size got into his field and whether he could just roll over them.

Kids, he decided, teenagers partying in the fields again, probably hauling in wood for a fire and a keg. He remembered those days. Good parties. Good memories.

As he inched closer to the wood, he saw an even larger chunk of the tree. It was dirtier and misshapen.

The sun hit it just right and a light reflected back. Odd.

He stopped.

The farmer stared at the reflected light, and then figured out that it was shining off of a large silver belt buckle.

His eyes followed the edge of the dirty stump as it tapered down. At the end of the stump, he saw a pair of cowboy boots.

"What the hell?"

CHAPTER TEN

Deputy Maus sat and waited at the modern E.C. Honour gastropub off of Thirteenth and Bickell in downtown Miami. There was a lot of dark wood, leather, and shiny brass fixtures. About 250 people fit comfortably in the place. There was a wall of glass separating the bar from the brewery. The gastropub was set up for patrons to eat food and socialize while watching the hops and barley turn into something magical through the window. In an hour, the pub would be bustling for lunch, catering to all the suits with expense accounts. but for now, it was quiet.

Maus sat alone. Most of the restaurant's staff prepped for the lunch service. A few waiters wiped down menus. Others rolled bundles of silverware in red cloth napkins.

Maus didn't want to be there. He had predicted that it was going to be a mess. He just had a bad feeling that the guy was going to be trouble.

Maus thought about his dad. His dad was a Marine. He was so proud that his son was a Sheriff's deputy. "My son the cop," is how his dad introduced him at the Jesser VFW hall. "Still not a Marine, but pretty good."

Maus thought about his wife and two kids. She would ditch him in a second at the first sign of trouble. And divorce was the

49

best-case scenario. He ran his hand through his cropped hair. *Cops don't do well in prison*, he thought.

It was typical for cops like him to have another job working security. Businesses liked having off-duty cops in uniform hanging around. They were a deterrent.

So when Maus had started working for Jolly Boy on the side, it had been for the same reason that other cops get a second job. He wanted the money. It paid for the extras that made life worth living. It kept his wife out of his way. It paid for vacations and for any sporting event he wanted to see. It also paid for the toys: a big screen television, ATV, guns, and the boat. *I love that damn boat*, thought Maus. Now it could all be gone.

Maus ran his hand across his scalp again. He was in rough shape. Being in the big city made it even worse.

Unlike in Jesser, the big city people didn't respect him. They didn't fear him. The nerds and freaks ruled Miami. He looked around at the skinny waiters and the even skinnier waitresses. They all had piercings, gelled hair and at least two visible tattoos.

It wasn't natural. Strength and size were supposed to dictate who had power. Power shouldn't be given to the wimp who wrote the best computer code or a chick with glasses who could speak funny languages.

Big cities were filled with the people like the ones that he used to harass in high school. They fled Jesser; he stayed, and Maus liked it that way. It was natural.

Maus ordered a Lone Jack Golden, because the bartender said it was the closest thing to Budweiser that they served. He prayed that Dylan wouldn't take too long. He needed to get back to Jesser. The Sheriff was going to be looking for him. There weren't too many murders in Jesser. Lots of bar fights and drunk drivers, but murders were rare. Everybody at the station was excited to catch the killer except him, for obvious reasons.

What a mess.

Dylan McNaughten arrived with a burst. His black hair was slicked back. He wore a tailored pale Michael Kors suit with a white open-collared dress shirt. He also wore black sunglasses to hide his bloodshot party eyes.

He looked around the gastropub. His attitude was one of entitlement. He was born rich, raised rich, and expected to become even richer.

His title was "Senior Vice President of Operations" for Jolly Boy, but he didn't know much about the business. He and his brother had inherited the company.

His brother, Brian, ran it, and Dylan just did the dirty work. In short, Dylan was in charge of finding and housing the immigrants that worked the fields. He didn't care if Dylan kept regular office hours and he didn't really care how hard Dylan partied, as long as he got the fields picked.

Dylan simply needed to keep the workers in line, pay them as little as possible, and ensure that there was no paper trail, no e-mails. The company always needed to be able to deny actual knowledge and thereby avoid responsibility.

That was the thing Brian insisted that Dylan understand – the company can't know what happens in the fields. And for Dylan, his knowledge was the only thing that kept the easy money from his brother coming. His secrets gave him power.

"Mausy." Dylan put his hand on Deputy Maus' shoulder. "We should get a booth."

Maus nodded, and got up. Maus took his beer in hand, and the two walked to a booth in the corner. They were an odd-looking couple.

As soon as they sat down, a waitress came over with two menus. She eyed Dylan, knowing who was in charge.

Maus watched as the waitress purred at Dylan. Dylan took the menus from her. He winked, she giggled, and Maus was ignored. *The world was upside down in the big city*, Maus thought.

Dylan handed a menu across the table to Maus.

"Just transfer my friend's tab from the bar over here, and we'll order in a minute."

A big, perfectly white smile stretched across the waitress's perfectly tanned and perfectly smooth face.

"I'll do that."

The waitress turned and walked to the bar to transfer the tab. Dylan watched as she went. She knew his eyes were on her – in that way that all women knew when they were being watched – and so she gave Dylan a little extra bounce.

"Nice girl," Dylan smiled, and then turned back to Maus. His smile went away, but the confidence and flash did not. "What's the big emergency? I had to ..." Dylan tried to think of something better than the truth, which was that he usually partied late and didn't get up until noon. "Uh, I had to cancel, like, two appointments and, uh, rearrange my whole morning for this."

Maus leaned in. He looked around, confirming that nobody was nearby.

"They found him."

Dylan's eyes narrowed; his mind already working the angles.

"I thought you took care of it." Dylan played it cool. He made eye contact with the waitress across the room and gave her a smile and a nod. Then he looked back at Maus. "You get paid really well so that we don't have problems."

"I must not've dug deep enough." Maus bit his lower lip. It was his mistake, and he thought it would be better to admit it. He cracked his neck, and then took a sip of beer. "Animal dug him up and pulled him into a farmer's field. The farmer found pieces."

"Anybody identify him?"

Maus shook his head. "Not yet."

"But it's not like you left his wallet on him. Right?"

"Of course I didn't leave a wallet on him."

Maus wasn't that dumb, but there were other ways to identify a body.

Dylan shrugged, still playing it cool.

"I think you're blowing this up," Dylan let out a little laugh. "We got nothing to worry about. Nobody cares about these people. Nobody is going to claim him, and even if somebody wants to, it's too expensive and too complicated. They won't be able to figure it out."

Dylan thought about some of the crime shows he'd seen on television.

"It's not like he's got dental records. He probably never even went to a dentist."

Dylan flashed some more of his sparkle, trying to calm down Maus. Dylan needed Maus on his side. They were The Keepers Of The Secrets.

"Cheer up, Mausy. He was just a wetback. I bet his face was all messed up, too, like rotted, right? Nobody is going to identify him." He laughed a little more at the thought, and then waved the waitress over.

"I gotta run, honey, but put whatever my friend wants on my tab."

Dylan got up. He took out a credit card and one of his business cards. He handed the credit card to the waitress, and then he wrote his cell phone number on the back of his business card. "And here's my number if there are any problems."

The waitress took the card. She read the front, and then turned the business card over to read the cell phone number on the back.

"Like what kind of problems are we talking about?"

"Like if you get lonely." Boom, and a little more flash.

The McNaughten brothers waited for Harrison Grant in the firm's main conference room. The conference room was on the top floor of the Millennium Tower. Green and Thomas, LLP, had the top 25 floors of the tower's 50 stories.

The conference room had all the accoutrements that one would expect. A large oak conference table surrounded by two-dozen high-back, black leather chairs. One wall had all of the gadgets necessary to conduct video-conferencing around the world. Another wall featured the obligatory, inoffensive piece of abstract art. And the outside wall was floor-to-ceiling glass, which provided a picturesque view of Biscayne Bay.

Biscayne Bay defined Miami – a beautiful marine ecosystem stretching along the ocean's coast and out for hundreds of miles. It was a place of recreation and fishing, but it was also under constant pressure from the millions of people living in Miami as well as one of the largest shipping ports in the world.

"Where is he?" Dylan McNaughten stood-up and walked to the window. He stuck his hands in his pants pockets while he paced the room.

Brian McNaughten, Dylan's twin, rolled his eyes.

"Calm down. I just want to run this situation past Grant. I want to make sure we're prepared if this worker is traced back to us. He'll figure it out. He always does."

"I told you." Dylan glared at his brother. "It isn't coming back to us."

"But it might," Brian said. "An ounce of prevention, brother. We need to protect ourselves."

"I don't have time to wait in conference rooms." Dylan looked around, and then looked back at his brother. "Does he understand who we are?"

Dylan's face was getting red, and he was getting more jumpy. He had wanted to be sober for his meeting with Maus, but after a few hours of work, he needed a hit. Dylan needed the confidence that only cocaine provided.

"I'm sure he knows who we are." Brian pulled a chair out from the table and patted the back of the chair. "Have a seat."

"I'm not sitting down." He wasn't going to be polite and cautious any more. Dylan took a small plastic bag and straw out of his pocket. "Why can't he come to us?"

"Because that's not how it works, and I don't want to pay a lawyer $600 an hour to drive to our office."

"Who cares? We got money." Dylan poured a little bit of his cocaine out on the conference table and cut a few lines. He needed the hit, but he also did it to piss off his brother.

Brian looked around; making sure the door was closed.

"You think you could do that in the bathroom?"

"This is as good a place as any." Dylan stuck the straw in his nose and drew in the white powder. He put the straw back in his pocket, and then Dylan let the drugs work him over. He loved cocaine. He had always loved cocaine.

Brian tried to stay calm. His brother made him nervous. One trip to Hazelden and two trips to Betty Ford hadn't made one bit of difference, mainly because Dylan didn't care. The only reason Dylan went was because Brian had threatened to cut him off and lock all of his money away in a trust fund.

"I know we have healthy bank accounts," Brian said, "but I want to keep it. You don't accumulate wealth by paying for things you don't have to." Brian talked slow, like he was explaining something to a child. "And I figured you'd have other ways to spend $600."

Dylan looked at his brother. His eyes were bugged, and he sneered at Brian while he thought it over. $600 would buy a nice bit of coke, he thought, that was a pretty good point.

CHAPTER ELEVEN

I called in a favor to get this meeting," Jane said. "So let me do the talking."

"What do you mean?" Michael found a meter on Fourth Street in downtown Miami and parked under a palm tree. "You're making me nervous."

That was true. Sweat rolled down Michael's neck, and then down his back. His stomach turned somersaults.

He had been in Florida for less than three days, and Michael knew the feds were already tracking him. He wanted to help Pace and his family. He also liked and wanted to help Jane, but now she'd asked him to do something crazy.

Michael didn't think that Jane knew what she was doing to him. He didn't think there was any way that she could know. But Jane had purportedly scheduled a meeting with somebody at the U.S. Attorney's Office in Florida. Michael was about to walk into the offices of an organization that had been investigating him for years.

"Besides meeting with the feds – who are constantly trying to deport your clients, by the way – how exactly does an Assistant United States Attorney owe you favor?"

Ignoring Michael's question, Jane grabbed her notebook and large purse off the floor of the SUV. Then she unlocked her door.

"Are you going to answer me?" Michael repeated the question, before Jane got out.

"Maybe. … It's a long story."

"I think I should know before we go in there." Michael looked up at the tall building, while Jane sighed.

"Well, if you have to know." Jane stopped fiddling with her purse. She turned to face Michael. "We were sort of engaged to be married."

"So you're not exactly calling in a favor," Michael said. "More like exploiting a personal relationship."

Jane opened the door.

"That's a more cynical way of looking at it."

The United States Attorney's Office in Miami was in the James Lawrence King Federal Court Building. It was a modern building built in the 1980s with lots of white stone, and then after the 1995 Oklahoma City bombing, accented with the hasty addition of concrete barricades.

Jane and Michael made it through the metal detectors and past a probing wand.

Michael thought that the guard was particularly thorough in patting down Jane. He expected a remark, but Jane didn't say anything. He realized that she was nervous, too.

They got into the elevator. The doors slid shut, and they were alone.

"When was the last time you talked with this guy?" Michael asked.

Jane paused, thinking. A bell rang. The doors slid open, and they stepped out into the hallway.

"It was the night I called off the engagement."

"*You* called off the engagement?"

Jane pursed her lips, thinking.

"Well, that may not be entirely accurate. There was a lot of yelling. I think he may believe that he called off the engagement. It was sort of mutual."

"Does he even know we're coming?"

Jane shook her head.

"No."

"But you said that you made an appointment."

"I lied."

###

They waited in a plain government conference room for 20 minutes. The walls were barren except for two large poster-sized photographs hung side-by-side. One picture was a portrait of the Attorney General in front of a flag. The other one was a nearly identical photograph of the President of the United States. The two giant heads with their four gigantic eyes peered down on them while they sat.

Eventually their unsuspecting host arrived.

Both Jane and Michael stood up.

On another day, the Assistant U.S. Attorney who entered the room would have been an attractive guy. At the moment, however, he looked like death. He was too thin. His hair was disheveled, and he had large, dark circles under his eyes.

His whole body tensed when Jane gave him a stiff and awkward hug. Then he noticed Michael and Michael caught the look. His eyes looked at Michael's wrinkled khaki pants, short-sleeve shirt, and sandals. His expression was: Who the hell are you?

"I'm Michael." Michael extended his hand, trying to be warm and friendly.

"Michael?" He hung on the last syllables of Michael's first name. He wanted a last name and Michael didn't want to give it to him. But there really wasn't a choice.

"Michael Collins." They shook hands in the way that men do; two dogs sniffing one another.

"I'm Justin Kent." He gestured to the chairs. "Please sit." And they all sat down.

Kent looked at Michael.

"So are you volunteering or working for Jane?"

"Volunteering," Michael said, thinking that was the least complicated explanation for his presence.

"That's great." It was obviously meant to be a compliment, but the tone was flat. Kent turned to Jane.

"Jane does ..." his voice cracked. Kent looked her over before finishing. "Jane does good work."

There was another lull in the conversation. Everyone wanted to be polite, but the silence lasted a little too long. There was frost in the air.

"So the receptionist said that you're working on a case," Kent said. "What do you need me for?"

Michael was thinking the same thing.

"It's Tommy," Jane said. "He's been missing for a few weeks. He's sick, and I wanted to know if you could find out whether immigration has him in custody."

"I shouldn't do that."

"Come on," Jane said. "Tommy was a good source for you. He trusted you and you trusted him."

"Why don't you call ICE? You don't need me for that." Kent checked his watch.

"Justin, you know how they are." Jane started to continue, but stopped short. Jane took another tack. "Maybe you should explain to Michael what you do."

Kent shifted in his seat. It was clear that he was trying to figure out how to act. Should he be mad, friendly, or business-like? It appeared as though he had settled on mildly irritated.

"I'm pretty busy, Jane," he said. "I don't have time for this anymore." Kent shook his head. "I don't even know why I agreed to this. I'm not going to get sucked into your schemes again. The last one almost cost me my job."

"I thought the information was good."

"But it wasn't good," Kent said. "We came up with nothing." Kent started to continue, raising his voice, but then stopped himself.

It was then that Michael realized why he was there. It was going to be harder for Kent to say no when there's a witness, an outsider. Michael was being used as a shield.

Jane tried to keep the meeting going, ignoring the digression.

"Michael," she turned to him, "Justin Kent is one of the nation's experts on modern-day slavery. That's what he prosecutes here. He investigates human trafficking, everything from sex rings to maids to farm laborers. Immigrants who are brought here illegally to work for little or no pay. That's how we met. We were on a panel together at a conference."

"Two attorneys tilting at windmills," Kent said, "but I'm not doing it any more. Politically nobody wanted me to do it from the beginning. Now it's time. Time for a transfer." Kent looked at Jane. His voice softened. "I'm thinking about going to Washington D.C."

"We just need a phone call," Jane said. "Just a quick look at whether anything new has come in."

Kent looked back at her, thinking.

"We've got nothing, Justin." Jane pleaded. "Not just with Tommy. I got another call from Jolly Boy's attorney. The negotiations are cancelled. We've got no funding. We're about to be evicted from our office. The board meets tomorrow. If I can't show them something, the board is going to vote to shut us down." Jane reached out and took hold of Justin Kent's hand.

"Please. I'm begging you."

Michael and Jane sat alone for another hour.

"How long do you think it's going to take?" Michael leaned back in his chair.

Jane didn't respond. She stared out the window, instead. It wasn't much of a view, only the side of another office building across the street, more glass and stone."You told me things were bad, but I didn't know about the board meeting."

He waited, but only got more silence. Jane sat with her arms crossed, staring off at the distance, tapping her foot.

"It doesn't make sense. They should be lining up to give you a grant. Justin was right about that ... you do great work."

Jane turned to him.

"Thanks." She had tears in her eyes. "I shouldn't cry. Lawyers don't cry. Lawyers are supposed to be tough, right? You've seen me beg and plead more in the past three days than ..." Her voice trailed off.

Michael countered her pity.

"I think you're pretty tough."

Jane wiped a tear away from her cheek.

"Lawyers are cheap bastards."

"Yes they are."

"But weird too," Jane said. "They drop $100 on lunch. They spend all this money for the top floors of whatever building seems the most prestigious. They buy oak desks, fancy suits, and expensive cars. But then when it comes to donating to legal aid ..." Jane shook her head. "Nothing."

Michael nodded, remembering his own time at the firm.

"At Wabash, I wasted so much money, pissed it away. I was stupid."

"Our board wants us to have an annual fundraising dinner at this hotel in downtown Miami. They want to have all the firms sponsor the tables, bring in a famous speaker, and then have the speaker praise them all for their commitment to legal services for the poor."

"I've been to those." Michael thought back to the various functions he had attended as an associate, excuses to drink at an open bar and be seen.

"The firm buys the table. I get to drink heavily and I don't give the organization a dime. The firm pays for everything."

"And when you subtract the costs, the organization barely raises a thing." Jane's voice hardened.

"You know I sent a letter to every lawyer in Miami, Naples and Fort Myers last year. I personally bought the list from the bar association, put it on my credit card. All I was asking for was $25 – they probably had three times that much in their wallet – and we sent out the letter and waited, and waited, and waited, and then three weeks later I get one response. It was a donation for $50 from a law school classmate of mine who works at Florida Legal Aid. She probably makes less than me, which is about one-fourth the salary of a first-year associate at any of those firms."

"Lawyers." Michael shook his head.

"Cheap bastards."

Michael eventually found a water pitcher and Styrofoam cups in a government-issued credenza. He filled up the pitcher from the hallway drinking fountain, and then returned to the conference room.

"Water?" Michael began pouring himself a glass.

Jane nodded, and so Michael poured another and handed it to her.

"So when did you break off the engagement?"

Jane took the glass of water. Michael could see that she didn't want to talk about it.

"Come on," Michael said. "I'll tell you about mine if you tell me about yours."

Jane raised an eyebrow.

"You were engaged?"

Michael nodded. "It was the happiest six hours of my life."

"Seriously?"

"Seriously." Michael took a sip of water. "But I made the mistake of being honest."

"You're saying honesty isn't the best policy?"

"Perhaps honesty isn't the best policy ... all at once." Michael smiled, finishing his water. He poured himself another. "Once upon a time, I was a pretty good lawyer. I dropped out, and I thought she deserved to know the reasons why."

Michael was surprised at how good it felt to talk to her. Jane was somebody who might understand.

"I knew she'd be upset, but I thought it'd be fair to let her know upfront. Full disclosure."

"Sorry." Jane didn't ask for more details, and Michael wasn't ready to tell her more. Not yet.

"So how about you?"

"I love my job," Jane said. "It drives me crazy, but I love my job and what I do. I got out of law school and decided to blaze my own path. I harassed all of these foundations to give me money to start, but after a few years they lost interest. Immigration was a big deal in the mid-1990s, then things shifted to charter schools and wrap-around services for inner-city kids, then it was about giving everybody who's poor a laptop computer, and now it's all about childhood obesity. I ask for money and they're like, 'haven't you solved that problem yet?' and 'why are you still around?' or 'what are your benchmarks for effectiveness?'"

Jane looked up at the ceiling, brought her focus back down, and then continued.

"We went from a staff of 10 to five and now it's just me. It's a slow death."

"Justin mentioned a raid?"

Jane nodded.

"So I get a tip that New Harvest foods is housing about 20 illegal immigrants in a pole barn on one of their big farms a little south of here. I convince Justin to get a search warrant and raid the place at the same time as their corporate human resources department, but when the raid happened there was nothing in the barn, only equipment."

"That happens." Michael shrugged his shoulders. "Why would it almost cost Justin his job?"

"Well," Jane scrunched up her face, embarrassed, "I kind of told some local television reporters."

"You think they tipped off New Harvest?"

"Probably, inadvertently," Jane said. "I had a big grant application in at the Miami Foundation. I thought the publicity would help. It didn't."

"And the feds thought Justin tipped off the media?"

"Exactly," Jane said. "They thought he was an ambitious young politician trying to make a name for himself. I mean, why else would anybody care about immigrants? Must be somebody running for office, courting the Latino vote."

"There's never any shortage of politically ambitious assistant U.S. Attorneys."

Jane shook her head.

"Justin isn't like that. He's a true believer," she paused, "or *was* a true believer. ... Anyway, I begged him to rat me out, but he didn't. We just got into a huge argument and the engagement was called off."

Justin Kent finally returned after another hour. Michael and Jane had thought about leaving, questioning whether Justin was really going to come back and wondering if it would be best just to move on. But the truth was, they had no other leads. They didn't have any place else to go.

Kermit was off on his own. He was busy talking with people in Jesser, likely scaring them more than obtaining useful information. They were prohibited from going to Tommy's trailer, and going to the other trailers hadn't prompted anybody to come forward.

"Did you find anything out from immigration?" Jane asked as Justin sat down.

"I talked to three people over there, and they hadn't picked him up. He's not in detention and hasn't been deported."

Justin set a folder onto the table. He opened it, and then removed a few pieces of paper. They looked like color printouts, photographs.

"What's that?" Jane asked.

Justin slid the photographs over to her.

"I don't know," he said. "But the timing worries me."

Michael rolled his chair closer to Jane. He looked over her shoulder as she stared down at the photographs.

"What are we looking at?" Michael looked and it appeared to be a pale object in the dirt. "Is that a bone?"

"An arm," Justin said. "It was badly decomposed, but what makes it more difficult is that some sort of animal got at it."

Jane placed first picture underneath the second.

The second photograph was of another object. This object was darker and thicker than the first.

Justin walked over to Jane, joining her and Michael. Justin pointed at the middle of the photograph with the tip of his pen.

"That's the torso and leg."

Jane took the second photograph, and then placed it on the bottom of the stack.

Justin began to narrate.

"No identification was found. No tattoos or anything else that could be used to identify him. We got a DNA sample and we'll run it through our database, including our database of convicted felons. But the next picture is probably the only thing that could be helpful."

Jane put the third photograph on the bottom to reveal the final photograph. It was a close-up of a shiny piece of metal. It was the metal that had reflected the sun, and had caught the farmer's attention.

"It's a belt buckle," Justin said.

Jane and Michael looked at it. The large buckle was silver with small turquoise stones surrounding a Mexican eagle.

Jane looked up and pushed all the photographs away.

"That's Tommy."

CHAPTER TWELVE

The coroner led Michael and Jane through a maze of cubi-cles. It was the administrative portion of the county morgue.

"Here we are." The coroner pointed at a gray metal door on the back wall. He was a slight man with pointed features that were beginning to round as he neared retirement.

"You get used to the smell, but it can be a little unsettling at first." He smiled, and then stopped in front of the door.

The coroner turned the knob, opened the door, and a cold plume of chemicals escaped. He let the initial burst of foul air pass, and then the coroner led Michael and Jane inside a large windowless room.

The space looked like a combination operating room, meat locker, and 1970s elementary school gymnasium.

"When I heard you were coming to make an identification, I set him up in the back." The coroner pointed at a stainless steel table pressed against a green tiled wall. A metal lamp with an adjustable cord hung above the long black body bag.

Jane and Michael stopped a few feet from the table. The coroner began to unzip the bag, but stopped.

"I do apologize for the condition, but given the investigation, I cannot clean the body for now, only preserve it in the exact manner in which it was found. That is why some of the clothes are still on."

Both Michael and Jane nodded, and then the coroner finished unzipping the bag.

Once open, the coroner carefully pulled back the edges of the bag to reveal its contents.

He stepped away, giving Jane and Michael space.

They each took a step forward, and looked down at the table.

It looked like an unfinished jigsaw puzzle with a lot of missing pieces.

The coroner had arranged the parts of the body in roughly the places where they should be – but disconnected.

Even the parts that were there still didn't look right. The head was simply a mass of black hair, mud and bone. The tissue and features had either decomposed or had been consumed by whatever animal dragged the body through the field. The individual body parts below the head were the same.

"Tomorrow, after everything has been photographed and documented, we can do a little more thorough examination. I thought that such activity would be premature, however, until an identification was made and the family could be consulted." The coroner waited for a response, but Jane and Michael continued to stare at the body in silence.

In time, Jane looked up. She was tense. Her eyes focused hard on the coroner.

"Did you do any bloodwork?"

The coroner shook his head.

"It wasn't possible."

"Tommy had cancer. That would maybe show up in any bloodwork." Jane looked back at the body parts on the table. "But I know that's him."

The coroner nodded his head.

"We could take a sample from bone marrow, the cancer might show up in that sample, but DNA is the most appropriate."

"I'll get you a sample from his cousin, Roberto," Jane said. "He's in town. We can get that quickly."

CHAPTER THIRTEEN

Kermit was already at their table at The Box. Jane and Michael entered and were, once again, greeted with open arms by Tyco. Filled with freaks and fringe, Michael liked The Box because it reminded him of The Sunset. He also didn't like The Box for the same reason.

He missed Hut No. 7. Whenever there was a lull in conversation or a few minutes of silence, his mind often drifted back down to the Mayan Riviera in Mexico. He could hear the blue Caribbean crash on the Sunset's pearl beach. He could feel the cool, salty air breeze pass through him, and then he thought of Andie. The thought of Andie Larone left him hollow. He felt sort of like the way Justin Kent looked.

Michael wanted closure, but closure had never been something that came easy for him.

"Yo, bro-ha, come back to the present." Kermit snapped his fingers in Michael's face. Then he got up and guided Michael the rest of the way, escorting him into the booth. Kermit then put his arm around Jane and guided her into the other side of the booth where he had been sitting.

"Right here next to me, sexy."

Jane smiled. "I wouldn't want it any other way."

Kermit waved over the waitress. She still walked with the weight of the world pressing down on her, but it looked like a little of the weight had been taken off.

"What can I get for you, Kermie?" She smiled a crooked grin.

"A round of your cheapest beer. And can I get your Juicy Lucy with a side of fries?"

"Of course." Her eyes sparkled.

When she left, Michael leaned in.

"Are you two an item now?"

"Maybe, *mi amigo*." Kermit bobbled his head. "She's a special girl with special gifts in linguistics. She's helping me with my new theories of advanced general semantics."

Michael nodded as if he understood. Advanced general semantics at least sounded a little less kooky than the teachings of Dr. Moo Yung Song. After enough time passed to be polite, he asked, "What the hell is a Juicy Lucy?"

Kermit began to answer, but Jane interrupted.

"It's their specialty. Two hamburger patties melded together with a chunk of molten, melted cheddar cheese in the middle."

"Like a jelly doughnut," Kermit added, "but with meat and cheese."

Michael shrugged his shoulders, confused. "Isn't that just a cheeseburger?"

Both Jane and Kermit laughed.

"You know little, my friend. The ingredients may be the same but the process transforms it into something ethereal, heaven-like."

"Then we better order a few more," Michael said. "I don't think I'll be getting any heaven when I'm gone."

Kermit's new lady friend slapped the plates of fries and greasy Juicy Lucys down on the table. After a few bites, carefully avoiding second-degree burns from the molten cheese, Michael concluded that they lived up to the hype, although he was pretty sure a few arteries had clogged by the time his plate was clean.

While they had eaten, Jane had filled Kermit in on their meeting with Justin Kent and their trip to the morgue.

"That's tough, yo. I'm sorry." Kermit froze for a few seconds, thinking, and then pounded the remaining half of his beer. He slid the empty glass toward the table's edge. His head twitched, and then Kermit connected his thoughts. "Today I found out some stuff. You know what I mean. I was workin' the Guillardo magic and getting a sense of Jesser's WIGO."

"WIGO?" Michael asked.

"General semantics, *mi amigo*, an off-shoot of applied linguistics," Kermit said. "It's the first step in understanding and analyzing complex societal problems and communicating with the public." Kermit raised his hand. "W-I-G-O," he numbered off."What.Is.Going.On, here? That's what I'm doing, and that's what you should do, too."

"We *are* doing that." Michael finished off his own beer, and made eye contact with their waitress for more.

"No, *mi amigo*," Kermit said. "You're approaching this situation with your own baggage, with your pre-constructed framework based upon your own life experiences and assumptions. WIGO means you identify your own filters, wipe them away, and start from scratch. You listen to people. You identify their filters, and communicate at their level. It's a basic foundational tool to obtain solutions and direction."

Michael nodded.

"Fine. I'll do that." The waitress approached, and Michael ordered another round of beer for the table. Once the waitress left, he turned back to Kermit. "So, you want to tell me the WIGO or what?"

"I will spare you the commentary on the socio-economic culture of exploitation that has been created here in Jesser."

"Thank you," Jane said. "I'm depressed enough."

Kermit ignored her.

"I learned that our friend Deputy Maus has a pretty nice side-job for Jolly Boy, and that he was the last person to see Tommy alive. As you all know, every day a van comes and picks up workers for the Jolly Boy fields. The van does a circular, going to the usual spots; the Home Depot parking lot, an apartment complex over on the edge of Fort Myers, and then the various trailers. The driver was at the one where Tommy lives, picking up the workers. They waited for Tommy for a while, but Maus waved them on. People know Tommy was sleeping in the trailer when they left. They know he was in there when Maus was knocking on the door. Nobody saw Tommy after that, though. They came back and his sleeping bag and his mat were gone." Kermit paused.

"We gotta watch Maus. That's why I'm thinking of picking me up a police scanner on the B.M."

Michael and Jane exchanged looks, both thinking of the abbreviation for bowel movement .Jane finally asked, "B.M.?"

"Black market." Kermit smiled. "We could listen to the radio dispatches and track him so we can figure out his buzz patterns."

"And you've got people who'll actually speak up, tell their story?" Michael asked, already figuring out how the testimony would be presented in court. He couldn't turn off the lawyer part of his brain, even though there was no case and he was now a fugitive beach bum.

"When we all went to the trailers, after talking with Roberto, that was what we were looking for, but nobody came forward," Jane said. "Now you're saying you have people who'll talk."

Kermit smiled.

"Of course, my lady. We've got a van full of them."

Jane shook her head.

"I'm not so sure. From my experience, they aren't going to testify. They're afraid."

Kermit picked at the last of his fries. He found one, drowned it in ketchup, and popped it in his mouth. Then his eyes got big.

"There's also that one dude we saw outside the first day at your office." Kermit snapped his fingers, remembering his name. "Miggy. He sounds promising. He'll testify for sure. I talked to him today for a long time. He says he's seen the dead."

"Miggy is crazy," Jane said. "Miggy has been telling people for years that he's seen the spirits."

"I know." Kermit nodded. "Pretty cool."

Michael decided it was time to move on.

"What else you got?"

"Just one other thing." Kermit raised an eyebrow. "One of Jolly Boy's boys, well, he's a really bad boy."

"Who?" Jane asked.

"*Muchacho* named Dylan." Kermit's narrowed his eyes and touched his nose. "We got to find out more about him."

Jane picked up her beer.

"Sounds like a plan," she said, taking a sip, "assuming I don't get shut down first."

And I don't get arrested, Michael thought.

CHAPTER FOURTEEN

Michael sat at the cheap desk in his motel room. It was late. He was tired, but not tired enough to fall asleep. He was drunk, but not drunk enough to pass out. So he sat and stared at the photograph of his namesake, the Irish revolutionary Michael John Collins.

As a boy, his mother had three pictures hanging on the wall of their old apartment. The first two were pictures of Pope John Paul II and President John F. Kennedy. The third photograph was of Michael John Collins. After his mother died, Michael took it with him. Then he kept it when he left everything else behind for Mexico. It was one of the few things that he had kept from his former life.

There was something about the photo that gave him strength.

The Michael John Collins in the photograph spent most of his life on the run, fighting the British and trying to unify Ireland. After he negotiated the peace deal that split the country in two, allowing the British to keep control of Northern Ireland, he was killed by one of his own.

Michael stared at the photograph and wondered how long he was going to last.

Michael wasn't a fan of Jesser, but felt himself getting sucked in. He wanted to help, but what could he really do? He wasn't going to anonymously give money to Jane's little non-profit. He had done that already donations almost cost him Father Stiles and Father Stiles had still almost lost his parish. His secret bailout of the Sunset had cost him Andie. He couldn't go down that path again, not with the feds getting so close.

It'd just turn all bad. Bad luck followed him.

Michael looked up from the photograph. He opened the window shade a crack.

Across the street sat the dark blue Ford Taurus with two people inside. It was the same car he had seen the first night he and Kermit checked into the motel. It was the same one he had seen down the street from Jane's office.

He had to get out of Jesser. He had to go home.

Michael looked at the photograph on the desk. He took a deep breath and closed his eyes.

I'll leave, he thought, *just not yet*. A few more days.

CHAPTER FIFTEEN

The view was lovely. The lawyer was late. Brian and Dylan McNaughten sat on the deck of the Everglade Boat and Yacht Club, overlooking Naples Bay.

It was breakfast time at the club, which was Dylan's favorite, but he was still in a bad mood. He ordered another Bloody Mary and headed to the omelet station where a young Hispanic woman was waiting to serve. She had 15 different ingredients to choose from. Each one – from green peppers to ham to broccoli florets – were meticulously displayed on the table in front of her.

He looked them over, never a smile. Dylan barked an order, and then he returned to his seat.

"I'm hung-over." Dylan looked around. "And where's my bloody?"

"It's coming." Brian exhibited patience that only came from experience. "So I take it from the way that you're dressed and your current condition that you are not coming in to work today."

"Is that a statement or question?"

"A statement, hoping for a response."

But Dylan didn't respond, and so Brian continued.

"You know," Brian said, "the way to avoid being hung-over is simply not to drink heavily the night before."

Dylan rolled his eyes.

"Whatever." He waved his brother off. "I do my thing and you do yours." Dylan saw a waiter with his drink. He held out his hand, and the waiter dutifully handed the glass of vodka and tomato juice to Dylan and disappeared.

Dylan took out the decorative stick of fruit and drank. Now satisfied with the day's first taste of alcohol, he continued.

"You're not capable of doing half the stuff I do for this company, so get off my back."

Brian bit his tongue. He knew it was true.

They were twins. They were connected, but different. They instinctively looked out for one another. That was how it had always been. When they were kids, their dad had been too busy running Jolly Boy to have much to do with them and their mother had been too busy with her tennis pro. So they had relied on each other growing up. Now, with their dad gone and their mother moved away, it wasn't too different.

Brian looked at his brother and tried another approach.

"I appreciate what you do, but it's getting complicated and you're starting to get a little sloppy."

Dylan shook his head. He shot his brother a dismissive look.

"We're fine." Dylan threw his napkin down on the chair, and then got up to see what was taking so long with his omelet.

When Dylan was out of earshot, Brian mumbled, "We'll see."

Harrison Grant eventually arrived. Once upon a time, Jolly Boy had been the client he milked for 40 percent of his annual billables. Back then, he would've walked on broken glass to keep Jolly Boy as a client, despite Dylan McNaughten's increasingly crass and erratic behavior.

Now, however, Grant had bigger clients. He was bringing cases to trial and winning. His reputation was growing.

Maybe it wouldn't be so bad if they fired him, Harrison thought. Things were getting tricky. Every business walks a thin line between ethics and illegality. Being unethical was fine, but breaking the law could result in everybody going to prison.

"Where have you been?" Dylan pushed his plate of half-eaten omelet away. "I got things to do."

"Things?" Harrison smiled. "Like what? I thought your brother was the one with the job." He sat down at the table.

Brian appreciated this little jab at Dylan. He gave Harrison a pat on the back, and the attorney's tardiness and inflated billable hours were momentarily forgiven.

"You wanted to meet with us?"

"I did." Harrison directed his attention at Brian, ignoring Dylan's tantrum. "I got word today from a contact that the do-gooder lawyer identified the body."

"You said they wouldn't be able to identify it," Brian said to Dylan accusingly.

Dylan shook his head.

"I said they *probably* wouldn't be able to identify it. No guarantees."

They all sat for a moment.

Silence.

Nobody wanted to say anything further. Brian thought of all the spy movies and cop shows featuring tiny recording devices. *Keep up the wall*, Brian thought. *Deny everything*.

Dylan, on the other hand, took the silence as an opportunity to finish his drink.

Harrison raised his hand.

"There's nothing for Jolly Boy to worry about," he said. "You didn't do anything, so there's no link. Legal liability requires a link. No link, no liability and without liability there are no damages."

"Nor should there be any connection to Jolly Boy," Brian added, thinking about the recording devices. He looked directly at his brother, and then continued with a loud, clear voice for the benefit of all of the imagined recording devices. "Jolly Boy had nothing to do with this person. He was merely an employee."

Dylan shook his head. They were all being stupid, overreacting. He could fix this.

"So why are you telling us this? Do me and Maus gotta knock off this lawyer chick?"

"No," Harrison said. He didn't appreciate the mess that Dylan was making for him. Dylan thought it was just a game, but Harrison was forced to advise him. Harrison cleared his throat.

"Do not knock off any person or any thing."

Brian added, "Because nothing needs knocking off."

Harrison continued.

"I'm telling you this so that you can be prepared for the press inquiries," Harrison ticked through the basics of an appropriate response. "Express condolences. Admit that you only just discovered he was here illegally after a detailed review of his fraudulent documents after the body was found. Say that he was no longer an employee of Jolly Boy."

There was silence.

Dylan shook his head.

"That's it," he said. "How much did that little bit of advice cost us?"

Dylan stood. He stretched out his arms, and then looked out at the dock.

"My boat is calling me." He grabbed his crotch. "I got two babes waiting for a ride."

Before he walked away, Dylan leaned over and whispered in Brian's ear.

"The lawyer chick has got to go."

Brian nodded his head. "It's taken care of."

"Really?" Dylan asked, standing. It was strange for his brother to be involved in a thing like this.

"Really," Brian said. "Today is her last day. Her nonprofit no longer exists."

Dylan nodded.

"It's about time you got your hands dirty." He patted Brian on the head. "I'm proud of you."

"What's that about?" Harrison asked as Dylan walked off. "I thought I told you it was best to stay away. No connections. Don't get involved. Ignore her."

Harrison slid his chair a little closer to Brian, as if he was about to impart great wisdom.

"In the 1960s General Motors started investigating Ralph Nader, and Nader sued them. Nader became famous and a major pain in the ass. If General Motors would have ignored him, Nader would just be a weird law school professor who writes books about cars that nobody reads."

"I agree," Brian said, but then he looked around, still imagining the listening devices. He lowered his voice. "Attorney-client privilege?"

Harrison considered it, and then nodded.

Brian allowed a brief smile. He thought the plan was quite clever.

"Tonight the board is going to vote to shut her down."

"You know this?" Harrison asked.

"I know this," Brian said. "The head of her nonprofit's board belongs to the Miami University Club with me. Our kids take riding lessons together."

Harrison nodded. He couldn't see how shutting down an insolvent nonprofit was illegal. It was actually a clean resolution. The Community Immigrant Legal Services had been a nuisance, although it had also been a great source of billable hours over the years.

"You're sure?" Harrison asked.

"I'm sure," Brian said. "The chair says he has no choice, actually sounded a little sad about it, as if he cared about these people." He shook his head. "I played along, of course, to get more information."

"Then what?"

Brian smiled wide.

"This is the best part." Brian paused, looked around again before continuing. "In a few days, I've arranged a little grant to a legal aid organization in Orange County, California. She'll be offered another job. Seems there are migrant farm workers everywhere, and the further away from here the better. She won't come back to Jesser. The California strawberry and spinach people will have to deal with her, instead of us."

Harrison picked up his glass of ice water from the table. He leaned back and smiled.

"Very nicely done, Brian. I believe that would be checkmate." Harrison raised his glass. "Very nicely played, indeed."

CHAPTER SIXTEEN

It was dark by the time Michael, Kermit and Jane arrived at the office. Earlier in the evening, Jane had made a spaghetti dinner for them after work at her apartment. Kermit wanted to go to The Box, but neither Michael or Jane could handle another batch of grease.

The meal was supposed to be a thank you and maybe even a goodbye.

When they walked up to the door, Miggy was waiting for them, just like he had been waiting on the day that Michael and Kermit had first arrived.

Jane hadn't seen him at first, distracted by the people she saw through the window. They were the members of her board, milling about her office, chatting.

Miggy coughed. His skinny body was folded up by the door. Next to him was his Army surplus backpack and sleeping bag.

He looked up at Jane.

"Wondering where you was." He took a drag off of one of his hand-rolled cigarettes. "I seen the lights on and a little action inside, so I figured you'd be here. Can't pull one over on ol' Miggy." His small laugh turned into a fit of coughs.

"We've got a meeting tonight." Jane crouched next to him. "So you can't show me your secret. No spirits tonight."

"It's important." Miggy's eyes got wide. "When you gonna come with me? The spirits are telling me to bring you there. I don't want to make the spirits mad."

"I'm sorry, Miggy." Jane put a hand on his shoulder, squeezed, and then stood. "It can't be tonight. Those people inside might shut us down tonight, so it's a big meeting."

"Them people in there now?" Miggy sat up further, and then pulled his slight body to his feet using the crutch. He looked into the window at the men and women in suits. "You need me to talk to 'em. I'll talk to them for ya. Put in a good word."

"Thanks," Jane put her arm around him, "but I'll take care of it."

Kermit stepped forward.

"You and Michael go in," he said. "I'm not much of a corporate-meeting type. Me and Miggy will go find a place for a hot meal and I'll find him a good place to spend the night."

Miggy licked his lips, excited about the possibility of a meal.

"Thank you," Miggy said, and then to Jane, "I don't want to leave you, though."

"I'll be fine." Jane turned to Michael and put on a brave face. "Let's do it."

The office felt heavy. *This is the end*, Jane thought. There were stilted conversations and forced laughter, but underneath it all, there was undeniable sadness.

Jane sat at one end of the table with the board members sitting in the rest of the chairs. Michael sat off to the side, merely observing the confessions and apologies.

"I've been with you from the beginning, Jane." A middle-aged woman with clunky red glasses put her hand on her forehead, and then she began rubbing one of her temples. "I don't understand the foundations. I don't know why we can't get the grants, but I do know that we can't function without money. We've got nothing. It's upsetting to me."

"Is that a statement in favor of the motion?" The board chair asked. He was a silver-haired man in a dark, tailored suit.

The chair waited, and eventually the woman with clunky red glasses nodded her head.

Another man spoke up, and the chair recognized him for the record.

He was bald with half-rimmed glasses.

"Jane, I know I speak for everyone when I say that this is not personal, but all of these foundations are looking for objective measurements of success. They want a big impact for their dollar. They want to know how many people you helped and how you helped them."

He shook his head and looked around the office. It was the first time that Jane felt embarrassed by the mess of files.

The man with half-rimmed glasses continued.

"The organization hasn't been and wasn't ever designed to do that. The days of wandering around the fields and asking workers what they want are over. We needed a strategic plan to improve their lives with measurable benchmarks. Frankly, I think Miami Legal Aid is in a better position as an organization to fill that role. They grasp the new normal. So I vote in favor of the motion."

The chair scanned the other individuals sitting at the table.

"Anyone else?"

There were no further comments. The seven board members sat in silence.

"Do I have a motion to end discussion and vote on the motion?"

There was a motion from the woman with red glasses.

"And a second?"

A few other board members seconded the motion.

The board chair paused, and then cleared his throat.

"We call the motion and it's time for the vote. Assuming that the motion passes, we'll begin the wind-down procedures for the organization. The office will officially close immediately, but we still need to assess assets and outstanding debts."

Jane sat stoically at the end of the table. She knew that this day had been coming. She had thought about it, but still wasn't prepared for the moment when it actually happened. She had been in denial.

She thought back to the beginning, and then she thought about now. Ten years of her life about to be ended by a vote. *No measurable results. No objective benchmarks of success.*

Jane thought about the half-dozen early agreements that she had negotiated with growers in Jesser, improving working conditions. She got little things, like a place for some workers to go to the bathroom. Another grower built a shaded place for the workers to eat lunch. She blocked deportation proceedings, obtained green cards for family members and reunited husbands and wives. She made sure that the children of the workers were allowed access to the public school system, the hot lunch program, and health care.

No measurable results. No objective benchmarks of success.

Jane wanted to ask the board, "How do you measure the success of poverty lawyers when there will always be poverty? Every day there are choices. Do you work on the systemic or do you work on the problem staring at you right now and asking for help? Giving Miggy a hot meal wasn't going to cure his mental illness or make him employable, but it was going to give him some dignity. That should count for something. There's a balance."

But Jane never asked the questions. She never made the argument. She was too tired to fight her own board of directors. Jane closed her eyes and reminded herself to breathe.

The meeting adjourned. The board members stood, stretched, and gathered up their things.

Jane remained seated. Each of the board members came up to her to express their sadness and disappointment that they had just voted to close the organization that she had started. Eventually they all left.

They had their own lives and families to take care of. They had their own careers to further, and ultimately the Community Immigrant Legal Services had been too much of a burden.

She watched them through the window. They got into their cars and SUVs that collectively cost more than the nonprofit's annual budget. Each car and SUV was worth more than Jane's yearly salary.

"Lawyers are cheap bastards," Jane said to nobody in particular.

Michael stood.

"Can I buy you a beer?"

Jane allowed a tear to escape. It rolled down her cheek.

"I did my best." She wiped her cheek dry.

"I know you did." Michael put his hand on her shoulder. "Everybody knows you did." Michael took Jane's hand and pulled her up from her chair. "But, you still didn't answer my question: Can I buy you a beer?"

Jane put her arms around Michael and pulled him in.

"You can buy me a beer." She kissed his cheek, and then whispered in his ear. "I'll even let you buy me more than one."

CHAPTER SEVENTEEN

Word spread quickly of what had happened to Jane and Community Immigrant Legal Services, Inc.

Tyco, the owner of The Box, wrapped her in a big bear hug. He declared that her money was no good – all drinks were on the house. So, Michael, Kermit, and Jane settled into their booth and didn't expect to leave until they were kicked out.

Jane gave Kermit a detailed description of the board meeting, and then the conversation wound around to other topics.

"What's with Miggy?" Jane asked. "I saw him sitting outside the bar when we came in."

Kermit grabbed a handful of popcorn and shoved it in his mouth.

"I told him to join us, but he said that being indoors freaks him out. He sleeps in the fields."

Kermit shrugged his shoulders and grabbed some more popcorn.

"His choice." Kermit pointed at Jane. "But he really wants some alone time with you, my dear. I think that's why he's really hanging around."

"So he can show me the spirits?"

"Exact-a-mondo," Kermit said.

Jane smiled and shook her head.

"He should know that ghost hunting isn't my job any more." Jane finished her pint of beer. "I'm not sure it was ever part of my job, but that's all theoretical now."

Michael picked up the pitcher of beer. He filled Jane's glass, and then topped off his own. He set the pitcher down, and then Michael slid out of the booth. He stood, picked up his glass, and raised it high.

"A toast," he said. "To unemployment."

They all clinked.

"To unemployment."

The Box started to really rock at three in the morning. It was officially closed. The doors were locked, but Tyco allowed Kermit, Michael and Jane to stay while he cleaned up.

With the other customers gone, Kermit jumped over the bar and found the stereo. He turned the dial until the radio tuned into a Miami salsa station.

"This is what we need." Kermit clapped his hands, turned the music up louder, and then pulled Jane out of the booth. "Time to groove."

They spun around the dance floor, laughing through a few songs, and then the music slowed.

Kermit looked at Jane and smiled.

"Sorry, darling, I think this other lady is the next one on my dance card." He walked over to the waitress – otherwise weighed down by the world – and lightened her load.

Jane, now standing alone, looked over at Michael.

"A dance?"

Michael got up out of the booth.

"I was afraid you'd never ask."

The radio station kept the music slow for another hour.

Michael and Jane held each other, rocking back and forth. Occasionally, Jane would kiss Michael's neck, his chin, and then his lips, working her way around.

Michael didn't stop her.

It was the first woman he had held and had kissed since Andie. It felt good to be with someone again. It felt good to be close.

Jane rocked up on her tip toes.

"I'm tired," she whispered in Michael's ear.

Michael kissed her, and then told her that he was taking her home.

"That's what I was hoping for," she said.

It was one in the afternoon by the time Michael and Jane woke up, but even then, neither wanted to get out of bed.

Jane put her hand on Michael's chest.

"It's nice waking up with you." Her voice was soft, still sleepy.

Michael smiled. "It is nice."

"We don't have to go anywhere do we?"

Michael shook his head. He then pulled the thin bedsheet up, covering them. Then he pulled Jane's naked body close to his. "This is yet another of the many advantages of being un-employed."

They didn't leave Jane's apartment for two days. If Michael and Jane hadn't have run out of coffee or depleted most of their food supply, they probably wouldn't have left the apartment at all.

As they stood in the checkout line at Kwik-E-Mart, Michael put his arms around Jane and kissed the top of her head. He hadn't felt this good in a long time, almost forgetting the people tracking his movements and searching foreign bank accounts.

"You want to go to Miami for a few days?" Michael asked. "I could get a room on the beach. We could sit in the sun and turn ourselves red. Maybe we could read trashy books or gossip magazines." Michael pointed to the row of magazines by the cash register. "Looks like that one has a three-page spread on botched nose-jobs."

Jane smiled, and then her smile faded away.

"I probably shouldn't."

"Why?"

"I still have clients," Jane said. "I need to wrap up cases and transfer the ones that I can't finish to another attorney, wind down the organization."

"Just a few days." Michael started to unload their groceries, putting them on the small conveyor-belt to be scanned.

"The DNA test should also be done, so we need to inform Tommy's family of the results and figure out what to do about the funeral." Jane nodded, mentally going over the lists in her head.

Michael knew what she was doing, because he used to do the same thing. The to-do lists, and then the lists of lists, and the sub-lists within each list. It was never-ending.

Jane looked at Michael. She bit her lip, thinking.

"I know what the vote did. I know what the board said. I'm 'closed immediately,' but I can't just drop it." Then Jane looked away, frustrated. "I'm still a lawyer. I've got professional obligations, and I need another job some day. I can't just leave a wreck behind me."

"I know," Michael said, although he had certainly left a wreck behind himself many times.

He let Jane have her moment, but then he regrouped.

"It's just a few days to play. What's another day or two?"

Jane didn't respond. She was thinking.

"I'll make a deal with you," Michael said. "I'll track down the DNA results and talk to the family about funeral arrangements for Tommy, while you pack your bags for a little getaway."

"You'll do that?"

"I promise." Michael kissed her, again. "Then you can do whatever you need to do." She smiled and he melted a little bit. It felt like they had been together forever. It was almost too easy being with her.

CHAPTER EIGHTTEEN

The sun rose high over the Thomas Dewey National Nature Preserve. Maus sat in his black Arctic Cat 150 ATV four-wheeler. He wore full camo. A long, polished pump-action rifle laid over his lap.

He watched the edge.

There was a clump of brush where the swamp turned to scrappy forest. His eyes narrowed when a few branches rustled.

Maus smoothly and silently took the rifle off his lap. He took the safety off and put his finger on the trigger.

He kept the gun pointed at the rustling brush. Maus felt his heartbeat quicken. He tightened his grip, and narrowed his focus even further.

Then he heard a warble, and then another. Two wild turkeys were about to emerge from the brush into the open; a clear shot.

He took a shallow breath as the first bird's foot and then its entire body came out of hiding. Maus smiled. Gotcha.

It was going to be an easy shot, he thought, and then Maus' cell phone rang.

The noise startled him as he pulled the trigger and the shot went high.

The combination of the shot and the loud ringtone sent the wild turkeys into a panic. The birds scattered, and Maus blindly fired six shots into the brush until he didn't have anything left to fire.

He may have hit them, maybe not. He'd have to check.

Maus put the rifle down, picked up his cell phone.

He pressed a button on the phone.

"What the hell? You're late." Maus shouted. "Where are you?"

He walked over to the scrub brush on the edge of the swamp. He held the cell phone to his ear, listening while he searched for signs of the stupid birds.

"Well, after you enter, take a left and follow Token Trail. It's not that hard." Maus turned off his cell phone and shoved it in his pocket. He had found them. Two turkeys were hit. One was dead, the other was still breathing.

He knelt down onto the soft ground. Crouched over the bird that was still breathing, Maus studied it. The turkey's breathing was slow and forced. Its head twitched.

He altered his position so that he could get his hands around the bird's neck without being pecked or bitten. Then in one quick movement he gripped the bird's neck, stood, twisted, and tore the bird's head off.

It felt good.

Dylan didn't like the swamp, but he appreciated the privacy.

He parked his black Aston Martin DB9 convertible and got out. Maus was waiting at a lone picnic table in the clearing between the road's turnaround and the trail head. His ATV was parked nearby. It had two turkey carcasses roped to the back.

"Never too early to kill something," Dylan smiled, as if he knew about the joys of hunting and the outdoors. He stepped over a small puddle, careful not to dirty his polished Kenneth Cole loafers as he walked over to Maus.

"Best time to hunt is always in the morning," Maus said. He unscrewed the top of his thermos and poured himself a cup of coffee. If his boss wanted to pretend to be a woodsman, he might as well play along.

When Dylan finally arrived at the table, he didn't sit. He wasn't going to hang out with a man like Maus. They weren't friends. It was business.

Dylan put an envelope of cash down on the table.

Maus set down his cup of coffee, took the envelope, and shoved it in his front jacket pocket.

"What's the status?" Maus picked the coffee back up and took a sip, feeling better. He always felt better when he got paid.

"It's done." Dylan was smug. His confidence in himself never failed.

"What do you mean?" Maus shook his head. "It's not done. The test came back yesterday. They matched the cousin's DNA. They confirmed what the lawyer chick's been saying. I don't think she knows yet, but she will."

"The lawyer is gone." Dylan folded his arms across his chest, smiling. "Believe it or not, my good-for-nothing brother actually did something useful. The board voted to shut her down immediately. She'll be clearing out of that shithole of an office and leaving town."

"She's leaving town?" That part sounded good to Maus, made him feel even better.

"Not confirmed," Dylan said. "But my brother arranged for her to get offered a job far away. I have a feeling that it won't be long. She's got no reason to stay."

Maus finished his coffee, and then shook out the remaining drops of liquid. He screwed the plastic cup back onto the top of his thermos and stood.

"Well, we'll keep in touch then?"

"We will," Dylan said. He slapped Maus on his big shoulder as if they were in a locker room after a big game. "How about a smile? How about a thank you?"

"I still got a bad feeling." Maus shook his head, trying to stay cool and not get too excited. "True believers don't quit easy." He walked over to his ATV. Maus put his thermos into the ATV's back compartment, and picked up his gun. "I know about true believers," he said, "because I am one. Just don't believe in the same things, that's all."

CHAPTER NINETEEN

Michael woke up early. He slid out of bed, grabbed a pair of shorts and T-shirt off of the floor, and then put them on. After writing a quick note to Jane, Michael took one of the room keys off of the table, found his flip-flops, and walked out the door.

The days away in Miami had been great. Michael and Jane had declared the historic Hotel Astor their home away from home. The Art Deco masterpiece was a white three-story jewel box on the corner of Washington and 10th Street. It was a quiet place to decompress, just four blocks from South Beach's famous Lummus Park and the ocean.

Michael rode the elevator down and walked through the hotel's sleek lobby. When he stepped outside, he could tell it was going to be a hot day. It was early. The sun was still low in the sky, but there wasn't a cloud and its rays already beat down on the asphalt, softening it.

He walked down10th. A few minutes later, he was at the beach. Michael ditched his flip-flops near a palm tree and stepped onto the sand, finding the cool underneath the top layer of white powder. It felt good. Michael imagined he was back at the Sunset.

Soon, he thought. *A couple more days.*

Michael took a few steps, slow at first, and then he started to run. His feet dug into the sand, found a spot, and pushed him forward. Michael's breathing became heavier. His quads started to burn, and he ran faster.

He passed one jogger, and then another. His eyes slackened, and Michael fell into a rhythm. He kept running for miles, until he finally reached the park's northern boundary. He stopped, touched the ground, and started running back, even faster than before.

Michael pushed himself hard. His shirt turned wet with sweat. His body begged him to stop, but he kept going until the end.

When he had reached the finish, Michael fell to his knees. His body folded in on itself as he tried to catch his breath. Beads of sweat ran into his eyes. The salt stung. His eyes started to water, and he closed them.

Blinking, the different blues of the ocean and tans of the beach cascaded in and out of overlapping dots of color. As his vision started to clear, Michael saw Agent Frank Vatch a hundred yards away. Vatch was watching from his wheelchair on one of the paved bike paths that ran along Ocean Drive.

Vatch seemed so small, almost harmless.

Michael blinked, and Vatch was gone. The consequences for his actions would be delayed for yet another day.

Michael got up, found his flip-flops, and began his walk back to the hotel. His head was light from the run. The appearance and disappearance of Agent Vatch didn't concern him, and Michael didn't know why. *Maybe it wasn't real*, Michael thought. *Maybe I'm imagining things*. Michael ran his hands through his hair and focused on the run.

He needed a good run, and it was good, hard run. The return to Jesser, however, was not as good.

CHAPTER TWENTY

As they pulled up in front of the office, they knew something wasn't right. The front door was wide open. It blew back and forth in the wind. Jane saw it first. She was out of the car before Michael could turn off the engine.

She surveyed the damage, unable to speak.

The window of the Community Immigrant Legal Services office was destroyed. Shards of glass laid on the sidewalk as if something in the office had exploded. Inside, tables and chairs were overturned, papers strewn on the floor. The file cabinets were tipped over. Jane's computer and monitor were smashed into scattered pieces.

They walked through the open front door, slowly.

Glass popped underneath their feet.

They turned in a circle, looking. The entire office was trashed.

Along the back wall there was a message scrawled with red spray paint:

THANK YOU.

HATE TO SEE YOU GO.

LOVE--

THE ILLEGALS

Irony was always the trademark of the youngest generation.

"I'm going to kill those redneck kids." Jane's jaw clenched tight. Her days of relaxation were gone, as if they had never happened. All of the feelings she had during the final board meeting were back.

Michael put his hand on her shoulder.

"We can get this cleaned up."

"When?" Jane asked. "How? Look at this place. This isn't just a shit-bag thrown at a window."

"I'll call Kermit. He can help." It sounded weak.

Jane pulled away from him.

"I should have been here. I should have been working. I shouldn't have been with you. What was I thinking?"

Jane sat down on the floor, put her hands on her face and began to cry.

Funny thing about a small town like Jesser, people care more than one would think.

The first person to arrive was the minister from the First Baptist Church down the block. He'd driven past Jane's office that morning on his way to the men's breakfast at the Prairie Diner. He said that three of the men he had eaten breakfast with would be arriving shortly with garbage bags and tools.

About 20 minutes later, another truck pulled up with six Hispanic men in the back.

Kermit got out of the truck's front cab with Miggy. He clapped his hands.

"Okay men. Let's get started. Who's got the plywood?"

Miggy translated, and soon a large piece of plywood was lifted from the back and brought over to the broken window.

"We gotta measure that sucker, and then, when everything is swept, we'll put it over the broken window. *Comprende*?"

Miggy translated and the men nodded their heads.

Within an hour, 50 other people were milling about. Somebody had brought a radio and music was playing. The music bridged the conversations and laughter.

A group of elderly women brought bread, meats, and cheeses for sandwiches along with three large boxes of classic ripple potato chips.

The pastor and another man set up a few of the office's folding tables outside. One of the women spread out a red and white checked tablecloth on top of the table, while another unloaded a bag full of paper plates, napkins and plastic utensils. A large Tupperware container filled with sliced watermelon was placed next to the cold cuts and chips, and soon people were taking breaks, munching for awhile, and then getting back to work.

Jane stood off to the side. She directed the activity, determining what could be thrown away and what needed to be saved.

Michael walked over to her with a can of soda and a sandwich.

"For you." He handed the plate to her, and Jane took it.

"Thank you." She took a bite without taking an eye off of all the people. "Can you believe this?"

Michael put his arm around her.

"Yes," he said. "I totally can."

"Last thing to do." Kermit stirred a bucket of white paint with a wooden stick. "Can you hand me a brush, Mr. Miggy?"

Miggy nodded his head, and dutifully located a paintbrush in a corner filled with various buckets of cleaners and other supplies. He hobbled back on his crutch and handed the brush to Kermit.

Kermit dipped the brush into the bucket of paint, but Jane stopped him.

"Hold on," she said. "I gotta do something first." Jane gave a pixie smile and bounced over to her purse. She dug around and found her iPhone, which also happened to be the most valuable thing she owned.

Jane came back over to where Kermit and Miggy stood.

"Thanks," she said. "And where's Michael?"

Jane looked around as Michael came through the front door after dropping off the last group of volunteers and delivering the last batch of garbage to the dump. The party was over, and it was just him, Jane, Kermit and Miggy.

"What's going on?" Michael asked. He had a six-pack of beer in his hand, and he raised them. "I got some cold ones."

"Perfect," Kermit said. "Jane is recording this for posterity. But first we must toast."

Kermit relieved Michael of his beer. They all smiled as Kermit dramatically unscrewed the caps on each bottle and distributed each one.

"Okay, Miss Jane," Kermit said. "Let's hear it."

"A speech?" Jane asked.

"Of course," Kermit said. "It was a great party."

Jane smiled and nodded her head. She started to speak, but then stopped and slowly looked around the office. Eight hours earlier it had been a disaster, now it was cleaner than it had been in years. The floors were scrubbed. The files were alphabetized, boxed, and ready to be moved. And in many ways, Jane was ready to move too.

"This was a terrible day," she said. "It started in the most horrific way. It was as if somebody was just trying to crush me, grind me into the ground. But I couldn't think of a better way to end it. I wondered if anybody would notice if we were gone, whether I was the biggest chump in the world. Whether 10 years of my life had been wasted when I should have been earning money, starting a family, and paying off my student loans." Jane took a deep breath, and then pointed her bottle of beer at the message painted along the back wall.

"They really do thank me. They really will miss me. And that feels good." Jane lifted her bottle higher. "To the illegals."

"To the illegals," Michael, Kermit and Miggy parroted back.

Then everyone took a drink.

"God, that tastes good." Jane took another sip. She set the bottle down on the floor. "I'm taking a picture of this before it's painted over. I want to frame it."

"Here, here," Kermit said, as Jane took a few pictures of the message that had been painted on the wall. It was intended to intimidate and mock, but it, instead, became an odd source of humor and inspiration.

THANK YOU.
HATE TO SEE YOU GO.
LOVE--
THE ILLEGALS

CHAPTER TWENTY ONE

Agent Frank Vatch sat at his desk. He had converted the small second bedroom in his Hoboken apartment into a home office. Vatch flipped open his notebook and started reviewing his notes, and then he began writing additional thoughts about his time in Florida.

For years he had tracked Michael Collins, and he knew it was finally going to end. The attorneys had said that they were close to reaching a deal with some of the foreign banks where Michael had purportedly stashed Joshua Krane's money. Vatch's supervisors wanted him to move on, but Vatch wouldn't let it go. He wasn't going to allow loose ends. He wanted Michael Collins.

Vatch looked at the framed picture of his dead partner, Agent Brenda Pastoura, on the corner of his desk. She was killed the same night Michael's client Joshua Krane was murdered. The FBI had placed Krane under 24-hour surveillance, fearing that the corporate executive would run.

Late at night, they followed Krane to the Bank of America building, watched him go inside, get the account numbers and passwords for Krane's offshore back accounts, and then get back into the car with Michael. A few blocks later a man on foot fired on the car, and Agent Pastoura chased after him. There was no way he could help. Vatch's wheelchair was in the trunk, and there wasn't time. He radioed for back-up, but it was too late. In an alley two blocks away, both Agent Pastoura and the man who shot Joshua Krane were dead. Nobody ever found the account numbers.

There was a knock on the window. Vatch looked away from the photograph, and saw Anthony on the fire escape.

"Open up," he said. Anthony knocked, again.

Vatch rolled back from the desk.

"A little late, isn't it?" Vatch opened the window, and Anthony jumped inside.

"You really should start using the door," Vatch said, but Anthony didn't respond.

Anthony pointed at the notebook on the desk. "Still working the case?"

"Always," Vatch nodded.

Anthony smiled.

"You look tan," he said. "How was Miami?"

"Okay," Vatch sighed.

"Any response from the subpoenas?"

"Still waiting," Vatch said.

"You gonna wait forever, huh?"

"Yes," Vatch said.

"You want to play cribbage, then? While you wait?"

Vatch looked at the clock. It was a quarter past eleven.

"Only if you let me win."

Anthony smiled. Even though he was growing into a young man, his smile still revealed the boy inside.

"Never," Anthony said. "If I let you win, it won't mean anything. You gotta earn it."

Vatch smiled and nodded.

"That's exactly right."

CHAPTER TWENTY TWO

Father Pena led the way down the dusty streets of San Corana. The setting sun cast the small stone city in an orange light. The coffin of Tommy Estrada – covered with a finely pleated cream cloth – was held high.

Brass band music bounced off the mud walls around San Corana's city center as they marched. The air was thick with the smell of earth and sweet Copal, a ceremonial incense used for more than 500 years.

The processional wound through the narrow passages into the town center, and then out again toward the cemetery just on the edge of town.

Michael, Kermit and Jane were not last, but toward the back of the crowd. Elana, Pace and the other children were in front. Close friends and family were in the middle.

Michael hadn't seen Jane since leaving Jesser, about three weeks earlier. They had talked a few times while he had helped make the funeral arrangements. When the arrangements were final, Michael had wondered whether she would come. At first, she wouldn't commit. Then, Jane arrived.

He watched her as they walked; Michael was happy she came. He wanted to spend time with her, but it wasn't like Florida. Memories of Andie were all around him. They competed with the present, pushing her away. He wasn't sure if he could move on from Andie or even if he should.

A man tapped Michael's shoulder. He pointed at his plastic bucket, showing Michael. Inside the bucket there were three bottles of Mezcal tequila on ice. It was the Mexican equivalent of Kentucky moonshine. The man gave Michael a toothless grin, and then he filled a small plastic cup with Mezcal.

Michael took it. He emptied the cup with a swift throw back.

The man laughed as Michael cringed. The Mezcal was jet fuel, but it was tradition.

Men and woman alternated between cries of mourning and celebration. Mexicans had always embraced death as a part of life. There was nothing wrong with celebrating someone in the moments of loss.

Jane took a plastic cup full of tequila. Kermit took two. Jane smiled at Michael, and he smiled back as the funeral parade progressed.

After the procession, Catholic service, and interment, Michael and Jane were finally alone together. The sun had set, and a dark cool had settled along the shore. During the day, the sky above the Mayan Riviera was arching and vast, but at night, the sky seemed to lower itself, creating a more intimate space. Even with others strolling along the beach, it was easy to feel close.

They sat out on the Point, a narrow streak of rocks that curved out into the Caribbean. It was Michael's favorite place at the resort.

He laid a thick blanket down on the rocks. Jane laid down on top of it.

"Having a good time?" he asked.

Jane nodded her head, cloudy from the shots of Mezcal.

"As much fun as an unemployed lawyer can have at a funeral."

"You're not setting a particularly high bar." Michael sat down behind her. He kissed Jane's neck. He teased her, trying to make Jane admit that she liked it. "Come on," he said. "Tell me you love this place." He kissed her neck some more.

"Okay," Jane said in her best lawyer-voice. "I'll stipulate to the sole fact that this is a lot more fun than an unemployed lawyer usually has at a funeral. Agreed?"

"Agreed," Michael said.

Jane pushed away from him, laughing.

"Now please stop molesting me."

Michael kissed her one more time, and then rolled onto his back.

He looked up at the night sky.

"I'd like to get lost up there." Michael stared at the stars, making constellations of his own design. "Any interest in staying for awhile? Maybe you could push your return flight out a bit."

Jane didn't respond for a long time.

"I don't know." She took in a deep breath, thinking. Then she said, "What's not to love about this? But I'm not sure what *this* is."

Jane turned and looked at Michael. Her eyes softened.

"I don't mean it in a bad way. I don't even know how I mean it. I just don't know."

"I don't know either." Michael was honest. He really didn't know, and Michael left it at that. Jane didn't push, either.

She stared up at the sky. They watched the stars together, tracked the satellites moving above them, and listened to the waves fall on the beach.

"You know I got a job offer?" Jane said after awhile.

"No," Michael said. "When?"

"Just after you left." Jane sat up a little. She rolled her shoulders, letting some of the tension out. "I got a call from Legal Aid in Los Angeles. Doing the same thing I was doing in Jesser – working with immigrant farm workers – but with more support and a little better salary."

"Sounds good," Michael said. "But ..."

"But ..." Jane answered. "I don't know. I feel like I committed myself to Jesser. The way it ended," Jane paused. "It didn't end the way it's supposed to. The bad guys got away. We know Jolly Boy did it, but nobody –"

"So go back," Michael said.

Jane shook her head.

"I can't. How?"

"I don't know." Michael sat up and started looking at the smooth rocks all around him. "Maybe you just need a break to think about your next move." Michael stopped looking. He found a rock and skipped it into the water. "Everybody needs a break." Michael found another rock and skipped it, thinking. "But I'm not like you. I never wanted to right wrongs and fight for justice."

Jane leaned over and whispered in Michael's ear.

"I think you're lying."

She kissed him on the lips.

When Michael didn't say anything, she did it again, a little harder.

"Okay, maybe you're right. Maybe I had a little fire for justice," Michael said, laughing. "Now please stop molesting me."

Jane grabbed his crotch and gave it a squeeze.

"You wish."

CHAPTER TWENTY THREE

Deputy Maus wanted to see it for himself. He parked his police cruiser, unlocked the door, and got out.

The faded sign for Community Immigrant Legal Services, Inc., was still there, but, as he got closer, Maus could see that she was gone. He put his hands up to block the reflection as he pressed closer to the glass. He peered inside.

No lights were on. The computers, telephone, and file cabinets were gone. The folding tables were stacked in a corner, and there was nothing hung on the walls.

Maus could hardly believe it. *Had he won?* The immediate relief felt good, but he still doubted it could be true.

Maus turned. He saw Miggy standing there, propped up by his crutch with his faded green backpack slung over his shoulder. Miggy had been watching him, intruding on his private moment.

"What the hell you looking at?" Maus started walking back toward his police cruiser.

Miggy didn't say anything. Miggy just watched, his eyes hard.

"Freak." Maus kicked out Miggy's crutch as he walked past.

Miggy tried to catch his balance, but he fell to the pavement.

Maus walked around the front of his cruiser. He started to open the door, but stopped. He looked down at Miggy. Miggy was still on the sidewalk, curled and holding his shoulder.

"You got something you want to say to me?" Maus asked.

Miggy struggled, turning his head so that he could see Maus. Maus waited a second for him to speak.

"I didn't think so." He got into his cruiser, turned the vehicle on, and then drove away.

The shooting pain in Miggy's shoulder wouldn't stop. He put his head down on the pavement. It felt rough, but cool.

Miggy took a breath, trying to control the waves of pain and keeping his breathing shallow. "I know who you are. The spirits tell me," he said quietly. Then he closed his eyes and waited for someone to help.

CHAPTER TWENTY FOUR

A week passed, and the topic didn't come up, again. Michael could tell that she was thinking about it – trying to map out the rest of her career or lack of a career – but Jane didn't say anything and Michael didn't push.

In the meantime, they were having fun. Their days fell into a routine. They'd wake up, have a little breakfast, and then swim, surf or kayak. Then they'd crash on the beach for the afternoon, and take a long walk along the shore in the evening.

They talked some, but not a lot. They enjoyed having each other's company. They enjoyed not being alone.

Michael started to imagine a life without Andie. Whether Jane was part of his future, he didn't know. But he felt himself starting to heal. He started to move forward.

Then the idea came.

Michael got out of the shower at Hut No. 7 and walked into the main room. Michael was naked, except for a towel wrapped around his waist. He dripped, but didn't care. He wanted to tell her.

"What if you could start over?"

Jane stirred, and then sat up in bed. She was wrapped in a sheet. Her hair was mussed, but she still looked good.

"What are you talking about?" Jane looked over at the clock, checked the time, and then back at Michael.

"What if you could go back to Jesser, start over," Michael said. "You saw how the community loves you. They need you. They want you back."

"But I have no money to start over," Jane said. "A nonprofit needs money. It needs funders. That's why we closed, remember? No grants."

"I remember," Michael said. "But maybe you had the wrong business model."

"It wasn't a business," Jane said, starting to get annoyed. "We were a nonprofit."

"Exactly," Michael said. "Maybe that was your problem."

Michael loaded his flour tortilla with scrambled eggs and chorizo sausage, and then topped it with salsa and sour cream. He walked over to the bar.

Kermit was back at his old job, tending bar at the Sunset and doing random maintenance jobs around the resort. As a drop-out with a doctorate degree in mathematics, Kermit was likely the most educated handyman in Mexico, if not the world.

He handed Michael a freshly squeezed orange juice, and then Michael walked back over to the table.

The table was on the far end of the deck that wrapped around the Sunset's thatch-roofed bar and restaurant. A nice breeze flowed through, and the water provided an easy rhythm as it beat the shore every few seconds.

Jane was already there, waiting for him. She pecked at a plate of fresh fruit and watched two pelicans resting on the tip of a red fishing boat that was anchored just 20 yards from shore.

"Still like the view?" Michael put his plate down on the table, and then sat. "Kermit says he lets the waves roll in and pull his troubles back out to sea."

Jane turned and looked at Michael. She smiled, and then shrugged.

"Not sure how well that's working for me."

"You'll figure it out." Michael took a sip of orange juice, and then started eating his breakfast burrito.

Jane set down her spoon, and then pushed the bowl away.

"So I was thinking about what you said about going back to Jesser. And I guess I don't get it."

"Maybe I don't either." Michael shook his head. "I overstepped. We were having a good time, and then I decided to meddle."

Jane picked up her mug of coffee, blew on it, and then took a drink. She waited a second, and then asserted herself.

"Don't do that. Don't go back into your shell. I'm glad you said it. The initial bath towel presentation could've been better, but it wasn't that bad." She smiled, giving Michael a break.

Jane took another sip of coffee, and then put the cup back on the saucer. Jane leaned in, showing that she was serious.

"I guess what I'm trying to say is that I want to hear more."

"Rambles and all?" Michael asked.

"Rambles and all," Jane said. "I've got nothing but time."

They finished breakfast, kicked off their shoes, and pulled out a pair of kayaks. They pushed them out into the Caribbean. It was a perfect day along the Mayan Riviera. The temperature was warm, but not too hot. Looking out, there were only shades of blue. The calm blue water and the clear blue sky perfectly mirrored each other.

Michael and Jane paddled out, and then followed the shore-line south. After a few minutes, they stopped paddling, leaned back, and just drifted next to one another.

"So you know how Kermit's been talking and talking about general semantics and filters and narrowing the scope of abstraction?"

Jane nodded.

"I think I've heard a little bit too much about that since you two arrived in my life, so yes," Jane said. "I now know about general semantics, although I don't really want to."

"That's what got me thinking – "

"Which frightens me," Jane added.

"I know, me too," Michael said. "But hear me out. We're all caught up in this IRS definition of nonprofit and for-profit. We've accepted the fallacy that an organization has to be one or the other, but when you think about the word 'nonprofit,' what does it really mean?"

"It means I don't get paid."

"No," Michael continued. "It's about mission. And you can be a for-profit with a mission. Your work has value. Your clients have money, maybe not a lot, but they have some. They can pay you a little, maybe not what a typical private practice attorney charges, but they can pay you a little. And you can take some cases on contingency. Instead of doing what you were doing for free, you can take a percentage of the damage award. You can keep some money, pay yourself. Forget the grants. Fund yourself."

"But they're poor," Jane said. "They should keep whatever they get. I shouldn't take a cut."

"But if you're not there." Michael paddled a few times to get himself back in the current. "If you're not in Jesser, who's going to take the cases at all? Who's going to step in and do them for free? You were all they had, and now you're gone."

"But –"

"There isn't anybody there at all," Michael said. "It's a great sentiment to do the work for free, and it would be great if the foundations would pay for it. But they've all frozen you out."

"But charging clients." Jane shook her head. "I've never done that before. I don't even have malpractice insurance."

Michael shrugged his shoulders.

"Do you think your clients really care about that?"

"What about bar association dues and annual license fees?"

"Why do you need to belong to the bar association?" Michael asked. "And your license is still good for a little while."

"It makes me nervous." Jane turned her kayak. She pointed it away from shore and paddled. Michael followed, and then they found some big waves to ride for the rest of the morning.

CHAPTER TWENTY FIVE

The Roja consisted of a boat, a net, a fire, and 15 tables on the beach.

The Roja's chef and owner grew up in Popolnah, about 70 miles northwest of Playa del Carmen. He trained at the Culinary Institute of America, bounced around a few top New York restaurants for 15 years, did a stint at a Rick Bayless' XOCO in Chicago, and then came home to work at the big resorts in Cancun.

Like most of the people in Playa, he had gotten burned out. He had needed a change, and so The Roja was born.

Jane and Michael sat across from one another. A white candle burned inside a small terra cotta pot painted with blue and yellow flowers. They started with the sweet corn soup with clams, and then the server brought out the main course: a whole grouper cooked over the fire stuffed with lobster in guava sauce.

"Looks amazing." Jane watched with wide eyes as the large tin platter was placed on their table.

Michael thanked the waitress, and they began the main course after refilling their glasses of wine.

Jane had been quiet all day. Michael knew she was close to making a decision. He was excited for her, even though it would probably mean she'd be leaving no matter what she decided.

"So what are you thinking?" He asked.

Jane considered the question.

"I'm thinking I don't have much money." She flaked off a piece of the fish with her fork and ate it. Jane closed her eyes and let the flavors rest, and then she took a sip of wine. Jane opened her eyes, came back to the present, and continued.

"The idea of going off on my own is growing on me, but I need a big case with real money. I can do some little stuff to keep the lights on, but I need one case that's going to pay the bills and give me the resources to really make it happen."

"So you're going to do it?"

Jane set down her glass of wine. She leaned in toward Michael.

"I'm only going to do it if you help me."

Until that moment, he hadn't seen it coming. It took him by surprise.

Michael was silent. He shook his head.

"I'm sorry, Jane, that's ..." Michael looked around. He sputtered. "I just don't practice law anymore."

"Michael, I know you were a great lawyer," Jane said. "I did some research."

"You're doing a background check on me? What gives you the —"

Jane cut him off.

"I know it'd be hard. I know what happened in New York. It's on the web, just type in your name."

"There's more to it." Michael wasn't sure why he was so mad, maybe he was just frustrated. Frustrated and trapped, not really free to do whatever he wanted. Tired of having secrets, and yet, having no secrets at all.

He pushed his plate away.

The other people, seated at the tables around them, had stopped eating. They were listening.

Michael lowered his voice, softly.

"I need some space," he said. "I don't want to say something that I'll regret."

"Michael." Jane grabbed his hand before he could leave. "I need you to help me sue Jolly Boy. I want to represent Tommy and his family, but they don't trust me. They trust you."

Michael pulled his hand away and shook his head.

"I should go." Michael stood. "I'll see you later."

Jane stood up, confused.

"What the hell, Michael?" Jane watched as Michael starting walking away. Jane shouted at him. "This was your big idea. You started all this. Now you're taking off?"

Just like I always do, Michael thought, disgusted with himself, but not disgusted enough to stop walking away.

CHAPTER TWENTY SIX

Kermit took the empty bottle away from Michael, and then put a full one on the bar.

"Sounds insane, dude," Kermit said. "It's one thing to do a drop-in for a week or so, but it's another thing to step back into the world of black robes and gavels, like all full-time and such."

"Then why do I want to do it?" Michael picked up a cut lemon wedge, squeezed its juice into his Corona, and then shoved the wedge into the bottle. "It makes no sense. I was there for a few days and the feds were on me. Vatch isn't going to stop until he puts me in prison."

"But it's righteous, yo." Kermit let his dreadlocks dangle. "Even though you give the cool vibe, deep down you're a legal warrior. You can't stop it. You're addicted."

"I'm not addicted," Michael said.

"You're addicted." Kermit laughed. "You love out-foxing those dudes. You love making the feds crazy, and you love winning."

Michael shook his head.

"Sounds like ego."

"Sounds like you don't run from a fight." Kermit nodded, agreeing with himself. "Might be the only thing you don't run from, *mi amigo*." Then he turned, walked into the back kitchen and fetched a basket of chips and guacamole. He put it on the bar next to Michael, pulled up a chair next to him, and then started snacking.

The bar was closed for the night, so there were no other customers to serve. Kermit and Michael were alone.

"You want to help Pace and his momma, too, dontcha?"

Michael thought about it, and then nodded.

"My dad was gone when I was little. It was just me and my mom, and then cancer got her."

"Kinda like little Pace." Kermit grabbed a few chips and ate them. "Like I was sayin', you love to fight for the underdog. You want to do right. Nothing wrong with that."

"Except it's insane, which is what you told me a few seconds ago." Michael looked around and lowered his voice. "And I'd be jeopardizing this place if the feds get me."

"True," Kermit said. "But maybe not. The possibilities are infinite. Maybe this thing would just resolve one way or the other. It wouldn't hang over you, man, like a cloud when you want the Sunny D."

"I think you're the first person to suggest prison might be freedom." Michael took sip of beer while Kermit scooped up some guacamole with a chip and shoved it in his mouth.

"There's two types of freedom, *mi amigo*. The freedom of your body and the freedom of your mind." Kermit thought a little bit more about the wisdom he was imparting. "I'd say the freedom of your mind is the utmost, but you gotta decide."

They sat for awhile, eating and drinking.

"You know what Alfred Korzybski says?" Kermit asked.

"No, but I do know who he is, which causes concern."

Kermit ignored Michael's slight disparagement of the founder of general semantics.

"Korby says we are a time-binding people. It means that every day we learn from our experiences and the experiences of others. No other animal on the planet really does that. No other animal learns from its mistakes quite like we do or transfers knowledge from one generation to the next the way we do."

Kermit shoved the remainder of the chips and dip in his mouth, and then continued.

"The 'you' of today is different than the 'you' of yesterday. We change. We evolve. All of these concepts are not exclusive of one another, *mi amigo*. They can co-exist, like all the different colors in my Froot Loops. We have to adapt to the new you. I can't treat you like the Michael Collins I met when you stumbled into this resort. You're different now. So you need to treat yourself differently, think of yourself differently than you did in the past. All this angst is driven by your own desire to keep yourself within the same construct of the past. You need to live the now, man. Figure out what's right in the present not *would* have been right in the past."

"I actually think I need another drink, right now, in the present." Michael drank half of his beer, took a breath, and then took another long draw from the bottle.

"Get serious, yo." Kermit frowned. "I'm talking straight." Kermit stood up. His voice louder. "Does the Michael Collins of today want to do this or not? It doesn't matter what I think. It doesn't matter what the old Michael Collins would do. The logic and reasoning of the past is not the present. Break the construct of your mind."

Kermit was breathing hard. He was excited. They stared at each other, processing. A moment passed, and then Kermit said, "Dude, I'm really hot. Wanna shed these clothes and go for a moonlight skinny dip?"

CHAPTER TWENTY SEVEN

Elana Estrada lived in the lower level of a faded white build-ing in San Corana.

She and the family moved there after Tommy went to the United States and started sending money home. Even though Tommy wasn't paid anywhere close to minimum wage by Jolly Boy, it was still higher than the three dollars a day he had earned in the fields nearby. The extra money moved the family out of the tin shanties and into the main part of town. San Corana's center was often crowded, but it was safer than the shanties, closer to relatives, and had running water.

Pace opened the door. He was proud of where they lived, and he was proud that, as the oldest boy, he was making a little money at the resort and contributing.

"Tea?" he asked.

Both Jane and Michael accepted. A refusal would have been rude.

Pace nodded and smiled. He pointed to the table where he wanted Jane and Michael to sit, and he busied himself preparing the tea.

Elana came in from the back room. She wore all black, still mourning the loss of Tommy. She sat down at the table, and nodded at Jane and Michael.

Pace brought a pot of hot water from the kitchen, set it down on the table, and then went back and got cups and loose tea leaves.

Pace's younger sisters were playing in the back room. They started to get loud. Pace shouted at them to quiet down while he distributed the cups. Then he sat down next to his mother. Pace was the man of the house now.

They all exchanged pleasantries, and then Jane explained what she wanted to do in Spanish. Elana sat quietly, listening.

Michael wondered what she was thinking.

Elana Estrada had never lived any place else. She had never visited any place else. Her life had always been San Corana, and it consisted mostly of survival. When Jane talked about lawsuits, lawyers, witnesses, depositions, discovery, motions, it confused her. Elana didn't understand what Jane wanted her to do.

Finally, Michael stepped in.

He had agreed to arrange for the meeting. He hadn't promised Jane anything else. But now he was going to go further. Looking around, he knew that Elana wouldn't be able to afford the rent much longer without her husband, Tommy. He wasn't sure she'd even be able to afford food.

Michael thought about all the money in his bank account. He thought about all the food at the resort, enough to feed Elana and her family for months. What was he afraid of? Whatever was going to happen would happen, regardless. He needed to help whoever he could help.

"I'm going to hire Pace, full-time," Michael said. "I need an assistant manager at the resort. He's getting old enough and Kermit needs help cleaning and maintaining the place."

Elana didn't smile. She was reserved, but Michael saw relief wash across her face. Pace, on the other hand, nearly bounced out of his seat.

"But we also need justice for Tommy," Michael said. Elana understood justice. "You need to trust us." Michael looked at Jane. "Let Jane help you, and I'll help the both of you. Okay?"

CHAPTER TWENTY EIGHT

It took 13 months. Michael had known from the start that it would take that long. It wasn't like the movies or on television. There, the gorgeous actor filed the lawsuit and the next day they're in court, picking a jury and trying the case. In real life, it was a slog.

Along with their lawsuit against Jolly Boy, there were hundreds of thousands of other lawsuits. The underlying facts of these lawsuits related to any event in a typical life that had gone horribly wrong. There was no way for the system to handle that many trials, and so barriers had been erected. The Court's Rules of Civil Procedure had been designed to slow down litigation. Motions had to be filed. Parties were required to submit to mediation "in good faith." Information and documents must slowly be extracted from each party related to their theories of the case, witnesses, and proof.

It was all part of the dance. Michael knew it was two steps forward, one step back, and one to the side.

Michael and Jane weren't zealots. They'd settle if the price was right, but the price had never been anywhere close to being right.

"It's their best offer." Judge M. Vincent Delaney looked up at Michael and Jane with sharp crystal blue eyes. Judge Delaney didn't mind presiding over a trial. In fact, he enjoyed it, although he enjoyed leaving early and hitting the golf course a lot more.

Judge Delaney was in his late sixties with a shock of white hair. At one time, he had been an Olympic swimmer. He was tall and lean, still in fantastic shape. He had seen it all, and he knew how and when to exert pressure. In short, Judge Delaney was good at his job.

He pushed the piece of paper across his large oak desk.

"I know it isn't what you want," the judge said. "But settlements are never what either party wants. defendants want to leave without paying one penny and the plaintiffs want to leave with all the king's gold."

Jane lifted the piece of paper off of the desk. She looked at Michael. He nodded, assuring her, and then Jane turned it over.

The number and basic terms were written in black Sharpie ink: $15,000 plus costs and confidentiality.

"That's an insult," Michael said. "Those attorneys in the other room probably get paid $600 an hour. Win or lose, a trial like this is going to cost them a massive amount in legal fees."

Michael wasn't posturing. It was the truth. He knew the life of the big firm lawyer.

Michael vented some more, and Judge Delaney listened. The judge didn't betray a thought. He merely nodded his head, waiting for Michael to burn himself out.

Eventually Michael did. Judge Delaney waited another moment to be sure, and then he turned to Jane. He leaned back in his high-back leather chair.

"Thoughts?"

Jane shook her head.

"Michael's right." She closed her eyes. "It is an insult. I thought that they'd give us a little respect, but –" Jane tried to keep herself calm. She had put everything on the line when she came back to Jesser. Her student loans were in default. Her credit cards were maxed out. She thought of all the things that she needed to really get her law firm going, not just scraping by.

If accepted, the settlement offer would only allow her to pay her debts. The firm could limp along ... maybe. But, if they turned it down and lost the case, the firm would have to close. She'd also be in debt, and the debt would follow her.

Jane looked down at the piece of paper again, thinking.

She shook her head, pushing the piece of paper back across the desk toward Judge Delaney.

"I don't think we can accept this."

Judge Delaney nodded. He was smart. He knew what was at stake, and you could see the wheels turn in his brain. He was figuring out how to resolve this case. He was also letting the silence work the room.

Judge Delaney looked at Michael and Jane, and then he put both hands down on his desk, positioning himself for a final move. His eyes narrowed.

"That's your answer – no."

The judge nodded his head, and then he hit Jane and Michael with the reality of trial. It was a machine gun of dates, times, and obligations.

"So you both want a trial. We'll have a trial. I can do that, and that's your right," he said. "Tomorrow, you need to be here at 8:00 a.m. Don't be late. I will hear any final pre-trial motions, rule on them, and then we'll bring the jury pool up at 10:00 am. You will have no more than two hours for jury selection. I won't allow this to drag on. We'll take 30 minutes for lunch. Opening arguments will begin, and you'll call your first witness by the time we adjourn for the day. Then, we'll get up and do it again and again, every day, until it's done."

Judge Delaney took a breath. He held Jane in his sight, wait-ing for her to crack. He allowed the silence to work, again. He was comfortable in the silence. In a world in which people were constantly talking, texting, or tweeting, Judge Delaney projected an authority and calm above all of that.

He's a damn good judge, Michael thought. There were over 120 judges in the Eleventh Judicial District serving Miami-Dade County. They could have drawn somebody far worse.

Judge Delaney pushed himself away from his desk, and then he stood. He walked over to his window. It was 15 floors above the sea of people and cars stuttering their way down First Ave-nue. The Miami Art Museum was just beyond the pulsing traffic.

"How much do you have invested in this case?" Judge Delaney asked the question, but he wasn't expecting an an-swer. "Looks like you've done 10 depositions. I'd guess you've also had," he thought about it, rubbing his chin, but not turning away from the view, "about five discovery motions, summary judgment motions, and mediation. Then there's the future costs of bringing in those Mexican witnesses."

Judge Delaney turned, slowly, and walked back to his chair and sat down.

"Here's a chance to submit a bill to me for all those costs, which I will approve and they will pay for."

He smiled and leaned forward. Judge Delaney was about to share a secret.

"I think your organization did a lot of good, and I think your new law firm will do a lot of good. It'd be nice to get off to a strong start. You could get your debt paid, and then get $15,000 for Mr. Estrada's widow and kids. Fifteen thousand dollars is a big deal to them. That kind of money would go pretty far down there."

He paused, and then concluded with the biggest reason why they should settle.

"And I don't need to tell you that you've got a major causation issue and a major damages issue. I let it slide with the motion to dismiss, but this is a trial. The case is wrongful death. It's your burden to prove Jolly Boy knew and killed your client. And even if you do prove it, you've got a hell of a job convincing a jury that your client's life was worth much more than $15,000. He was an illegal immigrant. Don't get me wrong. *I* personally think his life is worth a million dollars, but that's just what I think. What matters to a jury is what you can prove, and you can't prove much more than $15,000. I had a case where a mentally disabled kid drowned in a hotel pool last year. The jury gave these parents $50,000. Can you believe it? Fifty thousand is all that the life of a child is worth. That's what you're up against, here."

Judge Delaney nodded his head.

"Think about it. Talk to your client. Then tell me what you want to do."

Elana Estrada sat with Pace in a small conference room.

On every floor of the courthouse there were two courtrooms, two chambers for the judges and their clerks, and, at the end of hall, there was also a small reception area with bathrooms and three small attorney-client conference rooms.

When Michael and Jane opened the door, both Elana and Pace sat up. Their eyes got a little wider. Their expressions hopeful that their attorneys had good news.

Michael and Jane sat down at the table across from them.

"Well," Michael said, "we have another offer, but it's not what we had hoped."

Elana didn't say anything, and then she looked to Jane for a translation. She understood some English, but not a lot.

Jane told her what happened, and her eyes dropped to the table. Her round heavy shoulders also dropped a few inches.

"That's it?" Elana shook her head. "No more?"

"Probably not," Michael said. "Once trial starts, there usually aren't any more offers." Michael tried to be positive, but his eyes betrayed him. Elana knew that there wasn't going to be an easy way out. She and her children were going to have to continue to struggle.

Michael had been working closely with Elana and the other witnesses for the past year from Hut No. 7 at the Sunset. He had talked with Jane over the phone and they corresponded a few times a day by e-mail, while she continued to investigate in Jesser and make court appearances.

Every few months Michael had flown to Florida to meet with Jane and help with the latest roadblock that the Jolly Boy attorneys had thrown in their way. Each trip was the same: work, argue about strategy, go to a nice Miami restaurant, and then have sex if they weren't too tired, which they usually were.

It wasn't a traditional relationship, but it wasn't bad, either.

"We have risks," Michael continued, pausing every few words to allow them to be relayed in Spanish by Jane to Elana.

"At first they offered us nothing, now they've offered us this money." Michael put his hand on Elana's hand. He looked her in the eye, because there would be no turning back. This was the final decision. "It's less than what we wanted, but it's something. If we lose, we get nothing so you need to consider it."

Elana looked at Pace, and then back to Michael.

"We going to win?"

She asked him like a terminal patient asking her doctor if there was a miracle cure.

Michael squeezed her hand, looked her in the eye, and then lied.

"Damn right we're going to win."

"What the hell was that?" Jane asked as the elevator doors opened into the main lobby on the ground floor. "You promised a client we were going to win?"

"Unorthodox," Michael said. "But what else am I going to say? She wanted me to say it."

"They always want you to say it, but you never do."

"You never do because of a malpractice claim," Michael said. "You really think she's going to sue us if we lose? We need her to be confident."

"If we lose? *If* we lose?" Jane pushed open the doors to the courthouse. She was starting to panic as they walked out of the court house's air conditioning. It was like opening an oven door and stepping inside. "You meant to say *when* we lose."

"We just have to make sure to pick the right jury." Michael reached into his suit pocket and removed a pair of sunglasses. He slipped them on. Initially, it had been odd wearing a suit, again, donning the lawyer costume. By the end of the day, however, it felt normal. It was easy to fall back into the old habits. He was an attorney again. An attorney being watched by the FBI for stealing over half a billion dollars, but still an attorney.

"We can do this," Michael said. "Just pick a good jury. That's all we have to do."

"The judge was dead-on. We don't have causation. We need causation. We need specific proof that Jolly Boy knew what was going on. All we have is a bunch of testimony about a bad subcontractor and rumors. We need to connect everything to Jolly

Boy. Jolly Boy is the deep pocket." Jane's face was tense. "What have you got on that?"

"Same as I had yesterday and the day before that –"

"And that would be, specifically, jack shit," Jane said.

"No, that's not true." Michael pressed a button on his key chain. The rental SUV's lights flashed twice and the doors unlocked. "I have stuff, but it just hasn't come together yet. What we really need is for your boyfriend to come through for us and work his magic."

"My boyfriend?" Jane shook her head. "You're purportedly my boyfriend, and you don't have any magic." Jane opened the door.

"I prefer the term, 'lover,'" Michael said. "When I say boyfriend you know who I'm talking about. Mr. Justin 'Justice' Kent. My lover magic got us through the summary judgment phase. That was pretty good. Now we need Kent."

Jane put one foot into the rental, but paused. She looked at Michael.

"We were lucky," Jane said. "We were very lucky at summary judgment. We should have been dismissed."

"But we weren't." Michael smiled. "Because Judge Delaney likes your spunk. Now we need Kent. It's the only way."

Jane wiped the sweat off her forehead and blew back the bangs that had fallen in her face.

"Fine," she said. "I will call Justin again, but he isn't exactly pumped to help me out."

"He still loves you," Michael said. "He'll do it."

"We can't bank on it."

"I can," Michael said.

CHAPTER TWENTY NINE

Maus drove past the Law Offices of Jane Nance, looking. She was supposedly in Miami for a final pre-trial settlement conference with the judge, but Maus wanted to make sure she was gone. He didn't trust anybody.

Since the lights were off, Maus confirmed that his information was correct. He looked down at the sheet of paper with the list of names. Both parties to the lawsuit were required to file a witness list with the court. Dylan McNaughten had given him a copy of the list and told him what to do. Maus didn't have a choice, but at least he got more money this time.

He took Main Street to Fourth, and then cut over to the highway. Within minutes, he was driving a gravel road cutting through the middle of Jolly Boy's fields.

Maus drove for another 15 minutes until he found Field No. 130. He pulled his police cruiser to the side of the road, and got out. A few minutes later the field supervisor was there.

"You got 'em?"

"*Si.*" The supervisor nodded his head. "They're at the picnic table. I told them they could take an afternoon break."

"Good." Maus put his big hand on the small supervisor's shoulder. "Take me."

###

The supervisor led Maus to a picnic table. Six Mexican migrant workers, three on each side, sat talking, drinking water, and eating a little bread.

One of them turned when they saw Maus and the supervisor enter the small clearing. The others sensed his tension, and the conversation stopped. They all turned to look.

Maus raised his hand in the air.

"We have some information that there are individuals working illegally here in Collier County," Maus said, lying. "I need to see some papers. Please stand in line, and then I'll take a look. If everything is in order, you can go about your business. If something's not right, I'll have to take you in and hand you over to the federal authorities."

Technically, a local police officer had no authority to do anything on behalf of the federal immigration services. But that didn't matter much to the supervisor and the migrant workers. Maus had a badge. That was all that had mattered, and Maus knew that they would follow his instructions.

The field supervisor translated the instructions, and the six Mexicans stood in a line. Each removed dirty papers and faded cards from their back pockets. Some of the papers looked more authentic than others, but all of the documents were fraudulent.

Maus took each in his hand, one by one. He made a good show of examining the papers. He squinted his eyes. He made guttural noises, as if the job personally pained him. He held the documents up high in the sunlight as if he were searching for a watermark.

Then, much to the surprise of the workers, one by one he handed the documents back.

"These look good. You can go back to work." Then to the next one. "This is fine." Then to the next one. "I'm not sure about this card, but I'll let it slide."

He did the same routine for all of the workers who had been brought to the picnic table, except the last one.

"Mr. Roberto Estrada." Maus shook his head. "I'm afraid these papers don't look quite right." Maus took his handcuffs off of his belt, and then cuffed Roberto Estrada's hands behind his back. "Everybody else is free to go, but I'm afraid Mr. Estrada needs to be taken in. Sorry about that."

Maus nodded toward the supervisor, and then started to lead Roberto Estrada back through the fields to his car. Roberto Estrada was in front. Maus behind him.

They walked for about 50 yards, and then Maus leaned forward and whispered in Roberto's ear.

"Now I'm afraid you're going to end up like your cousin."

Roberto Estrada lowered his head.

"I know."

Maus waited until the sun started to set. He'd prefer working in the dark, but he needed some light so that he could see.

Maus drove for 20 minutes. He turned off of one gravel road, and then onto another.

He drove another hundred yards, and then he slowed. Maus looked at his mother's house up on the hill. It was the house where he had grown up. Most of the lights were off, but the lower windows flashed with blues and greens from the television.

Maus checked his watch. Wheel of Fortune.

Then he looked at Roberto Estrada in the back seat. His passenger was quiet now. The fight was kicked out of him.

Roberto Estrada's forehead was bruised. His nose was broken. Red streaked from his upper lip, across his mouth, and down his chin. The bleeding had stopped for the moment and the blood was dry.

With his hands cuffed behind his back, Roberto Estrada had no way of stopping the blood or wiping it away. Probably not a good idea, breaking his nose like that, thought Maus. It was fun, but it was also a mess. *Always making messes*, Maus thought. *Gotta stop that.*

Maus pulled his police cruiser to the side of the road near a patch of Cypress trees. It was his spot.

He got out, popped the trunk, and got out a shovel. Then he went around to the back passenger side door of his cruiser. Maus opened the door and ordered Roberto Estrada out.

At first Roberto Estrada didn't move. He sat in a daze. Maus ordered him out, again.

This time Maus hit him in the nose. Roberto Estrada screamed in pain, and new streams of blood began to run.

"Get out now." Maus grabbed Roberto Estrada by the shirt and pulled. Estrada wasn't physically able to fight anymore. He was a rag doll.

When Maus got him to the edge of the back seat, Roberto Estrada fell head first onto the ground. Maus looked at some of the blood that had gotten on the back seat of his cruiser. He cursed, and then flipped Roberto Estrada onto his back with the toe of his boot. Estrada's eyes were clouded, but he was still alive.

Maus pulled him to his feet, and they started to walk. Roberto Estrada's knees buckled a few times, but Maus kept him moving toward a patch of trees.

"Since you're such a good worker," Maus looked at the shovel and tightened his grip. "I got one last job for you."

###

Miggy heard the car. There weren't that many cars in this part of Collier County, and the other spirits had told him that Maus would be bringing more. He hadn't wanted to believe it, but the spirits were always right.

Miggy crawled out of a small tent to get a better view.

The tent was actually a plastic tarp that he had fastened to one end of a picnic table with the other end staked to the ground. This was where Miggy lived when he didn't have business in town. It was a break area for the migrant field workers. Far better than the shelters in Miami, thought Miggy. Safer. He could sleep in the break area, and then clear out early in the morning before anyone arrived. If he timed it right, some of the van drivers would even take him back into town after dropping off the workers.

The break area one of the dozens that Jane Nance and Community Immigrant Legal Services, Inc., had fought for 10 years ago. They had been her first project when she got to Jesser.

Jane had also gotten the growers to create shaded spaces for workers to eat. Each space also had a place to go to the bathroom, a Porta-Potty.

Miggy used his crutch to pull himself to his feet. He grabbed his green knapsack, slung it over his shoulder, and then worked his way through the fields toward the grove. When he was about a hundred yards away, he saw the silhouette of two men. The big man was Maus. Miggy didn't know the other man. It looked like he was hurt, but he was also the one who was digging.

The spirits swirled around the cypress patch. They darted around the sky in bright yellow streaks, cutting toward Miggy and then back, again.

They howled in Miggy's ear, screaming at him to act, but Miggy stayed hidden. He waved them away, watching as he had done before.

After 10 minutes, the digging stopped. Miggy saw Maus take the shovel away and toss it to the side. Then he kicked the other man's legs, and he fell to his knees. There was shouting, but Miggy was too far away to hear.

Then there was a gun shot. It was a single pop that broke the quiet of the fields for a moment.

Miggy watched the man on his knees fall into the ground, and then the spirits went wild.

CHAPTER THIRTY

Food helped. Food always helped. Michael ordered two pizzas from Speedy's. One pepperoni and one Italian sausage, mushroom, and green pepper. The pizzas were loaded with cheese and greasy as hell.

Michael, Jane, and Kermit sat around the folding tables in the center of the room and ate in silence.

When Jane had returned from the Sunset Resort & Hostel, she had simply rented her old office. The board had been removed and the broken front window had been replaced. The painted sign out front for Community Legal Services, Inc., had also been replaced. It now read, The Law Offices of Jane Nance, Esq. Other than those two things, nothing else had changed.

While the case against Jolly Boy worked its way through the Miami-Dade County court system, Jane had quickly learned how to do personal injury lawsuits involving everything from car accidents to food poisoning. She had also learned how to do wills and adoptions, and had continued her immigration work. This other work generated only enough fees to keep the lights on and prevent her from being homeless.

The wrongful death lawsuit against Jolly Boy was her focus. It was the big case with a big payout that would theoretically stabilize the law firm and her life. That was the plan, anyway.

Over the past year, nearly every spare moment was spent building the Tommy Estrada case and responding to motions and requests for documents. Jolly Boy had an army of attorneys working the file hard. Harrison Grant and his minions at Greene and Thomas, LLP, had the dream job: a rich client with a lot to lose. It was the perfect opportunity for them to rack up gigantic legal bills, which would be promptly paid without complaint.

The slices of pizza disappeared one after another, and nobody talked until the pizza was about half gone. Everybody knew that they'd be working late. There'd be plenty of time to talk after dinner.

When Jane finished eating, she looked up, took a sip of soda, and set the bottle down on the table.

"Sorry I snapped at you," she said to Michael.

"Just a little stress." Michael winked at her. "I have a thick skin." He bit into his last slice of pepperoni. "I'll get over it."

Kermit smiled, looking back and forth between them. "You two make the cutest little couple."

It was 2:00 am when they finally arrived back at Jane's apartment. Michael undressed on the way to the bedroom, leaving a trail of clothes behind him.

He collapsed onto the bed. His head hit hard. The sheets and pillow were cool, and that coolness surrounded him.

Michael laid there with his eyes closed, listening to the faint sounds of Jane brushing her teeth and washing her face. He thought about whether he should get up and join her, but then thought better of it. Personal hygiene would come in the morning. He was too tired to move.

Michael heard the click of the bathroom light as Jane turned it off, and then she crawled into bed wearing only underwear and an oversized T-shirt.

Jane pecked Michael on the cheek.

"Good night."

Michael turned. He put his arm around her and kissed Jane's shoulder. Then he rolled back.

They laid still in the darkness for a minute, unmoving. Then Jane turned.

"Thank you," she said. "For your help. I couldn't have made it this far without you. I wouldn't be here, if you hadn't agreed to come back."

Michael turned, opening his eyes. He saw Jane laying next to him. She was mostly shadow.

"Don't thank me until it's over," Michael smiled. "You may not be so happy when it's done."

"I'll be happy, win or lose," Jane said.

"I don't believe you." Michael laughed. "You want to win just as much as me."

Jane smiled.

"That's true." She nodded. "I confess."

Michael closed his eyes. He turned away from her.

It was quiet, again, but then Jane put her hand on his head, playing with his hair.

"Hey Michael?" she asked, soft.

"What is it?"

"Where'd you get all your money?" she asked. "You said your mom died when you were in high school and you worked your way through with odd jobs and scholarships, so how are you paying for all these flights to Florida and for these witnesses to come up here?"

Michael didn't answer. He thought about the electronic trail of credit card transactions and withdrawals that he was leaving for Agent Vatch and an unknown number of additional federal agents. He also thought about Andie and how the truth had already cost him a woman that he had loved. *The truth doesn't always set you free*, he thought. T*he Enlightenment is dead.*

Michael rolled over and kissed Jane on her cheek.

"It's really late, and there's not much to tell." Michael looked at Jane. He told her that he'd talk to her about it some other time, but he didn't mean it. Some things were better left alone.

The sleep came on fast. The worries fell away, but not entirely. They swirled just below the surface like a riptide wanting to pull him back into the ocean, wanting to drag him below the water so that he couldn't breathe.

Michael hung there – weightless and twirling in the water. Problems pushed him further underwater. There was the money trail, the chase, his relationship with Jane; the worries were both present and distant at the same time. Then he was back in the rectory with Father Stiles.

He was in high school, again, and Father Stiles was in the rectory's study surrounded by books. Father Stiles worked on his sermon, while Michael was on the couch studying for his history exam.

Father Stiles looked up from his papers.

"It's late, Michael, mind locking up?"

Michael nodded. He set his book down on the floor next to the couch, and went out the door to the stairwell. He walked down the winding stone steps, lit only by candles.

In the dream, the steps were narrower and steeper than in reality. The steps were uneven, and with each one, Michael's foot turned slightly, keeping him off balance. He'd take a step, stumble, catch himself before he fell, and then repeat.

Michael wound down. His breathing heavy, echoing in his head. His heartbeat thumping, a kick-drum pushing him lower toward the door.

He made it.

Michael saw the old, solid door in front of him. Five thick, wide pieces of oak strapped together with a band of hand-forged iron.

He felt the pressure growing, and his pulse quickened. Every second mattered. Urgent, he reached for the lock. He turned it, and the click was immediately followed by an explosion of sound on the other side of the door. The knob shook. Scratching and shouting came from the other side of the door, screaming. Someone was trying to get in.

Scared, Michael thought of the other door on the other side of the church, still unlocked and open.

He ran down the hallway to the back door. The cobblestones, like the stairs, were uneven and slick. Michael quickened his pace, but, as soon as he did, his foot slipped out from under him. He crashed to the floor.

He shook it off.

He stood, got his balance, and then he started to run again. But, as soon as he made it to a full stride, his foot slipped out from under him again.

Michael fell to the ground.

A third time and a fourth time, the run and the fall repeated. His hands and knees bruised. Stone cut them open.

His heart continued to race. His hands were wet. He wiped them on his shirt. Michael looked down and saw that the wet stones were not damp with water. His hands were stained red. Streaks of blood covered his shirt where he had wiped them.

Michael got up, and ran, slower now, trying not to lose his balance. A few more yards to go.

He made it to the back door of the church.

Michael reached into his pocket to find the key. He fumbled them and the ring of keys fell to the ground. He picked them up. He found the right key.

Michael got it in the keyhole and turned, but he only made it halfway.

The door burst open.

Before he could react, a large body was on top of him. A dark blur pressed down on him. The air in Michael's lungs pushed out. He tried to take in more. He tried to breathe ... recover, but he couldn't get it back.

The air was gone.

His body shook.

Weight pressed down even harder on top of him, and the form put its hands around his neck. It squeezed. Two sharp thumb nails, claws, dug into his windpipe.

Michael bucked his body, trying to throw the faceless form off of him, but the weight only got heavier until his fight was almost gone.

Try again, he thought. *Try again.*

He thrust his hips as hard as he could into the air, attempting to throw off the thing.

When he arched back, the floor opened up. Michael fell. He drifted back into a hole. *This is it*, he thought. The bottom of the pit came as the hole narrowed. It was 15 feet away, then 10, then five, and then ... Michael woke up.

He was covered in sweat.

Morning sunlight came through the window in Jane's apartment. He smelled coffee brewing in the kitchen. He looked at where Jane had been sleeping. She was gone, but he heard the shower running. It was morning.

Time for the trial.

CHAPTER THIRTY ONE

The courtroom's back door opened at 8:00 a.m., as promised. The bailiff instructed everyone to rise, and Judge Delaney strode into the courtroom in his black robe. As he stepped up to the bench and walked to his large chair, Judge Delaney scanned the room with his ice-blue eyes, smiled, and shrugged. He waved the courtroom down with a practiced expression of humbleness.

"Please, you may all be seated, and thank you all for being here on time."

Judge Delaney set a large white binder down on the bench, and then he sat down.

"We've got a lot to do and we're going to do it." Judge Delaney glanced up at the ornate bronze clock in the back of the courtroom. Then he scanned the room, noting each of the faces.

When Judge Delaney's eyes met Elana Estrada, Michael felt his client tense. Still looking at Elana, Judge Delaney said, "We have an offer from the defendant. I assume that offer is still valid."

Harrison Grant stood; Brian McNaughten remained seated and watched his highly paid attorney work.

"Yes, Your Honor." Harrison Grant looked at Michael and Jane with pity. He shook his head.

Harrison Grant was in his prime. In a big firm world where lawyers rarely went to trial, that was now almost the only thing that Harrison Grant did. He traveled around the country doing one trial after another for whatever client was willing to pay him the most.

"But I should note, Your Honor, that my client will withdraw that offer as soon as we begin jury selection. We have to make an example of these people and take a stand. My client can't simply throw money at every nuisance lawsuit that is filed –"

Judge Delaney raised his hand, silencing the great Harrison Grant with a simple gesture.

"Thank you Mr. Grant." Judge Delaney turned toward Michael, Jane and their client. He smiled. His eyes twinkled. "And now you, Ms. Nance. Any thoughts related to the offer?"

Jane stood. She fiddled with her pen. Her voice was a little shaky.

"My client still rejects the offer."

"You're sure, Ms. Nance?" he asked."Yes, Your Honor," Jane nodded.

The twinkle went out of Judge Delaney's eyes just a bit, but soon returned. It was as if he remembered how much fun he was going to have at a trial.

Judge Delaney clasped his hands together

"Notify the jury office that they can bring up the pool, he said to his law clerk" Then he addressed the attorneys, "And in the meantime, here are some things to remember. Always stand when addressing me. Never approach a witness without asking permission. Never talk over me. Never surprise me. And never lose control of yourself or your client. If you do, you will regret it. If you violate these rules, I will embarrass you in front of the jury. That is a promise." Judge Delaney paused, a smile, then, slowly he emphasized each individual word. "And none of us want to be embarrassed, right?"

Six.

Six was the magic number. The jury would be comprised of six people. These six would hold the future of Elana Estrada and her family in their hands as well as the future of Jane's law firm.

The pool of potential jurors were led into the courtroom. Everyone stood for them and watched.

Of course, Michael and Jane tried to play it cool, but the reality had set in. They were about to accuse one of the area's largest employers of killing an immigrant, and then they were going to ask that the jury give the family an astronomical amount of money in return. Part of the money was to compensate Elana Estrada for her loss, but most of the money was to punish Jolly Boy.

It was called "punitive damages," and it was only available if Michael and Jane proved Jolly Boy acted in reckless disregard of the safety and health of others. Since Michael and Jane couldn't even prove that Jolly Boy had acted at all, any damages, at this point, were a long shot. Punitive damages were a fantasy.

The potential jurors sat down on the benches in the back of the courtroom. When they were seated, Judge Delaney directed the attorneys to sit.

"Let's get started." Judge Delaney smiled. He took in the mass of people that had just come through the door. They were young and old. Some wore T-shirts and others wore business suits. Nearly all of them carried big bags filled with paperback novels, magazines, notepads, and anything else that would fill time while waiting to be summoned up from the big jury room in the courthouse basement.

Now they had arrived.

"Good morning." Judge Delaney's charisma was turned to high. His deep voice filled the room. He exuded energy, as if to compensate for the sad mass of humanity that had just landed in front of him.

"Many of you have your own ideas of what jury service is or is not. My guess is that most of you were not happy about being here, disrupting your lives and inconveniencing your family and co-workers."

Judge Delaney waited until he received a few head nods in agreement. He wanted everyone to acknowledge that he understood the juror's plight. But, he also made it clear that he was in control. This was his show.

"I brought you up here this morning related to a civil case. Civil cases are different than criminal cases. Criminal cases are brought by prosecutors on behalf of the State of Florida and the defendants are charged with crimes that may ultimately cost them their liberty. In short, they could go to jail."

Judge Delaney paused again, waiting for a head nod or two.

"This is a civil case. Civil cases are brought by one person against another person. Liberty and imprisonment are not at issue. Civil cases are about compensation for alleged wrongs. For example, you get hit by a car and have medical bills due to the car accident. Therefore, you sue the driver of the car that hit you and seek payment for those medical bills. That's a civil case. And, that is what we have here. This is not a car accident case, but it is a civil case brought by one person against another person. It is a wrongful death lawsuit brought by the family of Thomas Estrada against Jolly Boy Farms."

Judge Delaney took a sip of water, and then set the glass back down on the bench.

"Our Constitution gives every party in a civil case the right to have a jury decide whether they are at fault and must pay. Those are big questions – important questions – and that is why you are all here. Our judicial system needs a jury to fulfill this constitutional mandate. We need you to be fair. We need you be willing to give your time and we need you to be just, acting without passion or prejudice."

Judge Delaney gave weight to each word. Not one of the people in the room would think it was an act or a show. It was authentic. In a world of phonies, Judge Delaney believed in what he was saying. They respected that.

"Will you help me?" Judge Delaney asked. "Let me hear whether or not you will do this, okay? I ask: Will you play this important part in our system of government?"

Every one of the jurors said yes. Some louder than others, but they all said yes.

It was amazing.

In just over two minutes, Judge Delaney took a sad, tired, and frustrated jury pool and transformed them into an army of patriots that would do whatever he asked of them.

Delaney was a damn good judge, Michael thought.

The selection process took the rest of the morning. Judge Delaney took the lead, asking jurors about general concepts of the law and their background. Then each of the attorneys had an opportunity. Finally, the pool was whittled down to 14.

They needed six jurors and two alternates.

Each side had the opportunity to strike some of the remaining 14, three each.

Judge Delaney excused the remaining jurors for lunch to give the attorneys privacy during their final selection.

The jurors filed out of the courtroom. Delaney's law clerk led them to a smaller jury room on the same floor. This jury room had a window and bottled water. The jurors were moving up in the world."Mind if we take the courtroom?" Harrison Grant asked Michael and Jane, gesturing back to a thin woman in a dark suit and black glasses and two young men behind her. She was a jury consultant from Los Angeles. Michael couldn't remember her name, but he recognized her from the glossy solicitations she'd sent out when he had worked at Wabash, Kramer and Moore."As you can see, we have quite a few people working on this," Harrison continued

"That's fine." Michael packed up his things. "But a consultant isn't going to save you on this." It was a small attempt at bravado, but Harrison Grant shrugged it off. He gave no response as Michael, Jane, and Elana Estrada retreated to the small conference room across the hall.

Kermit and Pace were waiting in the hallway, and followed them into the room.

"Don't like the teacher, man. She looks like she's been oppressed her whole life. She couldn't give a rat's ass about some Mexicano getting the shaft."

Elana looked at Kermit, and then back at Michael and Jane. She didn't understand all of what Kermit had said, but she was obviously concerned that they were going to pick a jury based on his advice.

Michael put his hand on Elana's shoulder.

"Let's just sit down and do this rationally, okay? Go through them one at a time."

He smiled at Elana.

"It's going to be fine," Michael said. "We'll get a good jury."

Lunch was nonexistent. The hour and a half felt like a five-minute bathroom break, and they were now back in the courtroom.

Even though it had already been planned, Jane was having second thoughts about doing the opening argument. Her confidence was low. During the break, they had debated again about who should do it.

Michael had more experience, but in the end, Michael had convinced her. It was Jane's case. It was her career. She'd do the opening argument.

Michael looked at her, and then he looked at the jurors. The original pool had filled nearly the entire courtroom just that morning. Now there were only eight sitting in the box, six jurors and two alternates. Michael always felt sorry for the alternates. They had no idea about their status – they rarely did.

About 20 years ago, there had been some studies that found that alternate jurors who knew that they were alternates didn't listen as well as the other jurors. The alternates in the study figured that the likelihood of them actually deliberating was small, so there wasn't any reason for them to invest themselves in the case. As a result, judges and attorneys decided it was best to keep the alternates in the dark. The alternate juror's surprise when he or she was excused at the end of the trial and their disappointment was now simply an unfortunate by-product of the law factory.

Michael put on a friendly face and made eye contact with each of the jurors. When he got to the end of the row, he saw the old, white engineer from the suburbs. Now he was Juror No. 5. He had snuck through. It was a tough decision. Maybe it was a mistake not to strike him, but nobody would ever really know.

With the parties and jurors settled, Judge Delaney arranged the papers in front of him. He called the case on the record, and then nodded at Jane. It was a prompt for her to proceed. As the plaintiffs, Jane was required to go first.

She was a little wobbly as she stood, but she found her confidence as she approached the podium. Jane set her notes on the stand and then took a step to the side. The jurors sat up. The men, in particular, were happy for the excuse to stare at Jane.

"Jolly Boy broke the rules." Jane gave each word a sense of importance, and when she completed this sentence, she waited. That was the theme of their case. It sounded simple, too simple, but simplicity won cases.

Lawyers always overestimated the capacity of a juror to take in the massive amount of information and facts that they had assembled. Lawyers also overestimated how interesting they were. Jurors got bored. Simplicity wins.

"My client, Tommy Estrada, is dead because the defendants broke the rules. Tommy Estrada worked in the fields that Jolly Boy owns. He picked tomatoes and anything else that Jolly Boy wanted him to pick. But in the end, he died because Jolly Boy didn't follow the rules."

"That is the testimony that you will hear," Jane continued. "You will hear about the rules, and you will hear about how Jolly Boy broke them over and over again. The first rule is that you give your workers a break. Every worker, under the law, is entitled to a break in the morning, a break for lunch, and a break in the afternoon."

Jane paused. Her tone was casual, but serious.

"The defendant broke that rule."

Jane stepped back to the podium. She glanced down at her notes, a rehearsed movement to show that she was moving on-to to the next point.

"The second rule is that you wait 24 hours after spraying the fields with deadly chemicals before sending your workers back into them. The defendant broke that rule, too. As a result, Tommy Estrada got cancer."

Jane took a sip of water, and then continued.

"The rules also say that you can't fire an employee simply because they are injured or sick, but the defendant did that all the time. They did that to Tommy."

Jane surveyed the jurors sitting in front of her, making eye contact with each one, and then holding eye contact with the old engineer, Juror No. 5.

"And then finally, you can't kill somebody. That's the biggest rule of all."

The courtroom was silent. Jane didn't sound shrill or like some activist chained to a tree. She sounded cool, like a professional.

"That's our case." Jane nodded, and then she pointed and turned toward the defendant's table. Harrison Grant stared at her, a practiced look of bemusement and pity. The Jolly Boy CEO, Brian McNaughten, sat next to his attorney. His head was down, scribbling notes in a notebook.

"This defendant broke the rules," Jane concluded. "My client died, leaving a wife and children to fend for themselves. And that's why we're here. I'm asking you to hold defendant Jolly Boy accountable for breaking the rules. Thank you."

Jane waited a moment, and then collected her things from the podium. She walked back to the plaintiff's table and sat down. Michael scribbled a note on his legal pad and slid it over to her: NICE JOB!

He meant it, too. Jane had set up the case beautifully. She laid out their theme. She previewed their testimony, but didn't allow it to get bogged down in details. Unfortunately, Harrison Grant had a response.

Jolly Boy's attorney stood and walked over to the podium, but he didn't give the jury a smile. Instead, he sighed. It wasn't an obnoxious sigh, nor did it appear fake. It was a simple, audible breath that would never appear in any court transcript, but the jurors certainly saw it and heard it. And in that brief moment, Harrison Grant landed his first punch.

Michael felt Jane tense next to him. She felt the punch, too, and it landed hard.

Harrison Grant had presence. His suit and tie, his haircut, his mannerisms, his voice – they all worked together to establish credibility. Although Jane Nance was pretty to look at, Harrison Grant was the one attorney in the room that any juror would hire, if given the choice. He had authority, and he leveraged that authority.

"I hope you listened carefully to what the Plaintiff just said, because at the end of this trial, you're going to have to hold her to her promises. She promised to offer proof that Jolly Boy broke the rules, but at the end of this trial, you'll realize that she doesn't have any proof that Jolly Boy did any of those things. All of the rules that these trial lawyers talked about ..." Harrison Grant said the word 'trial lawyers' with disgust, as if he was not one.

"All of those rules are good ones. Good rules that Jolly Boy didn't break. This is just a show. This is just an attempt for these people to get rich quick."

Harrison Grant's eyes dropped in sadness, and then he continued.

"Jolly Boy is a company that's grown the food that we all eat since the 1940s. You aren't in business that long if you're doing all the terrible things that it was just accused of doing."

Harrison Grant smiled and shook his head, belittling Jane and the case against them at every moment.

Harrison Grant raised his eyebrows.

"Killing people!" He shook his head. "If I sound upset, that's because I am. That's an outrageous accusation, and there's not a single shred of evidence to support it."

Harrison Grant looked around the ornate courtroom, taking it in.

"You have the task of listening to the evidence and doing what is right. That's what makes this place and your work so special."

Harrison Grant stepped closer to the jury box, and then continued in a whisper.

"Jolly Boy and Mr. McNaughten are good. They didn't do anything wrong. They didn't break the rules."

Harrison Grant stepped back. His secret moment with the jury over.

"What happened to Mr. Estrada is very sad," Grant continued. "But, these attorneys can't blame us for something we didn't do. There's no evidence to support it. But here's a quick list of the testimony that you actually *will* hear from the Plaintiffs over the next few days: First, Tommy Estrada lied to Jolly Boy about his immigration status. He lied and obtained a false identification card and used a false Social Security card to obtain employment with us. Jolly Boy didn't violate any immigration law. Tommy Estrada broke the rules. He may have had very legitimate financial reasons to do so. He may have wanted to support his family. But Jolly Boy didn't know about that, and if Jolly Boy had, my client wouldn't have hired him. This isn't 10 or 20 years ago. The stakes are too high."

Harrison Grant took a step toward the jury. He was just getting started.

"Second, Tommy Estrada never told Jolly Boy he was sick. I won't get into the details now, but keep this in mind: If a person doesn't know you are sick, then they can't fire you because you are sick. You will not hear one person testify that Tommy Estrada told Jolly Boy that he was sick, and you certainly won't hear anybody say that Mr. Brian McNaughten knew about it. Brian is the CEO of a major corporation. He has thousands of shareholders. He serves on four other corporate boards. He manages a multimillion dollar company. Even if he wanted to, Mr. McNaughten doesn't check to see who called in sick. Just think about that. Think about Bill Gates or the President of the United States keeping personal tabs on every single employee. This isn't the local gas station with fifteen employees. Jolly Boy employs over 3000 people and has even more independent contractors." Harrison Grant laughed a little, and Michael watched with dismay as a few of the jurors laughed along with him.

"Now as it relates to the spraying of fields and when workers are allowed to go pick crops after the fields have been sprayed, again," he paused, "it never happened."

Grant took a step to the side, drank a little water, and then continued.

"You may ask yourself, how can they be so sure? Because Jolly Boy knows that its customers want a healthy and safe product. So they've invested in sophisticated computer tracking system. This system tracks every field that supplies its produce, and every morning a list of fields goes out to its managers. It tells them what fields to pick and what fields to stay away from.

Managers are trained as to what to do and what not to do. Could a manager have made a mistake or misread one of these lists?" Harrison Grant tilted his head back and forth, as if weighing the possibility.

"Maybe. I'm going to level with you: Maybe."

He turned to Judge Delaney and pointed.

"But the judge will instruct you at the end of the trial that a mistake and error like that by a manager does not break the rules. You can't hold a big company or a person like Mr. McNaughten responsible for a mistake like that. You will never hear one person testify that Jolly Boy knew a field had been sprayed and deliberately sent workers into that field. It never happened."

He shook his head.

"In the end, Ms. Nance and the plaintiff may be able to tell us what the rules are, but they can't prove Jolly Boy and Brian McNaughten broke the rules. Why? Because they didn't."

Harrison Grant went back to the podium. He gathered up his things. And then, as he walked back to the defense table, he added, "And I apologize in advance for these people wasting your time."

Jane and Michael heard it, but couldn't believe it. Harrison snuck it in so quickly that they both hesitated. Michael wanted to object, but then he thought that wouldn't look right. Jane was the lead attorney, and, if he objected, that would under-cut her authority in front of the jury.

Jane looked at Michael and began to stand, but then sat back down in her seat. The moment had passed. They were too slow. The jury had heard the comment, and to object now would only look clumsy.

Both Jane and Michael realized that there was a reason Harrison Grant charged his clients so much money.

CHAPTER THIRTY TWO

The rest of the afternoon didn't go any better. Jane and Michael called two witnesses. They were former Jolly Boy employees that Kermit had found living outside of Cancun and working as maintenance workers at a mega-resort.

Both of them seemed scared. The confidence that they had in their initial interviews with Michael and Kermit was gone. They shifted in their seats. The pauses and breaks between words made them seem spacey and unreliable. And then Harrison Grant disposed of both of them in exactly the same way. He had five simple questions.

"When you applied for the job at Jolly Boy, you didn't tell them that you were illegal and you were using fake documents. Right?"

"And you never reported to anyone at Jolly Boy that you thought the fields were unsafe. Right?"

"And you never spoke to Tommy Estrada about his experiences and illness. Right?"

"In fact, you didn't even know Tommy Estrada. Correct?"

"You're just here because these attorneys somehow found you in Mexico, and said they would give you a free trip to Florida to testify. Is that what happened?"

It didn't matter what the answers were. The damage was done. Jolly Boy had won the first day of trial.

"Damn it." Jane threw her briefcase down on the conference room table. She folded her arms and looked up at the ceiling. Every muscle in her body was tight.

Going into the case, they knew that there were problems with causation and damages. They knew that it was going to be difficult to prove that Jolly Boy and Brian McNaughten knew what was going on in their fields and didn't do anything. But, there was always the thought that the jury would connect the dots.

It seemed obvious to Jane. Living in Jesser and personally seeing the workers in the fields, the problems were everywhere. They couldn't be avoided. How could anyone not know what was going on? If Jane knew what was happening, of course Jolly Boy knew how the crops were being picked at such a low cost.

But, sitting in a Miami courtroom with jurors who had never been to a farm and hadn't thought twice about where the food in their grocery cart came from, connecting the dots was different. It became harder. The courtroom environment was sterile. There was no context.

Jane and Michael saw it now. They saw why Harrison Grant was so confident.

If the jurors themselves were ignorant about the workers in the field, then it wouldn't be too difficult to convince them that Jolly Boy was ignorant about it too.

The underlying argument that Jolly Boy made was simple. It was in everybody's interest to ignore reality. Cheap food benefited everybody, and, if the working conditions and pay were so bad, the Mexicans would've stopped coming. But they hadn't. Every week the newspaper had another story about the wave of illegal immigrants and the so-called "browning of America."

Michael checked his watch. Judge Delaney wanted to see them. He didn't know why.

"You calm?" He looked at Jane, and then he looked at the door. "We have to go."

Jane put her hands together, trying to stop them from shaking.

"I can't believe I did this. I'm going to go bankrupt."

"It's fine. We just have to keep going."

Jane shook her head.

"It was a mistake."

Then there was a knock on the conference room door.

Kermit didn't wait for a response. He just opened it and stuck his head in.

"We got a problemo, yo."

Michael and Jane looked at each other. They tried to think of what else could go wrong, but couldn't.

"What are you talking about?" Michael asked.

"Roberto Estrada." Kermit shook his head. "Can't find him. I told him that I'd come and pick him up this morning at the Waffle House, since we didn't know when he'd testify." Kermit's eyes got wide. "But he didn't show. I been all over town, man. I can't find that dude."

Jane and Michael sat in Judge Delaney's chambers. They sat in silence. It was like they were still in elementary school, waiting in the principal's office. They'd been bad.

They heard the judge in the outer office. He told his law clerk that he was going to be working late, and asked her to order him a sandwich for dinner. Then he came into his chambers, took off his suit jacket and sat down.

He looked at Michael and Jane. The twinkle hadn't entirely left his eye, but there was a bit of sadness.

"They're willing to pay you $5,000 to go away with a confidentiality agreement." Judge Delaney looked at Jane. "I could probably convince them to give you a little something extra for costs, but that wasn't their offer. They offered to pay your costs *before* trial started. After this afternoon, I can't say that I'm too confident they'd offer it again."

"Did they say anything else?" Jane's voice was flat.

Judge Delaney nodded. "Two things," he said. "First, the offer is good until tomorrow morning at eight, and, second, no more offers. They mean it this time. They want to make an example of you. They say that, when you lose, they're going to be seeking sanctions and attorneys' fees."

"That's ridiculous." Michael shook his head.

Judge Delaney looked at him, but he didn't respond. He didn't tell Michael that it wasn't ridiculous at all. Instead, Judge Delaney stood, turned, and stretched while looking out his large window.

He waited a minute, watching the traffic below.

"The truth is, Mr. Collins, they didn't even want to offer you the five grand, but I sort of made them. I've got some golfing to do, and I also don't like good people like Ms. Nance going broke so early in their careers. You both tried to do the right thing, but you're coming up short. You know it. I know it, and Harrison Grant knows it, too."

Jane looked down, thinking about her unpaid bills and credit cards. She wondered if she should tell Judge Delaney that Roberto Estrada wasn't going to testify. They didn't have much causation to begin with, and Tommy's cousin was as close as they got. Now he had disappeared.

Judge Delaney turned away from the window.

"Why don't you two sleep on it? Come back tomorrow and let me know after talking with your client. I'll work on Mr. Grant some more to see if he'll pay some of your costs. God knows he can afford it."

Jane wanted to accept the offer. The first day of trial had been brutal, and with Roberto Estrada gone, their chances of success were that much worse. But, it wasn't her call. She and Michael could advise, but only the client could accept or reject a settlement offer.

Jane and Michael walked across the hall to the same conference room that they had been in before. It was also the same room where Michael had made Elana a promise of success less than 24 hours ago.

They opened the door. Pace was in the corner thumbing through the soccer magazine *4-4-3*. Elana Estrada waited by the window. Like Judge Delaney, she was watching the cars and people swirl below.

"Want to have a seat?" Michael pulled out a chair for her.

Elana eventually turned, looked at the chair, and then shook her head, no. She continued to stand, looking out the window.

"You know, I never been this high before. Never been in a building this tall before I come here." She looked up at the ceiling as if searching for her husband, Tommy.

"We didn't expect there to be another settlement offer," Jane said, "but they've offered $5,000, if you remain silent when this is done." Jane looked at Michael. She was resigned to their fate. "I know Michael said that we'd win, but ..." Jane shook her head. "I don't think that's going to happen."

Elana stared at her. She could tell that Jane was telling the truth.

"Why take it now?"

"Roberto is gone," Michael said. "We can't find him to testify. We needed him."

Elana pursed her lips. She looked at Pace, and then back at Michael.

"They kill him?"

Michael shrugged his shoulders.

"I don't know what happened. We can't find him, and he was our next witness."

"They killed him." Elana's jaw clinched. "I know it." Her face hardened. "If we lose, do I have to be silent? Can I talk about them? Can I talk about what they do to Tommy?"

Jane nodded. "Of course. You can say whatever you want."

Elana thought for a moment, and then she turned to Pace. They spoke to one another in Spanish for a long time, but it was clear that she wanted a trial. Elana wasn't going to settle. She had always been poor, and she had always survived. She wanted money, but she didn't need it.

"They can't silence me," she said. "That's not for sale."

CHAPTER THIRTY THREE

Kermit and the waitress at The Box were now on intimate terms. Despite the disturbing mental image of her and Kermit together and naked, both Michael and Jane were pleased with the more attentive customer service she was providing.

"Here you go." She set a pitcher of cheap, watery beer down on the table.

"Thanks sweet-cheeks." Kermit winked. She smiled and blushed. Then, Kermit gave her butt a gentle pat as she turned and walked away.

"I think you're creating a hostile work environment." Michael poured three glasses of beer.

"A hostile work environment for you?" Kermit reached out, grabbed a glass, and slid it towards himself.

"No." Michael nodded toward the waitress. "A hostile work environment for her."

"Don't think so, *mi amigo*." Kermit took a sip of beer and chased it with a handful of salty popcorn. "She's lovin' it, and I'm lovin' that." Kermit waved at her, smiling big. From across the room, she smiled and waved back.

"You're sick," Michael said. "I think you seriously have something wrong with you."

"Beauty comes in many forms." Kermit raised his glass and took a drink.

"Indeed." Jane nodded, took a drink and then set the glass down. "You want to talk about work now or later?"

Michael shook his head.

"How about never?"

"Yo, bro." Kermit's dreadlocks bounced. "You gotta keep it positive. We got the Miggs coming up."

"Miggy?" Both Michael and Jane said it in unison, pain in their voices.

"Miggs is a home-run." Kermit made a motion, pretending he was hitting a baseball out of the ballpark.

"My boy's going to get us a grand salami, my friends. You can take it to the bank."

"I don't know if we're going to call him as a witness." Michael looked at Jane, and then back at Kermit. "We had a rough day today, and —" Michael lowered his voice. "I'm afraid we're going to lose credibility. Miggy is going to start talking about ghosts and spirits, and then there's the drug thing."

"My boy Miggy is going to do you proud. He saw what he saw. It's all there."

Jane stepped in.

"But it's not credible. He's not credible."

"That's based on your own filters, yo." Kermit pointed at Michael. "Using Korby's model of general semantics, you just have to identify all the reasons you think he's not credible and then address each one. Ask yourselves, what would make this dude credible? Then do it."

Kermit stood.

"If you want to win, put some faith in Miggy. You all been dismissing him from the beginning." Kermit shook his head. "You're acting like arrogant lawyers."

He picked up his glass of beer and started walking over to the bar.

"Kermit, come back here." Michael started to stand.

"Let him go, Michael," Jane said. "We don't have time to explain it to him."

Then Jane's cell phone rang. She fished it out of her purse, turned it over so that she could see the screen.

"I have to take this."

"Who is it?" Michael asked.

"The ex," she said with a little bit of hope. Justin Kent had finally returned her call. "I have to go some place quiet and call him. See you later?"

Michael nodded, still looking over at Kermit.

"I have to talk with our partner over there," he said. "I don't think I've ever seen Kermit quite this upset."

"Fine," Jane said. "Talk to him, just don't drink too much and don't promise to put Miggy on the stand. I know Kermit wants to, but it'd be a disaster."

Jane kissed the top of Michael's head.

"And, if you have a moment, it would be great if you could say a quick prayer that Justin has some good news for us."

"I will," said Michael, watching her go.

CHAPTER THIRTY FOUR

The jurors looked bored and tired. It was the second day of trial and the novelty had already worn off. Each of the jurors had now realized that all they could do was sit and listen. They couldn't ask questions. They couldn't discuss the case among themselves until all the evidence had been presented and both sides had rested. The jurors also couldn't talk about it with their husbands or wives. They couldn't talk about it with their friends. They could only sit and listen. It was hard to listen.

The good news, however, was that Michael's third witness of the day was going to create a little excitement.

Michael approached the podium. He placed his notes in front of him, scanned his questions, and then looked up at the man sitting in the raised wooden witness box.

"For the record, could you please state and spell your name?"

Michael glanced back at Jane who looked at him with a flicker of panic. Her doubts made the room feel a little hotter. His hands began to sweat. He could stop, but without Roberto, they didn't have much choice. They had to push the rules.

The night before, Michael and Jane had talked about how they had nothing to lose. It had been brave talk after a long, tough day. Now, in the courtroom and in front of Judge Delaney, Michael didn't feel so brave.

He worked through the preliminary questions. Michael established that Antonio Sanz was a father of three, married 22 years, and currently living in Mexico. He established that Mr. Sanz came to the United States illegally three years ago to work for Jolly Boy, and then he was arrested and deported a year ago.

Michael stared at his notes. Time to roll the dice.

His body and his voice took on an edge as he pushed forward.

"When you were at Jolly Boy, did you ever make mistakes?"

"*Si.*" Mr. Sanz smiled. "I mean yes."

"When you say mistakes, what kind of mistakes?"

"I was away from home, lonely," Mr. Sanz looked down at his hands. "I drank too much, stayed out all night, and I brought a woman back to my trailer in the morning."

"Now when you say 'my trailer,' was it really your trailer?"

Mr. Sanz shook his head. "No, owned by Jolly Boy for the workers. We sleep probably 10 in the trailer. And Jolly Boy has rules about guests in the trailers."

"And what date are we talking about? When did this late night happen?"

Mr. Sanz shook his head.

"Don't know."

"Was it the summer?" Michael asked. He could sense that he had Harrison Grant's attention. Grant leaned forward in his chair, listening. Judge Delaney also edged up in his chair, eyeing Mr. Sanz with suspicion. Everybody prepared to pounce as Mr. Sanz answered that it was June or July.

Then Michael moved on to the next question.

"And when you arrived back at your trailer, was anybody there?"

Mr. Sanz shook his head.

"No, they all leave for the fields already. I missed the van that come to pick us up. The trailer was empty."

"And then what happened?"

"Objection." Harrison Grant rose to his feet. "Relevance and calls for a narrative answer."

Judge Delaney smiled. It was the objection that he had been waiting for. He turned to the jurors.

"I'm going to talk with these attorneys. I want you all to stand up, stretch, and admire our beautiful courthouse. You are encouraged to talk amongst yourselves, just not about this case."

He turned back to Michael and Harrison Grant, and then motioned for them to approach the bench. The two came forward, and Judge Delaney leaned in. He hovered over them."What's this about counselor?" he asked Michael.

"Same as yesterday, Your Honor."

Michael felt his stomach turn. It was never good to lie to a judge. "Just establishing the intolerable working conditions at Jolly Boy."

Judge Delaney turned to Harrison Grant.

"Do you know what this is about?"

"I have no idea." Harrison Grant looked at Michael with disgust. "If it is truly the same as yesterday, then this is getting cumulative and unnecessary. We had multiple worker witnesses yesterday, and then there have already been two this morning. I ask the court to stop it, and allow this case to move forward. The parade of illegal workers hasn't offered anything so far, and it's not going to offer anything in the future."

Judge Delaney raised his hand, stopping Harrison Grant from getting too far into the preview of his closing argument. He turned to Michael.

"Response?"

"Jolly Boy had an opportunity to depose this worker, and they chose not to. If there is a surprise, it's due to their lack of preparation."

Judge Delaney stared at Michael, evaluating what he had just heard. He turned to Grant.

"I overrule your objection, he can ask his questions."

Judge Delaney turned back to Michael.

"Get to the point. This better have something to do with causation."

"I understand, Your Honor." Michael returned to the podium. He waited until Harrison Grant and the jury were settled back in their seats, and then he continued his questions.

"As you were saying," he said, "you were with a woman, alone, in your trailer. Everybody else was at work, and you should've been at work, too."

"Yes." Mr. Sanz nodded his head. He looked at the jury, and then continued, "The woman and I began to kiss. We laid down on my mattress."

Mr. Sanz paused, embarrassed. The courtroom was silent, waiting.

"And then what happened?" Michael asked.

"A police officer burst through the door. Deputy Maus worked for Jolly Boy. He had a nightstick and he started to beat me with —"

There was an eruption of noise. Harrison Grant started to shout objections. Michael yelled at his witness to continue to answer the question. Judge Delaney brought his gavel down hard, trying to bring order back into the courtroom.

Judge Delaney stood. Because of the height of the bench and that he was already a tall man, Judge Delaney towered over the proceedings in his black robe. He pointed at Michael and Harrison Grant.

"You and you, in my chambers, now."

He turned to the jury, and managed a contained smile.

"We're going to break for the day," he said. "I'll see you all tomorrow."

Michael, Jane, Harrison Grant and Judge Delaney walked into his chambers.

"Door." Judge Delaney pointed. "Shut it."

His jaw was locked.

"I'm asking for a mistrial, Your Honor." Harrison Grant stared at Michael and Jane. His tone was sad, as if he was being forced to ask due to their irresponsible conduct.

"A mistrial?"

Judge Delaney ran his hand through his perfect head of white hair. He looked at Michael and Jane.

"No surprises, I told you two. No surprises is the rule, and now we have a surprise. There aren't supposed to be surprises."

Michael sat down in the chair across from Judge Delaney. He had been hoping the situation would de-escalate from the time it took for them to go from the courtroom to Judge Delaney's chambers, but clearly it hadn't.

"I know there aren't supposed to be surprises," Michael said, "but, as I told you at our bench conference, this witness has been identified and known to defendants for nearly six months. They chose not to depose him. He's establishing the working conditions at Jolly Boy."

"That's not true." Harrison Grant shook his head. "We paid to travel to Mexico and depose the witnesses we heard yesterday. After we returned and shortly before the discovery deadline, we got notice of this witness and a few others. They were playing games."

"We disclosed, Your Honor. I said I wouldn't oppose a discovery extension to allow them time to depose this witness. I have the letter." Michael opened his folder and gave Judge Delaney a copy of the letter that he had sent to Harrison Grant.

Judge Delaney read it, and then put it down on his desk.

"Your Honor," Harrison Grant saw that Michael was wearing down the judge. "I spoke with counsel, and I asked him what this witness was going to testify to. Mr. Collins stated that this witness was merely going to give testimony similar to the witnesses yesterday and about the working conditions at Jolly Boy. He didn't say that the witness was going to accuse a decorated law enforcement officer of assault."

Judge Delaney turned back to Michael.

"Is that true?"

"I didn't get into detail with Mr. Grant about the specifics," Michael answered. "But frankly that's not my job. I'm required to make my witness available under the rules, which I did. There's nothing in the rules that requires me to tell Harrison Grant what I think are the most important facts that the witness is going to testify about. I only have to provide a general statement. That's the law."

"It's dishonest," Judge Delaney said. "There are things such as professional courtesy, which you obviously disregarded. You omitted material facts in your discussions."

"Your Honor," Jane stepped forward. She had been standing against the back wall. "May I speak?"

"You may." Judge Delaney raised an eyebrow and bit his lower lip. "I want to know what you think. It doesn't seem like you'd be okay with this." Judge Delaney pointed at Michael. "He's not exactly acting in a manner consistent with your reputation."

"I know the rules, and the rules are clear that Mr. Collins does not have to identify the most important facts in the case. That's attorney work-product. It's like me asking in discovery, 'What is the most important fact related to your defense?' An opposing attorney does not have to answer that. Harrison Grant doesn't have to sift through his file and identify what he thinks are the most important facts in his favor. Similarly, neither do we. That's what Mr. Grant is upset about. He didn't do his job. He had an opportunity to find out what this witness was going to testify about, and he chose not to. And we're not required to tell him. The system is premised upon each side advocating for their own client. Harrison Grant should've advocated, but he didn't. He didn't take us seriously. He doesn't respect us. And he thought he could slide by. Now he's claiming we surprised him with a witness that he knew about six months ago."

Judge Delaney raised his hand, silencing her. He thought for a moment.

"Advocating is one thing, Ms. Nance." Judge Delaney looked at Michael. "It seems more like counsel tricked the other side. Harrison Grant asked him what Mr. Sanz was going to testify about, and Mr. Collins told him that he was going to be similar to the witnesses yesterday. But, obviously, he is not similar. An attorney has an obligation of candor."

Judge Delaney folded his hands together and brought them up to his chin.

"I'm not allowing the testimony to continue."

Michael stood. "Your Honor –"

"Is this witness going to say that Deputy Maus acted under the direct supervision and knowledge of Jolly Boy?" The judge asked.

"That's who paid him."

"That's not enough." Judge Delaney shook his head. "Do you have any witness that is going to testify that any executive at Jolly Boy told Maus to beat this worker with a night stick?"

"No," Michael said, "but I don't think that's –"

"Yes it *is* necessary," Judge Delaney said. "It's called causation, and you don't have it. This Maus person isn't on trial. You sued Jolly Boy. That's what this trial is about." Judge Delaney looked away in disgust. "It's done."

He took a deep breath, calming himself. Then Judge Delaney looked at Harrison Grant.

"And no mistrial for you. I'll strike the testimony, instruct the jury to disregard it, and we'll continue tomorrow."

He pointed at Michael.

"Unless you have a witness that is going to directly link Jolly Boy to what happens out in those fields, you should forget about it. I won't allow it. I won't allow any more similar worker testimony. If you try again to sneak it in, I'll find you in contempt. Got it?"

They regrouped back at the office. Michael set two square boxes down on the table, each filled with a hot Speedy's pizza.

"You get the Canadian bacon and pineapple for me this time?" Kermit leaned forward examining the boxes. "Sir Speedy fires up my old soul with the swine and pine, my friend."

"It's on the bottom." Michael slid the bottom box out from under the other. He handed it to Kermit, and then looked over at Jane. She hadn't said a word during the ride from the courthouse to the office. Once they were in the office, she just sat at her desk. She kept her back turned to them, thumbing through the papers at her desk.

"You gotta eat." Michael called over to her.

Jane slowly turned around.

"Sorry," she said. "I'm not that hungry."

She pushed the stack of papers away.

"I don't even know why I'm preparing any more. It's a train wreck."

"It's not that bad," Michael said. "We can still pray for the DOJ. Your ex might surprise you."

"Doubt it." Jane got up and walked over to the table. She grabbed a small slice of pizza and sat down. "Last night he didn't sound too hopeful. My guess is that he's heard how the trial is going and just wants to meet in person to let me down easy."

"You're meeting with him tonight?" Michael asked.

Jane nodded her head, and then looked at the clock on the wall.

"In a couple hours." She turned back to Michael. "What are you two going to do?"

Michael hesitated. He didn't want to tell her, but figured he should.

"Kermit has some ideas about Miggy's testimony. Ways to give it some credibility."

Jane narrowed her eyes, and then looked at Kermit.

"You're going to verify the spirits?"

"Maybe." Kermit smiled. He took a big bite of his slice of his pizza. "No guarantees, but I think I got a way to make the spirits more tangible to those that are less enlightened and judgmental."

Jane looked at Michael.

"Have fun." She grabbed a bottle of water off of the table and started toward the front door. "If you find enlightenment, let me know."

"I will," Michael said. "And if Mr. Justice offers you enlightenment tonight at your meeting, please let us know. I want in on that, too."

CHAPTER THIRTY FIVE

Brian McNaughten handed the drink to his brother Dylan. They were in Brian's basement. He had seen an article in *GQ* magazine about "man caves." They sounded cool, and so Brian had sent the article to his architect and had told the architect to make one for him. Three months and $150,000 later, Brian had his own man cave.

It was all dark wood. One end of the room had a flat screen television, big overstuffed leather chairs, and a pool table. The television was surrounded by thick leather-bound books that Brian had never read. He wasn't even sure they were real, since he'd never taken one off of the shelf. The other end was an exact replica of the bar at Maggie Malone's Public House, a tiny Scottish pub in Glasgow.

The two brothers sat on bar stools. They clinked glasses.

"You should have seen them today," Brian said. "Pathetic."

"When's it over?" Dylan took a drink, staying away from the cocaine during the trial had been hard. He wanted to get back to the clubs. He needed to get back to the clubs.

"Can't be more than a few days," Brian said. "They tried to get some stuff in about Maus. The judge wouldn't allow it. I don't know what else they've got. Can't be much."

Dylan nodded.

"That's good."

"However you got rid of Roberto Estrada was brilliant." Brian took another sip. "I knew he was gone as soon as they walked in the door. It was all over their faces."

Brian took an envelope of cash out of his pocket. He put the envelope on the bar.

"Here's a little insurance. You can take a cut for your other activities, but make sure most of it gets to Maus."

"Now?" Dylan wondered. "I thought you wanted me to stay low."

Usually his brother didn't care about the work that he did, lately it had been different. Brian was getting more involved, micro-managing. Dylan didn't like it. His brother was upsetting the balance.

Brian smiled, not picking up on Dylan's discomfort.

"Maybe your sense of adventure is rubbing off on me." Brian drank a little more of his beer. "I want to keep Maus tight, but only for now, and then we need to cut him loose when the trial is over. He's becoming a problem. People know too much about him. He's too high-profile."

Dylan put the money in his pocket.

"Then things can get back to normal, right?"

"Of course." Brian stood. "I'll get out of your hair after the trial."

"Good," Dylan said. "You make shit too complex."

Brian leaned over. He patted his brother on the shoulder.

"Nothing to worry about," Brian said. "This will be over soon."

CHAPTER THIRTY SIX

It was after hours, so Jane called up to be let inside. After a few rings, he answered.

"It's me. I'm downstairs."

Kent came down a few minutes later. He swiped his magnetic card. The door clicked and Kent pushed it open.

"Sorry about having to meet so late." He ushered Jane inside. "I just figured with the trial that it'd be easier."

Jane noticed that he wasn't making eye contact. Another sign that her case against Jolly Boy wasn't going to get any help from the Department of Justice. Kent was already ashamed, trying to let her down easy.

They walked together. They went past the empty security check points, and then to the elevators. Kent swiped his magnetic card again, and then pressed the button.

The elevator doors slid open. They got inside. Jane looked over at Kent.

"You know you didn't have to do this. We didn't have to meet in person. If you can't set it up … I mean, if you can't help our case, I understand."

Jane paused, expecting Kent to answer. He didn't, so Jane continued to fill the silence as the elevator rose higher.

"It was a stretch asking you ... probably even unethical. Maybe it would've backfired, too, but I figured you'd know why I was asking. It's a big case for me."

She was nervous and she was rambling.

The elevator reached the sixth floor. A bell dinged, and then the doors slid open.

They walked out into the hall, Kent leading and Jane chasing behind.

"So are you not speaking to me now or what?" she asked.

They took a few more steps down the hallway, and Kent stopped in front of the conference room door. He put his hand on the knob, but he didn't open it. Kent turned to her.

"This got complicated," he said.

Jane looked at him, searching, but Kent's expression was blank.

"What do you mean?"

"I mean it got complicated." Kent nodded his head, gesturing to what was waiting on the other side of the door. "There are other people involved now."

Kent turned the knob and opened the door.

Inside, it was a full house. More than a half-dozen people in dark suits crowded around the table with their clerks and assistants in the seats behind them. There were also two big guys, each with an earpiece, a badge, and a gun attached to their belts. They were federal marshals.

A man in a wheelchair rolled out from the far end of the conference room table, and then rolled toward her. He looked like a snake.

"Jane Nance, I am Agent Frank Vatch." He smiled; attempting to comfort her, but the smile was forced and made a chill run up Jane's back.

Vatch held out his hand. Out of habit, Jane took it, weakly.

"I've been hearing about your great work," Vatch said, gesturing toward an empty seat. "I think we have a lot to talk about. Please sit."

His tongue flicked out of his narrow slit of a mouth.

"Yes, we have a lot to talk about." He patted the back of the empty seat. "Please sit."

Jane looked at her watch. They had been going for an hour. She glanced down at her phone, laying on the conference room table. The screen had the date and time and, underneath, a summary: 2 new text messages, one missed call.

Vatch noticed Jane looking at her phone.

"I'm sorry," he said. "Do you need to go, Ms. Nance?"

"Michael is probably wondering what's going on."

Jane scanned the faces of the people in the room, all still pretending to be her friend.

"I should be going."

"And I hope you understand the need for this conversation to be private." Vatch spoke slowly for emphasis. "You could be charged with interfering with a federal investigation, if you tip him off."

"I think she understands," Kent said. "Jane knows what she has to do."

"Do you?" Vatch asked her. "Do you understand?"

Jane looked at Kent. Her eyes pierced him. Kent was a traitor. If ever there was a chance that they could get back together or even be friends, that chance was gone. He'd set her up.

"I understand the choice," Jane said. "But I don't know what I'm going to do. Like I told you, he's never said anything to me about where he gets his money or much about his past. We talk about work. We talk about our case."

"But surely you've wondered," Vatch said. "His behavior and his mysterious background is certainly suspicious."

Vatch leaned in, as if he and Jane were the only people in the room.

"Just find out the truth for us and we'll help you win your case. It's pretty simple."

The phone on the table began to vibrate. Jane picked it up and looked at the screen. The incoming call was from Michael again.

"I have to go."

She shut the phone off, and then put it in her purse.

"I've got some work to do."

Jane stood, steadied herself, and walked out the door.

Outside, the night air was crisp. Jane tried to get control of the growing pit in her stomach. During the meeting, she had tried to be calm. She had tried to play it cool, but now waves of nausea rushed over her body. She vacillated between fear and excitement, courage and guilt, love and anger.

Jane took a few more steps, stopping at the curb. She turned and looked up at the tall office building. *The Department of In-justice*, she thought. Jane closed her eyes, trying to center herself.

It was a deal with the devil.

Vatch wasn't lying when he said that they could help her win their case. She had given Justin Kent all the information that they needed, all the feds had to do was act on it.

The opportunity was there. If it worked, she would win. She could finally have the respect she wanted. She'd also get the financial reward that she deserved. It would be national news. She'd be a hero in the legal services community.

All she had to do was sell out Michael Collins.

A deal with the devil, she thought.

CHAPTER THIRTY SEVEN

Michael was asleep when Jane finally got back to her apartment. She walked over to the bed without turning on any of the lights. Her eyes adjusted as she stood in the dark, watching him.

Jane thought about what she would be doing if Michael had never come into her life, where would she be? He helped her take risks. He believed in her. But at the same time, he never let her know what was really going on inside his head.

Jane ran through the possibilities. She rationalized how she could live with herself if she turned Michael over to Agent Vatch. Then she pushed away the possibilities and focused on loyalty and trust. *Those counted for something*, she thought, *didn't they?*

Jane took a step toward her nightstand. The floor creaked, and Michael stirred.

"It's just me," Jane said. "Go back to sleep."

"Long meeting?" Michael asked. "I called a few times. I was getting worried." Michael pulled himself up, still clouded by sleep. "Anything good happen?" He reached out his hand and Jane took it, then he pulled her into bed with him.

"Maybe," Jane said. "Things are happening. I told Justin what was going on with the trial and what we needed."

"But he didn't commit." Michael rubbed Jane's back.

Jane shook her head.

"He needs more time to get approval." Jane lied. "We have to slow things down."

"We don't have too many more witnesses," Michael said. "Elana should go last. Once she's called, we should rest our case."

Jane was quiet. She laid next to Michael, still in her work clothes, but ready to close her eyes and fall back asleep.

Then Michael added, "There's Miggy."

Jane couldn't stop herself from laughing. With everything going on, the thought of Miggy had cut through the stress.

"Miggy," she smiled. "Did Kermit come up with a way to talk to the spirits?"

"Maybe," Michael said. "It's complicated, but it might work." Michael waited a beat. "But probably not."

"Will it delay the trial?" Jane asked.

"Most definitely," Michael said. "I'd need to call him now, wake him up, and get him started." Michael propped himself up higher on the bed. "I could kill the morning with motions while Kermit works on it, but I don't know what'll happen."

Jane rubbed her eyes. She tried to think about it rationally, but everything was a jumble.

"Worst case, I delay the trial a morning and piss off Judge Delaney," Michael said. "Best case, we cause enough disruption that Judge Delaney quits for the day."

"Or Judge Delaney throws you in jail for contempt of court," Jane added.

"Certainly possible," Michael smiled. There were approximately 500 million reasons why he should be in jail, but contempt of court had not been one of them until now.

"I think we're losing out minds," Jane said. "We're delirious."

Michael nodded. "So what do want me to do?"

Jane closed her eyes. She had to make a decision.

"Do it," she eventually said. "We need the time."

CHAPTER THIRTY EIGHT

Kermit had seen the dogs on Animal Planet. That's where he had gotten the idea. He'd been talking with the dog owners for about a week, but he needed Michael on board. All it took was some money, and, as soon as he got the "big dough ball" from Michael, Kermit got the dogs.

He watched them with a big smile on his face. The dogs were going nuts. Two handlers tried to keep them under control. Another three men trailed behind. They all walked a patch of ground underneath a large cypress tree on the edge of a soy bean field. It was about 10 miles west of Jesser, near where Tommy Estrada's body had been found.

Whenever the dogs barked, circled, and started to dig, a handler would shout. Then, another man would run up behind them and put a small flag into the ground.

Kermit stood off to the side with a very young reporter for Miami's Seven News. Kermit had called every newspaper and television station in town that morning. They had all laughed at him except Seven News. The reporter had just started. A few years back she had been third place in the Miss Florida beauty pageant. After graduating from Florida State, her rich daddy had gotten her this job. When Kermit called, the news producer had been ecstatic to get her out of the office and out of his hair.

"Can you believe this?" The reporter's blue eyes danced every time a flag went into the ground. "This is network," she said. "This is my break."

She grabbed Kermit's arm and gave it a squeeze.

"Easy honey, I bruise easy." Kermit's eyes were dancing too. He loved the chaos. "So I got you the story, now what's the plan?"

"We call the police, but get some footage before they get here." She started to count the flags, and then turned back to Kermit. "We have to get the footage first, and then we'll go down to the courthouse. That's where you have your witness, right?"

"Right-o, slim." Kermit watched the dogs go nuts again,

The reporter squealed as the handler called for another flag. It wasn't a professional, detached reaction, but it was honest. She started to count the flags.

"What is that? Are there like, 10 dead bodies out there?"

Kermit shook his head.

"Don't know," he said. "Maybe it's just one body that's been cut up into a bunch of pieces."

"Cut up!" The reporter gave Kermit's arm another squeeze. "That's even better."

###

Michael took the whole morning. Every attorney liked to hear themselves talk, but this delay was deliberate. This was Kermit and Michael's plan. They needed time to get the cadaver dogs out to the site where Miggy saw Maus and the spirits. Neither Michael or Jane were comfortable with just putting Miggy on the stand without some corroboration.

As Judge Delaney told them the day before, he was striking Antonio Sanz's testimony. The jury would be instructed to disregard his testimony related to Deputy Maus and were prohibited from considering any testimony he gave.

That was now the law of the case. And Michael took the first part of the morning putting his objections to the ruling on the record as well as laying a detailed "offer of proof" for any appeal.

An "offer of proof" was done outside the presence of a jury. During an "offer," an attorney described the testimony that would have been given absent the judge's decision to exclude it.

Michael stood at the podium with 15 pages of notes. As he continued on, Harrison Grant kept coughing and shifting in his seat. He tried to express to the court that he was both bored and annoyed with Michael's speech. Judge Delaney didn't look much happier, but the judge knew enough not to prevent Michael from finishing. If he interrupted an offer of proof and didn't allow Michael to finish, Judge Delaney knew that he would be flipped on appeal. Then he'd have to do the whole trial over, and he definitely did not want that.

Michael turned the page, ignoring a room full of people shooting daggers at him with their eyes. Then he glanced up at the clock. It was five minutes to 10:30. Time to wrap up.

"In conclusion, Your Honor, the testimony of Mr. Sanz is just the first piece in the plaintiff's case. These are facts. These are real events that a reasonable jury could use to conclude that Jolly Boy and its executives knew what was going on or created an environment in which they were deliberately ignorant of Deputy Maus' conduct. By knowing or ignoring these facts they are negligent in the wrongful death of Tommy Estrada."

Michael collected his papers and walked back to his seat. He looked at Jane, hoping for some reassurance, but Jane didn't look at him. She had been quiet all morning.

"Okay." Judge Delaney stared at Michael. "That was incredibly thorough." He spoke with sarcastic tone. "Off the record, let's try and be a little less thorough in the future."

Judge Delaney looked at his watch, and then looked back at the attorneys.

"We'll take our morning break, round up the jurors, and then continue with testimony for the rest of the morning."

Judge Delaney got up, and the bailiff instructed everyone remaining in the courtroom to rise. The court was in recess.

Jane sat back down in her chair. Michael looked over at her.

"Not coming?"

Jane slowly folded her arms across her chest and shook her head.

"I'll just stay here; you can take care of it."

Michael cocked his head to the side.

"You feeling okay?"

"Not really," Jane said. She looked over at Michael. "This just isn't how I thought it would be. That's all."

"Hang in there," Michael said. "Maybe DOJ will come around even if Judge Delaney doesn't let Miggy testify."

He put his hand on Jane's shoulder. "You needed to give the DOJ time, and that's what we're doing. That's all we're trying to accomplish."

Jane nodded, although she was the one who needed the delay. She needed the time to make up her own mind.

Outside the courthouse, Michael walked across the street to a bench while he read the text messages from Kermit. He stopped, re-read the last one, and then looked up. He smiled at

Miggy, who had been waiting for him. Miggy was clean. His hair was trimmed and combed. He wore khakis and a polo shirt, and he almost looked normal.

"Is it time?" Miggy asked.

"Showtime," Michael said. "You look great."

"Kermit made me look like a fashion model."

Miggy giggled, and then squirmed a little in his new outfit. It was clear that he wasn't used to wearing clothes that actually fit.

"You know we've got a lot riding on this." Michael sat down next to him. "We need you to pretend you don't hear the voices. Can you do that?"

"Kermit told me to be a regular dude like him."

Miggy looked at Michael, not realizing the absurdity of his last statement.

"I'll keep it like we practiced." Miggy twirled a few strands of his hair.

"Great." Michael typed the number for Kermit on his cell phone. A few seconds, and then Kermit answered. "Everything still a go?" Michael listened, nodding. "When are they coming down to interview Miggy?" He listened, and then hung up. "Are you going to talk about the spirits?" Michael asked Miggy.

Miggy shook his head.

"Kermit told me not to, so I ain't talking about no spirits today."

"Good."

CHAPTER THIRTY NINE

The plaintiffs call Miguel Vatale to the stand."

Miggy didn't get up. He wasn't used to being called Miguel. He hadn't been called Miguel Vatale since elementary school.

Michael turned to the seats in the back of the courtroom. He made eye contact with Miggy, and gestured for him to come forward.

Miggy stood, and then made his way to the witness stand. Before he sat down, Judge Delaney made him swear to tell the truth and gave Miggy general instructions about how the questioning would proceed.

"So you understand?" asked Judge Delaney.

Miggy nodded.

"Yes."

"Good." Judge Delaney smiled. "You may sit down."

Judge Delaney turned to Michael.

"You may proceed with this witness."

"Thank you, Your Honor." Michael looked at Jane, who was still lost inside herself, and then turned to Harrison Grant. Finally, he scanned the faces of the jury. It was the first time they had been in the courtroom that day, and they looked ready for the case to move forward.

Looking at Miggy, Michael felt his pulse quicken. There was a sinking feeling in his gut. He knew what Miggy was going to say, but he wasn't sure how Judge Delaney would react. The judge had been clear: no surprises. Now there was about to be a big surprise. It might cause a mistrial. It might result in sanctions. It might destroy their credibility with the jury. It might do nothing at all. Michael had no idea.

Miggy had talked about spirits and ghosts so often over the past year that it had become a joke among Michael and Jane. But Kermit wore them down, telling Michael and Jane to give Miggy a chance; they had to listen to him; it could help the case.

Michael and Jane had thought about it, and then laughed. Kermit had been brainwashed, they thought, but Kermit wouldn't let it go. "Hear him out," Kermit had asked them. "Just listen to what he has to say."

And finally they did, because they didn't have any other options. That decision had been the moment when the case turned.

"Mr. Vatale, could you tell the court where you live?"

"Jesser." Miggy smiled at the jury, and some of the jurors actually smiled back. The friendly response was probably out of sympathy. Michael was okay with that.

"Are you employed?"

Miggy shook his head.

"No," he said. "Was at one time, but not now."

"You're unemployed?"

Miggy nodded.

"I have some substance abuse issues."

Although most people would consider this admission to be terrible for Miggy's credibility, Michael had planned it. He wanted the jury to find out about Miggy's mental health and various addictions upfront, rather than waiting for Harrison Grant to expose Miggy's instability on cross-examination.

"You've been in treatment?"

Miggy smiled.

"Many times."

"But you're sober now, today?"

"Thirty days sober." Miggy looked up at Judge Delaney. "Not too shabby."

Some of the older, female jurors laughed. Miggy was charming.

"Let's turn our attention to the past," Michael said. "It was last summer, a little over a year ago. Do you remember where you were?"

"Outskirts of Jesser." Miggy started to go into a long, random monologue, but Michael cut him off. He raised his hand, and Miggy stopped talking. "Specifically, you saw something that was very significant. Is that true?"

Harrison Grant stood.

"Objection, Your Honor, he's leading this witness."

Judge Delaney rolled his eyes. He gestured for Grant to sit down, and then overruled the objection.

"Mr. Collins may continue, but now that we're getting into the substance of testimony, you need to be more careful."

"Yes, Your Honor." Michael looked down at his notes. "What were you doing?"

"I was getting high," Miggy said. "I knew these guys in a farmhouse outside of Jesser. They grow some weed in the national park nearby, and they cook some stuff in their pole barn. I hitched out there, got some smack, and then hunkered in a field."

"What do you mean by 'hunkered'?"

"I had my smack. I found a quiet spot in a field. It was a break area for the workers."

"Kind of like a picnic area?"

Miggy nodded.

"That's right. It had a table. I put down my stuff, and I sat down to shoot up."

Miggy shifted in his seat, uneasy. It was as if he just realized he had admitted to committing a crime, under oath, and in a court of law.

Michael continued, praying that Miggy would remember not to talk about the spirits.

"And then what did you see?" he asked.

"I saw a guy pull up in a pickup truck. I thought it was weird. I mean, I'm in a field. Ain't nothing around, and this guy stops. I'm thinking that maybe he saw me or something, but I don't know."

"Was it a man or woman?"

"It was a man," Miggy said, glad that Michael had stopped asking him about his drug use.

"And did you later figure out who this man was?"

Miggy nodded.

"It was Deputy Maus. He works for the Sheriff, but he also works for the farms, works for Jolly Boy, like an enforcer."

Harrison Grant stood.

"Objection, Your Honor. May we approach?"

Michael and Harrison Grant approached the bench.

Judge Delaney leaned toward them.

"Mr. Collins, what's going on?"

Michael tried to look innocent.

"I'm just trying to put in my case."

Judge Delaney stared at him for a moment, then looked at Harrison Grant, and then back to Michael. "Chambers."

###

They returned to their seats. Michael and Jane sat down on the left side of Judge Delaney's large oak desk. Harrison Grant and Brian McNaughten sat down on the right side of the desk.

Judge Delaney leaned back in his chair and closed his eyes. He was tired.

"Tell me again what this witness is going to testify about?"

"Mr. Vatale saw, on multiple occasions, Deputy Maus dig a grave, remove a body from the back of his truck or cruiser, and bury the body. We think that one of those times it was Tommy Estrada, since Mr. Estrada's body was found in a nearby field. We're building our case that Deputy Maus –"

"Your Honor," Harrison Grant interrupted. "You've previously ruled on this issue. Although I find it hard to believe that this testimony from a heroin addict is true. Deputy Maus is a police officer. He is not some sort of serial killer –"

"Nobody said he was a serial killer,"Michael interrupted, "but he takes care of problems for Jolly Boy, including problem people."

Grant shook his head.

"Ridiculous, and even if it is true, it proves nothing. Obviously Jolly Boy did not instruct this person to do this and there is no evidence that Deputy Maus murdered these people. Certainly, if that was the case, Mr. Collins and Ms. Nance would have reported that to the police."

There was a knock at the door.

Judge Delaney raised his hand, stopping Grant from talking.

"Hold that thought." To the person on the other side of the door. "Come in."

The door opened and it was Judge Delaney's law clerk.

"Your Honor, I wanted to let you know that a camera crew is here."

Judge Delaney shot Michael Collins a look. Then he waved the clerk to come further into his chambers and shut the door.

"What do they want?"

"They would like to set up a camera to record Mr. Vatale's testimony. They're doing a story about the Jolly Boy graveyard."

"The Jolly Boy graveyard?"

The clerk nodded. His face concerned. The clerk knew that his boss wouldn't be happy. Judges hated cameras in the courtroom almost as much as they hated surprises during trials. Every judge preferred to toil away in anonymity. Less publicity meant more job security.

"Your Honor, I strongly object." Harrison Grant, for the first time, exhibited true concern. "This false testimony shouldn't be broadcast to the world. It would damage the reputation of one of Florida's best corporate citizens, and –"

Judge Delaney held out his hand, again. He'd heard enough from Harrison Grant.

"What's the story about?"

The clerk waited a second, hoping that Judge Delaney didn't really want him to say it in the presence of the attorneys.

"Come on," Judge Delaney. "Out with it. What's the story?"

"The reporter said they were out at this field with cadaver dogs, following up on a tip from Mr. Vatale. They found a lot of bodies or body parts. Nobody knows for sure, but the police have the area sealed off. She says that they're going to interview Mr. Vatale when he's done, but they want some footage of him actually testifying."

Michael's heart skipped a beat.

Out of desperation and largely to get Kermit to shut up, he had given Kermit money to hire a guy that trains cadaver dogs for rescue teams. When the cadaver dogs confirmed that Miggy was telling the truth that morning, Michael violated a half-dozen court rules and another half-dozen canons of professional ethics. He withheld the information from Harrison Grant. He didn't call the police right away.

Judge Delaney looked at Jane Nance.

"Did you know anything about these dogs?"

Jane didn't say anything. She just shook her head."But I bet you did," Delaney said to Michael. "Certainly Mr. Vatale did not hire cadaver dogs and orchestrate a news crew coming into my courtroom."

Judge Delaney took a deep breath.

"Okay," he said. "I've got a number of concerns."

Judge Delaney's speech was steady, but his face was flush. A vein was popping out of his head.

"Mr. Collins, did you know about this television crew? And more importantly, did you disclose any of this to Mr. Grant?"

"The dogs were part of our ongoing investigation, and all we did was tell the news crew what we were doing. I had no idea what the dogs were going to find. It was just part of our due diligence. We couldn't ethically call Mr. Vatale without honestly believing his testimony was true. And we didn't actually think we were going to call him as a witness until yesterday, although he had been disclosed. It all unfolded very quickly this morning."

Harrison Grant edged up in his seat, prepared to be the voice of reason. When Michael took a breath, Grant stepped in.

"As you ruled yesterday," Grant said, "there is no connection to these alleged acts and the defendant."

"But the alleged acts seem to be piling up," said Judge Delaney. He had calmed down, and now he was thinking about the camera crew and how his decisions would be interpreted by the media. He had a reputation to protect. Although he wasn't supposed to take public opinion into consideration, he was up for re-election in the fall.

"Here's what I'm going to do." Judge Delaney put his hand down on his desk, collecting his thoughts. "I am not going to rule on the objection at this time. Mr. Collins, you will call the remainder of your witnesses. I will tell the jury that Mr. Vatale may be called later in the trial. In the meantime, I will listen for direct evidence that Jolly Boy and its executives actually authorized Deputy Maus to do what you allege. If I hear direct evidence, then I'll allow Mr. Vatale to testify and I'll even allow you to recall any other witnesses that want to talk about Deputy Maus. If I don't hear direct evidence about knowledge and causation that connects Jolly Boy, then I will not allow the testimony."

Judge Delaney nodded his head. The decision was made.

"Do you understand? I want to hear a witness or see a document that connects the dots. I want evidence that Jolly Boy killed your client, not evidence that they employ a bad cop. You need to connect the dots. Understand?"

Michael looked over at Jane. Her head was down. Her hands were still clasped. Michael looked back to Judge Delaney. He nodded.

"I understand, Your Honor. Thank you, but we don't have any more witnesses ready for the day. Can we start fresh tomorrow?"

Judge Delaney leaned back in his chair. He considered it. Figuring that the television crew wouldn't come back for a second day, he nodded his head in agreement.

"We'll do that. I think that's reasonable. Tomorrow at 9:00 am. I'll see you then, and we can also put some of these objections and arguments on the record at that time."

CHAPTER FORTY

Brian McNaughten sat across the conference room table from Harrison Grant. Lawyers didn't usually scream at their clients, but Harrison Grant administered verbal abuse that was usually reserved for first-year associates.

"What the hell else is going to happen?" Grant folded his arms across his chest. "I don't lose. I get paid because I don't lose, and the reason I don't lose is because I know everything before the trial starts. I figure out a plan, and then I execute the plan."

Brian didn't say anything.

"You convinced me not to depose these witnesses." Grant held up a copy of the plaintiff's witness list. He waved it in front of Brian McNaughten's face. "I always depose every witness on a list, but you convinced me to violate my own rule." He slammed the paper down on the table. "You said Jolly Boy wouldn't pay for the depositions. You told me they were unnecessary, that these other lawyers were broke and didn't have anything."

Grant shook his head in disgust.

"Now I've got television stories and newspaper stories about a Jolly Boy graveyard. You think a jury isn't going to hear about that?"

"They're instructed not to watch television or read the newspapers," Brian said. "I heard the judge say it."

"That's crap and you know it." Grant shook his head. "I just got two emails from my wife saying they found seven bodies out there. The jurors are sitting at home right now. They're free to do whatever they want. They can't avoid this story. It's everywhere."

"It'll be fine," Brian said. "You heard Judge Delaney. They need a connection, and they don't have one."

Grant started to scream again, but stopped himself. He needed to calm down. He had never let a client see him like this. He needed to bring his focus back. He was supposed to be unflappable.

They sat in silence for a few minutes while Grant thought about how to handle the rest of the trial.

"I'll move for a directed verdict in this case," Grant finally said. "Maybe we can prevent it from ever getting to a jury. If they have nothing, then there is nothing for the jury to decide. Delaney will dismiss."

"That's right." Brian nodded his head. He was happy Grant was starting to look at this rationally again. He and his brother had been careful. Brian knew there was no connection. The only issue would be if Maus testified against them. Maus was the problem. Dylan needed to take care of Maus.

Deputy Maus stood on his momma's front porch. The farm had been in the family for more than 60 years. They had never been rich. The land was too sandy and dry to make any farmer rich, but they had managed to scratch out a living.

Now they just rented out the land to Jolly Boy and a few other companies. His daddy was in a nursing home, and his momma spent her days watching television.

Even on the porch, Maus heard the muffled noise coming from the television. It was always on. His momma never turned it off. In fact, it wasn't unusual for her to sleep in the big recliner in the living room, watching television until her eyes fell shut.

Maus tried to block out the noise. He had bigger issues down below.

The house rested on a small hill. The locals called Jesser "poverty flats" for a reason. Its inhabitants were certainly poor, and Jesser didn't have mountain vistas. So from the top of that small hill, there was a pretty good view.

Down south from the house, about three-quarters of a mile, Maus watched the action just on the other side of their property line. It was marked by a cypress grove.

In the morning, it had just been a news truck. Now there were three cop cars, a couple of ambulances, and two more news trucks.

Maus wanted to get closer. He knew that they had found it, but he wanted to hear what they were saying and what they were thinking. It was his day off, and they'd ask him why he was there on his day off. He'd have to explain that he saw the activity from his momma's house, and that wouldn't be good. He didn't want them to find out that he'd grown up here. He didn't want them to find out that he had played in that cypress grove as a kid. That this was his real home.

Then Maus thought about the bodies and DNA. He went to a class once about DNA. A professor from the University of Miami came and talked to the Sheriff's department and some of the local police. Maus didn't understand it all. He thought the professor was a big nerd, showing off how smart he was, but the message at the end of the lecture was pretty clear: DNA was everywhere.

He didn't think that they'd find any DNA that would trace back to him. *It's not like he'd raped 'em or anything*, Maus thought. Plus, they'd have to get a DNA sample from him to compare it to. So if they found DNA, they'd just run it through a database of convicted felons and there wouldn't be a match.

Maus closed his eyes. He rolled his broad shoulders, trying to roll back his paranoia.

He continued to watch the activity down in the cypress grove awhile longer, wondering how they'd found it. It had to be his own bad luck. He thought about Tommy Estrada. That was just bad luck, too. He hadn't buried the body deep enough. An animal got at it and pulled it into the nearby fields. It was just bad luck.

I'm safe. I'm safe. I'm safe.

Maus looked in his hand. It was a subpoena to testify in the Tommy Estrada trial. The woman attorney said they'd call him and let him know if he was needed. Maus hadn't gotten a call yet. *That's good*, he thought. *I'm still safe.*

Dylan McNaughten cut a line of coke on a small pocket mirror. He held it in his hand, looking down at his fractured reflection. His hand trembled in anticipation of the shot of white powder. He'd been off cocaine for a week, and he couldn't hold off any longer. He needed the power.

Dylan took a cut straw out of his pocket and snorted a line.

He let the rush take him.

He leaned back against the cold wall tiles, enjoying the relative privacy of his brother's downstairs toilet. He may have sat for a minute or maybe three. Dylan didn't care. He just needed a little boost.

He wiped the mirror down, and then put the mirror and straw back in his pocket.

Before exiting, Dylan checked himself, and then returned to the bar in his brother's man cave.

"You don't need to start over." Dylan pulled out a chair and sat down next to his brother, Brian. "Just give me the bottom line."

"Bottom line is that Maus is a problem. If there's any evidence that Jolly Boy knew about what was going on with workers or ordered Maus to do this stuff, then all bets are off. Judge Delaney said he'd allow all the excluded evidence about Maus to come in and probably a lot more. The liability would be big."

Dylan sat up in his chair. Money always got his attention. He had a lifestyle to maintain.

"Like how bad?"

Brian shrugged.

"Grant wouldn't give a number. He's a chicken-shit lawyer. But I think it could break us." Brian waited. "Plus Grant told me there might be criminal liability, like anybody who helped Maus or helped him cover it up could go to prison."

Brian let that hang in the room, and they both thought about what that would mean to them. Brian knew what had to be done, but he didn't want to say it out loud. He was still imagining the tiny recording devices.

"So do you think you can handle this?"

Dylan nodded his head.

"I need some cash, though," he said. "Lots of it."

CHAPTER FORTY ONE

Michael folded a couple of dress shirts and put them in his suitcase. He picked up the framed picture of his namesake, wrapped it in a towel and laid it on top of the other clothes.

Jane came out of the bathroom and saw the suitcase.

"You're leaving?" She walked across the room to Michael.

Michael closed the top of his suitcase and latched it shut.

"You seemed like you wanted some privacy, so I got a room at the Stay-Rite with Kermit."

Jane folded her arms.

"I was just thinking," she said. "Women think. That's all I've been doing." Jane walked closer to Michael. Physically she got closer, but there was an emotional distance between them. Their conversations were flat.

"You did a good job today. I asked you to get me a delay, and you got me a delay."

Michael sighed. He knew they needed more. A delay was just a delay.

"We need causation," Michael said. "I can't get you that."

"No more tricks up your sleeve?"

Michael shook his head.

"Afraid not." He picked up his suitcase. He walked over to Jane, set the suitcase down and then kissed her on the cheek. "Any word from the feds?"

Jane stepped back.

"I don't think so."

"Well stay on Justin," Michael said. "That guy still loves you and there's still some time."

###

Jane sat alone on her ratty couch. It was the same ratty couch she had bought secondhand while in college. It was the same ratty couch she had during law school, and now, here it was. The ratty couch was in the middle of her sad, one-bedroom apartment in Jesser, Florida.

She was rapidly closing in on 40 years old. She had no husband, no real boyfriend, no kids, no house, and a failing law firm. She rubbed her hand on the frayed cushion.

What the hell am I doing?

Jane allowed herself a few more minutes of self-pity, and then she got up. She walked over to the kitchen, opened her freezer, and found the pint of Ben and Jerry's chocolate chip cookie dough ice cream.

Jane grabbed a spoon, and walked back into her living room. She sat down on her couch, took off the lid, and then resumed the pity party in earnest.

The ice cream went down easy. One spoonful came after another, until it was all gone.

She set the empty container down on the end table, and then Jane laid down on the couch. She closed her eyes. She laid in the silence; thinking. She ran over the options in her head. They were options related to both the case against Jolly Boy and her life.

After sorting and resorting the list, Jane came to the simple conclusion that her future largely, if not entirely, depended on the case against Jolly Boy. She had to win. She had to figure out a way to win.

Jane eventually sat up and got her cell phone out of her pocket.

She punched in a few numbers, stopped, and then finished dialing.

It started to ring. For a moment, Jane thought about just hanging up and forgetting about it.

Then, an answer.

It took Justin Kent about an hour and a half to get there.

Jane opened the door and let him inside. They gave each other an awkward hug, and then Kent stood near the door. It was his first time back to her apartment after their broken engagement, and he was unsure of what to do with himself. Kent knew every inch of the place, but he didn't think he should act on that knowledge.

Finally, Jane figured out what was happening. He wanted direction.

"I'll take your coat," she said. "Just have a seat at the table."

Kent half-smiled, relieved.

He walked into the small kitchen area, pulled out a chair and sat down.

Jane came back from her bedroom after putting his coat on her bed. She opened the refrigerator.

"I'm having a beer. You want one?"

"Sure." Kent folded his hands in front of him. As Jane pulled out the bottles and began to screw off the caps, he filled the silence.

"I'm glad you called me," he said. "I wasn't sure whether I should call after the meeting, but I wanted to. ... You didn't seem too happy afterwards."

Jane handed him an open bottle of beer, and then she sat down on the other side of the table.

"It's a lot to take in." Jane took a sip from her bottle, and then started to pick at the label. "Sounds like Vatch wants him pretty bad."

Kent nodded.

"He's been after that money for years. Probably won't ever stop."

"Well I was being honest in there. I really don't know anything."

Jane took another sip of beer.

"Of course I've asked a few times, but Michael always blows me off. In a way, I don't want to know. He's a good guy. He's a friend."

"Do you love him?" Kent asked.

The question took Jane back.

"I *like* him," she said, thinking about it. "I could love him, some day. Depends. There's too much going on right now to fall in love, too much unknown."

Kent nodded. He waited a moment.

"I miss you, Jane," he said. He played with the beer bottle in his hand, a nervous fidget. "We aren't getting back together right now, and I get that, but I still miss you. I miss seeing you in the morning when I wake up. You made me feel proud of what I do."

Jane picked at the label on her bottle a little more, and then managed to pull it off. She balled up the wet sticker, and pushed it off to the side.

"If we were to do this deal," she said, ignoring what Kent had just told her. "How long would it take?"

"Not long," Kent said. "We could set it up pretty quickly, but you need to tell us. You're the one running out of time."

"We've got our medical expert, and then there's Elana. She hasn't testified yet, but she's last."

Jane finished her beer, and then got up and walked the empty bottle over to the sink.

"But the judge told us we needed to connect the dots, and neither the medical expert or Elana can do that. That's why I need your help."

She rinsed out the bottle, and then Jane put the bottle in the recycling.

"And you're sure the feds aren't going to do it just because it's the right thing to do?"

"If it was me, I'd do it in a heartbeat with no strings." Kent smiled. "But this is the FBI."

Kent got up and walked over to Jane. He put his hand on her shoulder.

"Vatch knows he's got leverage. He wants something in return." Kent shrugged. "It's not my call. I'm sorry."

CHAPTER FORTY TWO

It wasn't even midnight and the club was already pulsing. Dylan could walk into any club on South Beach, but the T1M3 was where he spent most of his nights. He walked past the long line of tourists and posers that would never make the doorman's cut, and then slipped under the red rope with a nod and a hundred-dollar bill.

Inside it was already packed. The huge dance floor pulsed with the rhythm of DJ Politik. The domed ceiling erupted in bursts of smoke and light while 12 women in glowing bikinis pranced on raised platforms.

On a typical night he'd have already zeroed in on a woman for later, but not tonight. He made his way back to the VIP lounge by himself.

To the right, he went up a few stairs, and then past another bouncer. One nod and he was in.

Dylan found a seat in the back.

Within a few seconds of sitting down, a waitress brought him a Red Bull and vodka. He took a few sips, and then pulled out his cell phone. He sent a text: BATHRM IN 10.

###

The bathrooms at T1M3 were dark. Dylan walked to the third stall and sat down on the toilet. He didn't need to go, but that's where he needed to be.

A few seconds later a man came into the stall next to him. The man sat down, and then put a leather courier bag down on the floor. Dylan leaned over, reached under the stall just a bit, pulled the bag toward him, and then picked the bag up.

Inside the bag he found a loaded gun and a bag of cocaine.

Dylan took out a handkerchief, picked up the gun, and slid it into his jacket pocket. Then he picked up the blow. His heart beat a little quicker, and he cursed his brother for pretending to be better than he was. His brother never gave him the respect he deserved. The business only existed because somebody had to bend the rules. *You don't eat tomatoes in the winter without a slave or two.*

Dylan removed a large clip of cash from his wallet. He put it in the bag, and then slid the bag back under the stall with his foot.

By the time he flushed and exited the bathroom, whoever had brought the leather courier bag and its precious contents was long gone.

###

Dylan McNaughten had a pretty simple plan. He was going to meet Maus at the nature preserve, and then shoot him in the face. *That couldn't be too hard*, thought Dylan. He'd never killed anybody before, but it seemed easy.

After Maus was dead, Dylan was going to pick up one of Maus' dead hands and fire another shot high into the woods. The second shot was for the residue. He needed to make it look like a suicide.

Dylan had seen it on one of those cop television shows. Guns leave a residue on the hand and sleeve of the shooter when fired. He needed that.

Although Dylan figured there wouldn't be too many tears that Maus was gone, he wanted 'proof' of Maus' purported suicide. After the Jolly Boy graveyard had been discovered, reporters started calling about Maus. The reporters knew about the trial, and they knew about some of Maus' handiwork. A suicide would just mean the fat boy had snapped under the pressure.

It was a simple plan. Dylan stopped his car at the nature preserve's entrance. The preserve was closed, so the gate was closed.

Dylan unlocked the door, but, before he got out of the car, he opened his new bag of coke and did a few lines. He was coming down and he needed a fresh hit to smooth the edge. It felt good. He loved the feeling of cocaine. It was power.

Dylan sealed up the bag and put it in his glove box. Then he took out a pair of thin leather gloves. Dylan looked at the gun laying in the passenger seat. It was a beautiful weapon, elegant. He picked up the gun and moved it to the center console of his car.

Then he got out and walked up to the gate. The chain was in place, but it was loose and unlocked. That was good news. It meant that Maus was already inside the preserve, waiting.

Dylan unwrapped the chain, lifted the gate, and then went back to his car. He pulled it forward twenty yards, and then got out of the car and walked back to the gate. He returned the chain to its place, and then he was on his way.

He followed the winding road about a mile further into the preserve. It was pitch black, and he was concerned about an animal darting in front of him. He continued on until he saw a sign for the trailhead and then another. Dylan followed the signs to a small parking lot.

He slowed down and picked the gun up off of the center console. He kept it low in his right hand while steering with his left.

Dylan scanned the abandoned parking area. Maus was alone. He was outside his truck, leaning against the truck's passenger-side door and drinking a beer.

Perfect.

This was the time for improvisation, and Dylan knew immediately how it would go down. He felt a rush of confidence. There were certain things in life that couldn't be planned. He couldn't have known where Maus would park his truck, whether Maus would be in his truck or outside. He couldn't have known whether Maus would be angry, scared, or drunk. Maybe Maus would be holding a shotgun. No way to know, there were too many variables. So he had kept the plan simple – a rough outline that would be filled in at the moment of engagement.

It was going to work. Dylan felt good.

He slowed down even further. As he pulled into the parking space next to where Maus was standing, Dylan unrolled the window. It was a natural thing to do, and it was also natural for Maus to see and hear the window open.

When Dylan stopped the car, Maus put his hand on the roof and bent over to say something through the open window. When Maus opened his mouth, Dylan smelled the alcohol come off his breath.

"Evening, deputy," Dylan said.

As Maus answered Dylan's greeting, Dylan shoved the gun's muzzle into Maus' mouth and pulled the trigger.

The shot jolted Maus' head. The entire back of his skull blew off. Fragments splattered the side of his truck as his body fell to the ground.

That was easy.

Dylan put the car in reverse, pulling back about 10 feet. He decided to keep the car's lights on so that he could better see what he was doing.

He got out of the car, walked over to Maus' body, and then picked up Maus' right hand. It was the perfect combination of the planned and the improvised.

Dylan rubbed his nose, longing for another hit of coke, but he knew it would have to wait. He placed the gun in Maus' hand, manipulated the index finger over the trigger, and then fired a shot high and off into the woods. Stepping back, Dylan let the hand go and let the gun fall to the ground.

Dylan smiled. The cocaine had made him powerful. He stepped back and started thinking that he should be named the CEO of Jolly Boy. His brother didn't have the balls. He thought, *I'm fucking ready now!*

Dylan made it about halfway back to his car when he heard some movement. His first thought was that it was a deer or something. Then he heard the shouts. The light changed. He looked around and was blinded by high-powered flashlights on all sides.

"Get your hands in the air and get down."

Dylan tried to comprehend, but he couldn't figure it out.

He hesitated, and then his leg was kicked out from under him. Dylan fell. They were shouting instructions at him, but he still didn't understand. Somebody grabbed his hair and shoved his face into the dirt. Gravel cut into his cheek, and he felt a boot come down on his neck. His arms were pulled back. His hands were put together, and then a plastic zipcord looped around each one and pulled tight. The plastic edges cut his wrists and he started to bleed.

Another person shouted instructions at him, but Dylan laid still. This evidently made the person angry, because he received a quick kick to his side and a pain shot through his rib cage.

Multiple hands grabbed him, and Dylan was rolled over onto his back. A flashlight shown into his face, keeping him blind, and then he heard the words: "You're under arrest."

CHAPTER FORTY THREE

Jane and Michael sat and listened to the cross-examination of their medical expert – a tweedy man in his late fifties, a professor at the University of Florida-Miami and a general legal gun-for-hire.

His career had followed a path typical of medical experts. He had gone to medical school, gotten his degree, published papers and taught classes until he had received tenure. Once he had the security of academic tenure and a guaranteed pension, he focused most of his energy on testifying in as many cases as possible for $20,000 to $50,000 a pop.

Jane waited and then stood up, objecting to a question posed by Harrison Grant related to some obscure medical issue. Judge Delaney quickly overruled her objection.

Being overruled was expected. Jane only made the objection to interrupt Grant's rhythm and remind the jury that she still existed.

Harrison Grant continued, ending with three questions.

"You agree that Mr. Estrada's cancer was terminal, meaning he was going to die within a year, correct?"

Their expert agreed with that statement, as he had to, because it was true.

"And you don't know for certain what caused Mr. Estrada's cancer, right?"

The expert tried to explain that, based on his medical review, the cancer was caused by repeated exposure to pesticides, but ultimately Harrison Grant boxed him in. He was ultimately forced to admit that he didn't know exactly what caused the cancer, and that there were thousands of people who died of cancer who had not been exposed to pesticides.

Finally, Harrison Grant asked, "And you don't know who killed Tommy Estrada do you?" The professor shook his head. He didn't know who had killed Mr. Estrada. He only knew that Tommy Estrada was killed by repeated blows to his head with a blunt object.

Jane asked a few questions on re-direct, but she was anxious to get the medical expert off the witness stand. She wanted a break. It had taken everything in her power not to check her voicemail messages during the testimony.

She looked down at her notes, and then looked up at Judge Delaney.

"No further questions, Your Honor."

Judge Delaney nodded. He looked at Harrison Grant, and Grant stated that he didn't have any further questions, either. Then Judge Delaney looked at the jury and smiled.

"Okay, then I think this is a good time for us to take a break."

Everyone in the courtroom stood and watched the jury stand, stretch, and then file out the side door.

Jane immediately picked her briefcase up off of the floor. She set it down on the table, opened the briefcase, and pulled out her cell phone. Jane turned it on.

Michael watched her, wondering what was going on.

"Expecting a call?"

Jane nodded her head.

"Yes, I am." She stared down at the cell phone screen and waited for it to connect to the network.

"Somebody I know?" Michael asked.

"Justin. I'm hoping he'll call." Jane got up, punched the button for her voicemail, and then listened. "I got a message," Jane said.

"From him?" Michael asked. "He called?"

Jane nodded as she started to walk away.

"I think something happened."

Jane said goodbye to Justin Kent and hung up the phone. She looked at Michael from across the room. He was still sitting at their table. Jane wasn't quite sure what to say.

She knew she was going to win. She'd done it. But it had come at a cost. Her "win" was built upon the loss of three lives. First, Tommy Estrada was dead. Second, Roberto Estrada was dead. Late last night, the police had confirmed that Roberto was one of the people buried in the cypress grove. Now Maus was dead, too.

Michael saw that she was off the phone. He stood up.

"Okay, what's going on? What did he say?"

Jane didn't say anything. She walked across the room to Michael. She took his hand.

"We have to talk." She led him out of the courtroom. "Things got complicated."

"In a good way?" Michael asked.

Jane nodded her head.

"I think so." She opened the door into the hallway. They walked across the hall toward the small conference rooms.

They went inside the first one available. Once the door closed, and they were alone, Jane began to explain. She told Michael about Maus and Dylan McNaughten's arrest.

"He's going to testify for us. Tell us everything he knows."

"That's the deal?" Michael asked.

Jane shook her head.

CHAPTER FORTY FOUR

The judge's law clerk led the attorneys back into chambers. Judge Delaney stood with his back to them, looking out his window.

"Come in," he said without turning around. He continued to look down at the people and cars below.

"You know this is one of the highlights of my day, looking out this window. The contrast is hypnotizing. There's chaos down there, and then peace and quiet up here."

Judge Delaney turned; a smile crept across his face.

"Of course, there are moments of chaos up here as well."

Judge Delaney sat down behind his desk. He nodded at Harrison Grant, and then turned to Jane and Michael.

"Ms. Nance, something tells me that you're about to do something or say something that creates some chaos." Judge Delaney raised an eyebrow. "Correct?"

Grant turned to Jane. Brian McNaughten did the same. They didn't know what was going to happen. After the discovery of the Jolly Boy graveyard, however, they both knew that whatever it was, they would not like it.

"Your Honor," Jane said, "I'm not sure quite how to say this in a tactful manner."

Judge Delaney shrugged.

"I've heard and seen lots of things in my years on the bench." He glanced at his watch. "We don't have that much time before I want to call the jurors back from break, so enlighten us."

"Okay." Jane looked at Michael, and then she continued. "We were going to call Deputy Maus as our next witness." Jane paused. "But that's not going to be possible."

Judge Delaney nodded his head, slowly.

"You have my attention now, Ms. Nance. What's going on?"

"As you know, it is the plaintiff's theory of the case that Deputy Maus was corrupt. He was hired by Jolly Boy to be a henchman, an enforcer, and we believe he killed our client and others when they were not able to work or were otherwise causing trouble for the company."

"That's your theory," Judge Delaney said. "But I wanted to hear testimony of the direct connection between his actions and Jolly Boy."

"And that's where my objection would come into play, Your Honor," Harrison Grant said. He saw his opening, and he took it. "It's the defendant's position that —"

Jane interrupted. "But Maus is dead. He was murdered last night."

Judge Delaney froze, and then he looked over at Harrison Grant and Brian McNaughten. His eyes turned cold.

"Do you know anything about this?"

Harrison Grant shook his head.

"Of course not, Your Honor, this is the first we ..." He looked over at his client, Brian McNaughten. Brian's head was down. Grant calculated the angles and tried to figure out what his client may have done.

"Perhaps the label of 'murder' is a bit premature. Deputy Maus was a troubled man. He may have succumbed to the pressure and took his own life."

Jane gave Harrison Grant some space. They allowed the great trial lawyer to continue spinning his new theory.

Eventually Grant stopped talking, and Judge Delaney looked back at Michael and Jane.

"While I appreciate Mr. Grant's ruminations, I'd prefer to hear from Ms. Nance." Judge Delaney nodded toward Jane. "Please continue."

"Maus did not commit suicide, Your Honor. His murder was witnessed by at least a half-dozen federal agents investigating a South Beach drug ring."

Judge Delaney leaned forward.

"So they have the person who did this?"

"Yes." Michael nodded his head. He looked at Jane, and then together they said, "Dylan McNaughten."

CHAPTER FORTY FIVE

They went back into the courtroom and Jane made a record of the events that had occurred over the past 24 hours. The jury wasn't in the courtroom, so the attorneys and judge could speak more freely.

When Jane had concluded, Harrison Grant's first reaction was to ask Judge Delaney to declare a mistrial. A mistrial could be declared by a judge whenever there was a significant procedural error or statements by witnesses, attorneys, or the judge that unfairly tainted a jury.

Judge Delaney barely paused to consider Grant's motion. He didn't even ask Michael and Jane for a response.

"The only person who may have grounds for a mistrial is the plaintiff in this case, due to my own statements during this trial and repeated decisions to preclude important evidence from being heard by this jury. I was giving Jolly Boy the benefit of the doubt. That was an error on my part."

Delaney turned to Michael and Jane.

"I am, however, able to correct that error." Judge Delaney leaned back in his chair. "In light of recent events, I will allow all testimony related to Deputy Maus. I will give the plaintiffs wide latitude to argue for any inferences they want to be made from that testimony related to Jolly Boy's knowledge of Maus' behavior."

Harrison Grant didn't push back on the judge's ruling. He thought for a moment, and then he played the only card he had left.

"In that case, Your Honor, I would ask that this court grant us a continuance so that we can better prepare for this testimony."

Judge Delaney leaned forward, peering down at Grant from the bench. He stared at Grant, and then he looked at Brian McNaughten. Brian McNaughten still hadn't met the judge's eye. The judge looked back at Harrison Grant and narrowed his gaze even further. Then he finally gave his one word response, "No."

Grant raised his hand, surrendering.

"Your Honor, I—"

"I thought my ruling was clear. The motion for a continuance is denied."

Judge Delaney slammed his gavel down. The sound echoed off the courtroom walls. Judge Delaney continued to glare at Harrison Grant and Brian McNaughten. He didn't blink until Grant slinked back to his seat and sat down.

Once Grant was seated, Judge Delaney took a long breath and then exhaled slowly. Then he pointed at Grant.

"If I find out you had any knowledge of this, I will not rest until the board revokes your license to practice law. Understood?"

Harrison Grant nodded.

"I assure you, Your Honor, that I knew nothing."

"Good." Judge Delaney turned to Michael and Jane. "Okay, it's your witness. Let's get on with this trial."

"Thank you, Your Honor," said Jane. "When the jury returns, the plaintiff will call Dylan McNaughten to the stand."

CHAPTER FORTY SIX

Dylan McNaughten entered from the back of the courtroom. There were five extra bailiffs on the perimeter of the room, and another three bulky federal agents in plain clothes.

Dylan walked to the witness stand. He raised his right hand, and then he was asked, "Do you swear to tell the truth, the whole truth, and nothing but the truth?"

Dylan's eyes darted around the room. He was shaky and unsure. Telling the truth wasn't exactly what he had been known for in the past, but now it was one of his only ways of avoiding "Ol' Sparky." Ol' Sparky was the nickname given to the three-legged oak chair built by Florida inmates in 1923. It had a long history of malfunctioning. It had caused dozens of prisoners' prolonged and gruesome deaths. The previous year, a cop-killer's head caught on fire after the execution team used the wrong foam cushion in the electrified helmet.

After the oath was repeated a second time, Dylan answered.

"Yeah, I'm gonna tell the truth."

He sat down, and then Jane started her questions. They were soft, easy questions. Jane asked Dylan about where he grew up and where he went to school. She asked about his family, and his hobbies.

Those initial questions lasted about a half-hour.

Jane knew that the jury was getting bored, but she needed Dylan to get comfortable. She also needed everybody in the room to get comfortable with him.

Periodically, Jane glanced over at Harrison Grant and Dylan's brother, Brian McNaughten.

Harrison Grant was on the edge of his seat, waiting for an opportunity to object. He wasn't quite ready to give up, although he soon would.

Brian McNaughten sat next to Harrison Grant. Although he had a pen in his hand and a notepad in front of him, Brian McNaughten was still. He just looked down at the notepad. He only wanted to get out of the courtroom as quickly as possible.

"Turning our attention to Jolly Boy's growing operations." Jane cleared her throat. "Do you know how they work?"

Dylan nodded his head.

"I do. My brother focused on the front office, management, and sales. I got the product picked, sorted, and trucked."

"You mentioned your brother. Is he in the courtroom today?"

Dylan nodded his head.

"And could you identify and describe him for the record?"

Jane had asked these identifying questions because she figured that the jury members would have seen it done on television or in the movies. She wanted the jury to start thinking about Jolly Boy and Brian McNaughten as criminals, which they were.

"My brother, Brian, is the man in the dark blue suit, white shirt and red tie." Dylan McNaughten pointed.

"Let the record reflect, Your Honor, that Dylan McNaughten has identified Brian McNaughten, the CEO and President of Jolly Boy."

Harrison Grant stood.

"Objection to this, Your Honor."

Judge Delaney leaned forward.

"Sit down, counselor. Objection overruled."

The judge's message was clear, and Jane watched Harrison Grant deflate. Judge Delaney wasn't going to give Grant anything.

"Tell me about your brother's involvement with getting the product picked and shipped."

"He didn't really want to know how it happened," Dylan said. "Brian just wanted it done for a certain price. He told me the price, and then I had to make it happen."

The answer surprised Jane. It wasn't what she had expected.

A silence hung in the room as Jane scanned her notes, thinking of how to recover. It wasn't sufficient for Dylan McNaughten to act alone in the same way that it wasn't sufficient to have Deputy Maus act alone. The whole company needed to know and approve of what he was doing.

Jane looked at Michael, and Michael gave her an encouraging nod.

Jane took a deep breath and decided she should go for it.

"When you just said, 'he didn't really want to know,' my question is this – and it's the most important question in this case – did he *actually* know?"

Dylan McNaughten smiled. He was done being the only bad boy in the family. It was time for his brother to get his hands dirty too.

"Of course Brian knew."

"How?"

"I told him," Dylan said. "We were careful. There were no emails. There were no memos. We'd just talk about what was going on."

###

After another series of questions, Dylan started to enjoy himself. He wanted to talk. The apprehension was gone. He liked the attention and he wanted to please his audience.

"Maus and I were a team." He leaned back. "My brother would say that a specific field wasn't producing the way it should, so Maus and I would figure out what was going on. Sometimes we had workers who were too old or too sick. Sometimes we had workers that were just lazy. Whatever the problem was, we'd fix it."

"And was Tommy Estrada a problem?"

Dylan nodded his head.

"He was a big problem." Dylan looked over at his brother with cold eyes. He was being charged with murder, and he wasn't going down alone.

His brother was just as guilty as he was. Brian just never wanted to get his hands dirty. He only wanted to reap the rewards.

"I talked to my brother about him," Dylan said. "It was sensitive, because Tommy Estrada had you. Both of you were organizing the workers, so we all knew about him. We hated the bad publicity. So in the end, we decided to teach a lesson to the others."

"Who is 'we,' when you say we decided?" Jane clarified.

"Me, my brother, and Maus."

Brian McNaughten rose to his feet.

"That's not true. He's lying."

Judge Delaney pounded his gavel.

"Sit down, Mr. McNaughten." Judge Delaney turned to the jury. "You are to disregard that outburst. It is stricken from the record." Then he turned back to Harrison Grant. "Control your client or I'll hold you both in contempt."

Judge Delaney motioned with his hand for Jane to continue.

"Then what happened?" she asked.

"I met with Maus again." Dylan shrugged his shoulders. "I told him that either Tommy works or Tommy goes."

"And what does that mean?"

"It meant we wanted Tommy taken out."

There was a pause. Dylan waited for Jane to continue, but she didn't. She wanted him to say it, and he finally understood.

"You know," Dylan said. "We needed him killed."

"Like the others found in the cypress grove?"

Dylan nodded.

"Like the others."

CHAPTER FORTY SEVEN

Your witness." Judge Delaney pointed at Harrison Grant, and Grant slowly gathered his notes and walked up to the podium.

He looked exhausted. Years of hustling for clients, traveling all over the country, and building an impressive track record of winning was appearing to catch up with him. As he began to cross-examine Dylan McNaughten, Michael could see the hesitation. The wheels turned inside Harrison Grant's head. He was making a calculation. Harrison Grant was figuring out how hard he should fight. He was trying to figure out if he would get burned again, and how.

Then Harrison Grant took a breath, stood a little taller, and soldiered on. That's what attorneys did.

"Mr. McNaughten, you use drugs, correct?" Dylan agreed, and then they went back and forth about the types of drugs that Dylan McNaughten had used and abused. They talked about the circumstances of his arrest the evening before, and then about his decision to testify.

"You were offered a pretty good deal if you took the witness stand today, isn't that right?"

Dylan shook his head.

"No, sir. There's no deal."

Harrison Grant laughed. He saw the angles, and then worked them for his client.

"Come on, Mr. McNaughten, certainly you obtained legal counsel, correct?"

"Yes."

Dylan nodded his head and shifted in his seat. He glanced over at Jane and Michael, as if they could stop it.

"And your counsel told you that it would be in your best interest to testify, correct?"

Jane and Michael both stood.

"Objection."

Judge Delaney raised his hand, and then directed Jane and Michael to sit.

"The objection is sustained. The question calls upon Mr. McNaughten to reveal privileged attorney-client communication." He looked at Harrison Grant. "You know better, counselor. Move on."

Harrison Grant nodded. He didn't care if Dylan McNaughten answered the question. He just wanted the jury to hear it. He wanted to plant a seed of doubt about Dylan's credibility.

"Certainly you hope that your testimony today will lessen the sentence that you may receive for murdering Deputy Maus, correct?"

Dylan again looked over at Michael and Jane. He wanted to know whether he should answer, but he didn't have a choice. Michael and Jane didn't have a basis to object. It was a valid question about his motive for testifying.

Dylan eventually nodded.

"Yes," he said. "That's one of the reasons." Dylan looked at his brother. "And I want the truth to come out."

Harrison Grant let out another little laugh.

"Yes, the truth, and let's talk about the truth." Harrison Grant paused, and then started a lengthy cross-examination about Brian McNaughten's knowledge of what Dylan and Maus were doing.

Dylan did well.

He never backed down. Dylan stuck by his testimony, but Harrison Grant did quite a bit of damage. He tripped Dylan up on some dates and facts, and at times Dylan looked shaky.

After another 10 minutes of questioning, Grant stopped. He reviewed his notes, making sure that he had covered all of the areas that he had intended to cover in his cross-examination.

Then Grant made a classic mistake. Rather than just being satisfied with the damage he had done to Dylan McNaughten's credibility, Grant decided to ask one last question.

"Just one more thing." Grant paused for drama, believing that Dylan's answer to his final question would save his client. Grant knew Brian McNaughten had been careful. For years, he had advised Jolly Boy to wall itself off from the ugliness that occurred in the fields. Grant assumed that Brian McNaughten and Jolly Boy had followed his advice.

"And – besides *your* testimony –," Grant continued, "you don't have any other proof that your brother knew what was going on, do you?"

Dylan looked confused.

"What do you mean? We talked about it all the time."

"Yes, *you* say you talked about it. But you don't have anything else, correct?"

Dylan shook his head.

"Anything else?"

"Like e-mails or letters, text messages, anything like that?" Harrison Grant smiled. His confidence was growing. "You don't have anything at all to prove Jolly Boy knew anything, do you?"

Dylan paused for a moment, thinking.

"Of course I do," he said. "I called Brian from jail last night. We talked about everything. It's recorded. The cops should have it."

Jane rose to her feet.

"Your Honor, the plaintiffs do not have that recording. We'd like an order from this Court to require the police to release this taped conversation. It's relevant and I need it for my rebuttal."

Judge Delaney looked at Harrison Grant. He enjoyed the humiliation.

"The motion is granted, Ms. Nance. The police shall produce the recording for this court immediately."

CHAPTER FORTY EIGHT

"Tell it again." Kermit lifted his bottle of beer and banged on the table top. "Tell it again. Tell it again," he chanted.

"Okay," Michael said. "If Jane isn't going to brag a little bit more, then I'll do it."

Kermit and Miggy clapped. Kermit's dreadlocks danced as his head tilted back with laughter.

"I knew you wouldn't let me down, *mi amigo*." Kermit lifted his bottle up, and Michael clinked it with his own beer. "Carry on."

"Okay." Michael took a breath and held it for dramatic affect. "Picture it: The great Harrison Grant, standing at the podium. He goes like this –" Michael put his nose in the air, squinted his eyes, and pouted out his front lip. "You don't have anything at all, do you?" Michael relaxed, put his arm around Jane, and then Michael continued the recap much to the delight of Kermit and Miggy. "Then Dylan McNaughten goes, 'I called Brian from jail last night. It's recorded.'"

"Yes." Kermit laughed wildly, and then pounded on the table some more. "Justice." He shouted at the other patrons of The Box. "Never whisper justice, my friends, never whisper justice."

Jane looked around the bar.

"You're going to get us thrown out of this place."

Kermit waved her off.

"Nonsense." Kermit blew a kiss at the heavyset waitress. "My honey has got our back, baby. We're royalty here."

"Well, this princess has to go to bed." Jane checked her watch. "It's late, and this thing isn't over. Judge Delaney is letting us recall the witnesses he didn't let testify, and then we have to prepare for whatever Harrison Grant comes up with after that."

Michael nodded.

"Grant's probably got a dozen associates up all night, researching objections and motions," he said. "His client is desperate, and he's going to bill the hell out of them before they go bankrupt."

Jane slid out of the booth. She picked up her purse.

"I've gotta go to the bathroom. Meet me out front?"

Michael finished his beer, and put it down on the table.

"I'll pay up and see you in a minute," he said.

"Fine," Kermit said. "You two lovebirds go. Miggy and me'll shut it down." Kermit turned to Miggy. "You got any more party left in you?"

"*Si*." Miggy smiled. "Very much party left."

CHAPTER FORTY NINE

This night was just like any other night. The gang of losers sat around Frankie's basement playing Xbox. Frankie's mom was gone for her monthly ladies' night, which he didn't really want to know much more about. Frankie's dad was in a crappy studio apartment in Fort Lauderdale, trying to save money to pay his lawyer to get the divorce finalized.

The unsupervised group of six teenage boys sat in a semi-circle. They pretended to shoot people that flashed across the screen and they sipped glasses of vodka and Mountain Dew. They wanted beer. Beer seemed more like what real guys would drink, but there was no way they looked old enough to buy. And swiping beer from the refrigerator was too risky. They'd get caught. So vodka it was.

Before Frankie's mom would get home, he planned on refilling the vodka bottle with water. His mother would never know the difference.

Frankie sat there, swirling his drink.

The night wasn't bad. It was just the same.

"I'm bored." Frankie leaned back in his bean bag. He kicked out his legs and rolled his head, staring at the ceiling. One of the other boys suggested that they check out some porn on the computer, but that idea was rejected.

"I don't want to watch porn with a bunch of dudes," Frankie said. "I'll get blue balls if I get all worked up and can't ... you know."

Frankie finished his drink, and then started swirling the ice cubes that remained in the glass.

"We could go pay our friends a visit," Frankie said, thinking out loud. "We could mess up the place real good this time. Watch 'em all go nuts again."

The fat boy with glasses paused the game.

"Been there, done that." The fat boy pointed at the screen. "Plus I'm close to beating your high score."

Frankie waved him off as the fat boy resumed playing the video game.

"I'm thinking of something different this time, different than shit-in-a-bag or spray paint." Frankie smiled, watching the things blow up on the television screen. "Something big that'll get in the papers, maybe even get that hot chick reporter from News 7 back here."

The fat boy scrunched up his nose.

"The one with the big tits or the small tits?"

"The big tits, of course." Frankie shook his head at the absurdity. "Why the fuck would I want a chick with small tits?"

"I kind of like chicks with small tits," said the fat kid with glasses. "They're more ... manageable."

Frankie rolled his eyes.

"Like you would know."

Jane came out the front door of The Box.

"Mind if you drive home?" She put her arm around Michael, and pulled him closer.

"That's fine," Michael said. "I'm parked back at your office." They started walking across the gravel parking lot. "Want to leave your car here?"

"Sounds good," Jane said. "We can pick it up tomorrow on the way to court."

"The walk will be nice." Michael took a breath. "The fresh air will sober me up a little, too."

He looked up at the perfect sky. It was dotted heavy with stars. The nighttime temperature was perfect, not too cold and not too warm.

The streets of downtown Jesser were deserted. It was peaceful, and for a moment, Michael thought things were finally working out. They were going to win this case for Elana and Pace, and he was going to be able to move on.

They continued to walk, leaving the parking lot and crossing the street. It was about a mile from The Box to Jane's office on Main Street.

For the first few minutes, Michael and Jane walked in silence.

"When did you know Justin was going to come through for us?" Michael asked after awhile.

Jane shook her head.

"I didn't ever know for sure," she said. "When we initially asked them, Justin convinced a few agents to start talking to their sources about Dylan, but I didn't know that until this morning. He hadn't told me. Then I got the call that they were going to make the arrest, but I didn't know whether he'd talk. And I certainly never thought he'd do that to Maus."

"Why didn't you tell me?" Michael asked.

"You knew I was working on it." Jane shrugged. "And I was in a weird place. I didn't know where we were at."

Michael stopped, and then Jane stopped too.

Jane wasn't looking at him, and so Michael gently put his hand under her chin. He tilted Jane's head up so that they were looking at each other eye to eye.

"You should've told me." Michael kissed her softly on her forehead. "We're a team."

Jane closed her eyes.

"I know." She nodded her head, and then she and Michael started walking again. A tear escaped, rolling down her cheek. It was dark, and Michael never saw the tear.

The truck's horn sounded Dixie, and Frankie turned and shouted at them.

"Chill out."

He looked back at the stacks of boxes in the back of the garage. He rummaged through the stuff alone, looking for spray paint. He knew there was some in one of the boxes by his dad's workbench, but he couldn't find it.

The truck's horn sounded Dixie again, and the engine revved.

Frankie shook his head. They were getting impatient. He didn't want them to give up. He didn't want to go back into the house and start playing video games again.

He saw a box that looked about the right size. It was up high in the far corner. Frankie took a few steps toward it, but stumbled as he reached. One of the lower boxes fell and knocked a rake and planter off a shelf. The terracotta planter crashed to the floor and shattered.

Frankie cursed. He tried to get the box again, and reaching with his fingertips, he finally got it down.

He flipped open the top, but it was just filled with old National Geographic magazines.

One of his friends started shouting at him.

"Hurry up, Frankie. I gotta be home by midnight tonight."

Frankie felt his face get flush. He was frustrated.

Frankie took a step back and scanned the garage. He was looking for anything, now. He just wanted to go screw with somebody. Then, he saw it.

There was a can of gasoline next to the lawnmower.

Frankie smiled.

"Perfect."

One of the gang had snagged a pack of cigarettes and matches off his old man's dresser. They used one lit cigarette to chain light the others. They all smoked as they bounced around in the bed of the pickup truck, shouting and whooping it up as they went.

The nicotine and alcohol gave Frankie a buzz. His lips felt sort of numb, and for a moment he almost felt happy. He felt free – just him and his buddies raising hell. *Long live the South*, he thought.

Underneath the blare of the truck's radio, he heard the gasoline slosh in the can wedged between his legs. Frankie smiled, but it was a cruel smile. Time to make the news.

The truck stopped in front of the Law Offices of Jane Nance. The driver killed the engine and the music stopped.

Frankie stood up. He wobbled at first, but caught his balance. He lifted the gas can above his head.

"Who's ready to cook this place?"

Frankie expected a big cheer. He expected the rest of his boys to stand up with him, but they remained seated. A few of them smiled and laughed, but most of them just sat there, continuing to smoke their cigarettes.

Frankie clinched his fist, tightening on the handle of the gas can.

"Come on, who's with me?"

Still no response.

"I thought we had a plan," Frankie said.

The fat boy with glasses shook his head.

"Maybe you should chill out, man. I ain't going to jail for this."

Frankie felt betrayed.

"What did you think we were going to do?" He shook the gas can in front of the fat boy's face. "You can only throw so many bags of shit at a window."

Frankie put down the gas can, and then hopped over the side of the truck. He landed on the sidewalk, and turned to his friends in the truck.

"We gotta show these wetbacks who's in charge. We gotta send this femi-nazi a message." He pointed at one of the other boys in the back of the truck. "Give me the matches." The boy hesitated, and so Frankie repeated the command. "Give me the matches."

The boy handed Frankie his old man's matches. Frankie stuffed them in his pocket. Then he picked up the red metal gas can and spun, throwing the can through the glass window. Shards cracked and fell. The noise echoed off the empty downtown buildings.

Frankie kicked out more of the glass. Then he kicked it a few more times, until the hole was big enough for him to step through.

Inside, Frankie walked over to a filing cabinet. It was against the back wall where he had spray painted his message to the immigrant-lover last year.

He pushed the filing cabinet over, opened a drawer, and spread the paper files over the floor. Then he walked back to the gas can. He picked it up, unscrewed the top and started pouring it out.

Frankie pulled a blue bandanna out of his back pocket. He dipped it into a pool of gas on the floor, and then he lit it on fire.

He tossed the bandanna on the ground, and then turned. Frankie ran. As he jumped out of the broken window, a whoosh of flames went up behind him. The power pushed Frankie, and he fell to the sidewalk.

Frankie looked up at the truck.

"Start the engine!"

He got up, grabbed the side of the truck, and pulled himself in.

A fire alarm sounded. A loud bell clanged and white lights flashed.

"Drive." Frankie ignored his friends' stunned and silent faces. He pounded on the window on the back of the truck's cab. "Drive! Get out of here."

CHAPTER FIFTY

S o, where are we?" Jane looked at Michael. She pulled him a little tighter.

"I don't know." Michael's thoughts drifted back to Hut No. 7 at the Sunset. He was ready to go home. The novelty of practicing law again had worn off. He was tired of wearing a suit and tie. He was tired of the drama and arbitrary deadlines.

"If I'm being honest with myself … and with you, I don't think I can stay here." They kept walking together, but Michael felt the space growing. "I can't be a lawyer."

"But you *are* a lawyer," Jane said. "And you're good at it. You have a gift. You could help a lot of people."

Michael shook his head.

"There are other ways to help people." Michael stuck one of his hands in his pocket. "My problem is that I like to win too much, if that makes sense."

"No." Jane shook her head. "It doesn't make sense."

"Lawyers have rules they have to follow. I'm not good at following rules."

"You won this case. Tommy Estrada's wife is going to have a different and better life because of you. That's got to be worth something."

Michael disagreed.

"You won this case. You built it, you and Justin Kent. You got the feds to do the right thing. I don't know how, but you did."

Jane felt a knot in the pit of her stomach grow.

"You know the feds are still looking for that money. Justin told me about the money from New York." Jane rubbed Michael's hand, keeping him close. "You know I don't care. We can work through it, figure something out."

"There's nothing to figure out."

"It's a lot of money, "Jane said. "They have questions. They see you living in Mexico. They see you flying around. It makes you look guilty."

Michael knew she was right, but kept his mouth shut. He didn't just *look* guilty; he *was* guilty.

He had shared his past with Andie, and he had gotten burned. Now she was gone. He had shared his past with Father Stiles, and Father Stiles had almost ended up in jail.

Michael wasn't sure he was entitled to be open. It was better if it just remained bottled up, compartmentalized. Michael knew he needed to take the advice that he had given to too many clients: When in doubt, shut the hell up. "If you answer their questions, just go in and talk with them, maybe everything will just straighten itself out," Jane said.

Michael didn't respond. It was similar to what Kermit had told him back at the Sunset when he was deciding whether to help Jane with her case. He just wasn't as optimistic. The federal government wasn't known for forgiving and forgetting.

They walked another half-block in silence.

"You're not talking to me now." Jane stopped and grabbed Michael. She pulled him toward her. "After everything. You don't trust me. You're not saying anything." Jane shook him. "Say something."

Michael looked at her. He felt a weight pressing against his chest, a pain. He wanted to tell her everything. He wanted her to be close. He wanted the chase to be over. He wanted resolution.

But, Michael pushed the thoughts away. *In the real world, things don't work out like that.*

Michael took a step back. "I've got –" He started, but stopped.

There were sirens off in the distance. Michael noticed that the night sky was no longer clear. The stars were hidden behind a thick wall of smoke.

Michael pointed.

"Is that coming from your office?"

Jane looked up. She saw the smoke and started to run. Her office was just a block and a half away.

She ran down Second Avenue. Jane was in the middle of the street. She was in a full sprint. Michael chased behind her. He shouted at her to wait. He told her to get back on the sidewalk, but Jane wouldn't stop.

As she crossed Seventh Street, Michael saw her flooded with light.

Tires squealed.

Jane screamed and jumped.

A truck tried to swerve out of the way, but it was too late. The front left corner of the truck caught Jane square in the chest and threw her 15 feet in the air. She flipped over, a time and a half. Then she landed. Her head hit the curb, and Jane started to bleed.

Michael ran to her. He picked her up and tried to elevate her head to stop the bleeding. It didn't help much. Her warm blood ran through his fingers.

Michael looked at the truck. It was the same white pickup truck that he had seen on the first day he had met Jane. It was filled with the same group of small-town boys who had thrown a bag of feces at Jane's office window. Michael locked eyes with a fat boy with glasses who sat in the back.

Michael started to yell at them, but the words caught in his throat and the truck sped away.

Michael watched the taillights disappear, and then he looked down at Jane. He was helpless.

He found his voice and screamed for help. Michael held Jane close, telling her it would be okay. He felt the tears roll down his cheeks as he rocked her.

Time passed.

It seemed liked an hour, but it was probably less than a minute before Michael was surrounded. An ambulance, three squad cars, and a half-dozen suits appeared out of nowhere.

The EMT pulled Michael away from Jane. Another EMT slid a padded board underneath her, stabilized her neck, and then got Jane on the stretcher.

They tried to keep him away, but Michael wouldn't leave. He stayed with her. His hand gripped the side of the stretcher as it rolled toward the back of the ambulance.

They got her in, and Michael followed. One of the EMTs tried to stop him, but the other shook his head.

"It's not worth it. Let him ride."

They shut the doors, and the ambulance pulled away from the scene. One of the EMTs got an oxygen mask on Jane and the other cut away her shirt so they could get to work and figure out where she was hurt.

"What the hell is this?" An EMT pointed at a black box and microphone taped to Jane's side.

Michael leaned back. He knew exactly what it was. She was wearing a wire.

Michael looked out the back window at the crowd that the ambulance was leaving behind. In the middle of the crowd, Michael saw a man in a wheelchair. Agent Frank Vatch.

As they rounded the corner, Michael pounded on the back door of the ambulance.

"Let me out." He kicked at the door. "Get me out of here!"

"We can't do that."

Michael continued to rage against the door, trying to get it open.

CHAPTER FIFTY ONE

The boys screamed at one another when the truck squealed to a stop.

"You hit that chick! You hit that chick!"

The driver looked back. The woman was on the side of the street about 20 yards away. A man held her in his arms. He was screaming too, but the driver couldn't hear what he was saying.

One of the boys yelled at the driver to call 911, and another yelled at him to unlock the doors so that he could get out. Then Frankie stuck his head through the small back window.

"You gotta get out of here, man, or we're going to jail," Frankie hollered. The driver looked at Frankie, while the others continued to yell at him.

The driver thought about what his parents would do to him if he were caught. He thought about college and everything else that was supposed to happen over the next few years that wouldn't. He knew that Frankie was right, but he was frozen.

Frankie pounded on the top of the truck. He was standing behind the front cab in the bed of the pickup truck.

"Come on," he said. "Go."

And then it clicked. The driver pressed the gas and sped away.

He had to get as far away as possible. The truck was going over a hundred miles per hour. The boys in the back slouched down low. They tried to hold on. Every time the truck hit a bump in the road, they were tossed up and then back down again. Landing on the hard metal bed hurt.

They were 20 miles down Highway 29 toward Harker when the lights started flashing behind them.

"Cops."

It was a Florida State Trooper and he was gaining on them, fast.

The other boys started yelling at the driver again. The driver tried to think. He wished they would all shut up. He was trying to figure out what to do.

Frankie poked his head into the window. He was on his knees, trying to stay upright.

"Keep going," he said. "Keep going."

It didn't sound like a good idea. The driver knew it was over. He needed to slow down, but he was frozen, again. Fear roiled through his body, and he felt like he was going to throw up.

The state trooper caught up with them. His squad car was just a few feet off the truck's bumper. The trooper honked his horn and flashed his lights.

The driver stayed frozen. The speedometer's needle bounced around at 105.

"Keep going," Frankie said. "Don't stop."

Then the boy riding shotgun unbuckled his seat belt and jumped across the seat. The passenger didn't say a word – not one word —when he yanked the steering wheel as hard as he could, screaming, "Pull over!"

The sharp turn buckled the truck's metal frame. Its wheels came out from underneath.

Time seemed to stop as the truck floated through the air. They were all weightless, flying, and then there was the crash. It was a horrific crash.

The trooper tried to avoid them, but it happened too quick.

Two boys fell out of the back, smashing into the state trooper's front windshield at a hundred miles an hour.

Frankie, who had been kneeling and yelling through the back window, tried to hold on. But when the truck flipped, he was pulled underneath. Caught between the top of the cab and the pavement, the truck landed on Frankie, crushing his wiry frame as metal sparked all around him. Then the truck rolled over and over for another 20 yards.

CHAPTER FIFTY TWO

The ambulance pulled to the side of the road in a quiet residential neighborhood. The EMTs wanted him gone. Michael was interfering with their patient. Jane was their real concern, and Michael arguably shouldn't have been allowed in the ambulance to begin with.

When the ambulance stopped, they pushed Michael out the back. Once he was out, the EMTs shut the rear doors and sped away.

Michael watched as the lights got smaller and the sound of the siren grew quiet.

He was alone on the side of the road, dark houses all around him. Michael looked down at his hands in the dim of the streetlights. They were red, covered in blood. Then Michael looked at his shirt. It was also covered in Jane's blood. It stuck to his skin like a wet rag.

He had to move. He had to get out, run away. The feds knew. Agent Vatch had always known, but now they must have proof. Michael realized that he was going to spend the rest of his life in prison.

He commanded his feet to go, but they disobeyed. He couldn't move. Michael John Collins stood alone – nothing in sight, nobody around and then he started to cry.

###

The sun had just started to rise when Michael woke up. He was sore and thirsty. He looked down at his hands and arms. The blood had dried, causing his skin to itch and crack.

It took a moment to orient himself, but Michael quickly remembered the ambulance and the wire – Jane's betrayal.

He spotted a house about 200 yards away. Michael walked to it as casually as he could. He found the garden hose, followed the length of the hose to the faucet attached to the house, and then turned the faucet on.

The garden hose gurgled.

Water eventually spat out of the end of the hose, then a steady stream.

Michael took off his shirt. He sprayed the shirt with water, wrung it out, and then did it over again. Michael didn't stop until the water dripped clear. Then he sprayed his body with the frigid water, trying to clean himself up as best as he could.

He heard some movement inside the house.

He quickly turned off the water, threw the hose to the ground, and walked away.

Michael had only made it two blocks when he heard a car horn. He turned and saw the rental SUV race up next to him.

The window was rolled down. Kermit stuck his head out.

"Cops are coming, man. I been listening to the police scans." Kermit's eyes were wild. Michael stood silent in front of him. Michael was half-naked and dripping wet.

"Been looking for you all night and listening to those scans," Kermit said. "Then some woman called 911 and it went out over dispatch. She said a homeless man was taking a bath in her yard." Kermit smiled. "I figured that homeless person was you, *mi amigo.*" Kermit unlocked the doors. "Get in. You look like hell."

Still in a daze, Michael got inside the SUV. He shut the door, and Kermit sped away. After a few minutes, Kermit turned to Michael and smiled.

"I told you getting that police scanner was a good idea. You doubted, but I was right once again."

Michael didn't respond. He remembered that Kermit had wanted to get a police scanner to track Maus when they had first arrived in Jesser. Since the scanners were illegal, Kermit had planned on buying it on the B.M. How Kermit was able to locate a black market in Jesser, Florida, Michael would never know. That was just Kermit.

After a few more minutes without saying anything, Kermit laughed.

"I take your silence as an apology. Apology accepted, *mi amigo.* Apology accepted."

They drove for an hour in relative silence. Occasionally Kermit tried to get a conversation started, but Michael didn't have anything to say. He was lost in his thoughts, trying to figure out a future.

"I think the cops were staking out our hotel last night." Kermit glanced over at Michael, waiting for a response. Nothing.

"I sensed something was up, like that tingle in the dingle that Spider Man gets." Kermit snapped his fingers. "That's what I got. I got the tingle. So I packed up all of our stuff, and I had sweetie drive me back to Jane's office. I got the rental and I been driving around since then just looking for you and working the police scanner." Kermit shook his head. "Last night was a nasty night, bro-ha, nasty night. … Glad you're okay, though."

Kermit glanced back over at Michael, again, waiting for a question or comment.

When Michael said nothing, Kermit continued to drive.

Michael didn't know where Kermit was taking him. He didn't really care. He knew that Kermit understood the situation, even if Kermit didn't know the details or the exact truth about his past. He knew that Kermit was doing what he needed: Kermit was going to get him home.

He exited the highway. It was too early for any rush-hour traffic, so they had made good time from Jesser to Miami. Kermit got onto Twenty-Sixth, and then he took the Rickenbaker Causeway east. They drove through Hobie Island Beach Park and turned off at the Stadium Marina.

"I got us a nice boat." Kermit pointed at a 55-foot Californian motor yacht. "It's that one with the blue stripe." Kermit pulled into the parking lot outside the marina's main office,.

"I knew a guy who knew a guy who knew another guy."

Kermit unlocked the door, but paused before he got out. He looked at Michael.

"I figured, if they're really after you, the airports will be locked down tight. Your passport isn't going to be very good. ... So, anyway, a boat was the best way I could think of to get you outta here." Kermit paused, examining Michael, and then Kermit put his hand on Michael's shoulder.

"You cool?"

Michael turned to Kermit. He nodded, wordless.

CHAPTER FIFTY THREE

There was something about the water. Calm settled around them as they moved further from shore. The waves were small, and the yacht cut through them with an easy chop.

The early morning sun rose higher in the sky, but it wasn't hot. Michael had found an old pair of forgotten sunglasses near the life-jackets, so it wasn't too bright either.

He sat in a padded "fighting chair" at the back of the yacht. It was a chair designed for serious fishing; a cross between a chair found in a dentist's office and a birthing table with the addition of a few cup holders. When a big fish was snagged, whoever was fishing wouldn't have to stand. They just needed to put their feet in the stirrups and lean back.

Michael wasn't fishing, but he did have his feet up in the stirrups.

They cruised further from shore, and Michael watched the Miami skyline get smaller. Moving at a fast clip, surrounded by water and fresh air, Michael should have felt free, but he didn't. He was on the run. Again.

He thought about those stupid kids in the truck. He thought about Jane. He wondered if she was still alive. Michael closed his eyes, remembering the wire underneath her shirt; the reaction of the EMTs; his panic to get out of the ambulance.

The recording device explained why the feds suddenly "did the right thing" and why Jane had been acting so distant. Justin Kent and the U.S. Attorney's Office had been ignoring them for a year, and then, as the case fell apart, they leveraged it. They had gotten Jane to turn on him.

Michael shook his head. If he was in Jane's position, would he have done anything different? She had to have known that he was going to get caught. It was only a matter of time. Why not get something for it?

He'd have probably done the same. But still, it hurt.

Going forward, he was only going to be more paranoid, more suspicious.

The boat kept going further away from shore, and Michael thought about the Sunset. He probably shouldn't have been going back, but he had no place else to go. Then Michael thought about Elana and Pace. They were depending on him, and he was about to disappear. Michael shut his eyes as he imagined Elana sitting alone at the plaintiff's table in a full courtroom, abandoned by her attorneys in midtrial. He felt horrible, but didn't know what else he could do.

Michael heard the engine's motor cut and the anchor drop below him. Then he heard Kermit come up and through the door behind him.

"Figured you needed some sustenance, *mi amigo*." Kermit carried a Bloody Mary in one hand and a big bottle of ice water in the other. "They got some fancy cheese and crackers down there too, if you want it."

Michael took the water and Bloody Mary from Kermit. He put the Bloody Mary down, and then unscrewed the cap on the bottle of water. Kermit watched him and smiled.

"I did good, didn't I?"

"You did good." Michael smiled for Kermit's sake, although he was torn up inside. He smiled because, Kermit deserved the thanks. Michael took another drink of water.

"What's the plan?" he asked.

Kermit sat down in the chair next to Michael.

"Should take about two hours, maybe more, to get out of U.S. waters. I'm thinking of a stop in Cuba, because they don't really give a damn about your passport, but maybe we should just keep going until we get home, just anchor this baby right outside the Sunset."

"What time is it?" Michael took another big drink of water, and then he looked up at the sun as if he could determine the time from its position.

"I found you a little after five. The clock in the bow says it's now a little after seven in the morning."

Michael nodded, staring back at the coast. The skyline was tiny, a raised dash above the shoreline. The windows on the Miami office towers reflected back the light, so the dash was just a long streak of orange and yellow.

They sat in silence for a few more minutes, and then Kermit turned to Michael, laughing. He had been reading Michael's mind.

"The K-Man knows you, Michael-o. When were you going to tell me you were thinking about making it back in time for court?"

CHAPTER FIFTY FOUR

The conference room was crowded, and Agent Frank Vatch was being grilled.

He was at one end of the long conference table. Justin Kent sat next to him, and the rest of the seats were filled with local FBI agents, supervisors from the Department of Justice, and then there was the United States Attorney for New York, Brenda Gadd, leading the inquisition.

Gadd had flown into Miami from New York in the middle of the night.

"This is a major screw-up," she said. "Who the hell authorized this?"

Vatch looked at Gadd with contempt. He didn't say anything.

"Exactly." Gadd nodded. "Nobody authorized this. Everybody in New York thought you were on vacation."

"I was on vacation," Vatch said. "I was pursuing this investigation on my own time."

"Wrong," Gadd said. "You weren't on your own time, because you sucked in all of these people." Gadd pointed at the various people sitting around the table. "And I guarantee you that none of these people were on vacation when they were helping you. They thought this was an authorized ongoing investigation."

"It *is* an ongoing investigation," Vatch said. He wasn't going to back down, even though it was clear that he had violated multiple internal rules and procedures.

"These officials were presented with the facts of this case, and they independently chose to assist me in this matter."

Gadd shook her head.

"We've got multiple dead kids, a dead sheriff's deputy, and a lawyer in the hospital as well as the cop who was driving the damn squad car that chased the kids. The body count is rising."

Vatch shook his head.

"We had nothing to do with those kids, and if we hadn't been on this case, the deputy's murderer would still be at large."

Gadd took a deep breath. While she was still processing the information, Vatch continued.

"I'd like you to convene a grand jury to indict Michael Collins. We need to place him under arrest before he returns to Mexico."

"Arrest?" Gadd laughed. "For what?"

"For stealing nearly a half-billion dollars in client funds." Vatch looked around the table for support, but nobody said anything. He was going to have to do this on his own. "You heard the recording."

"I did." Gadd nodded. "There's nothing on it. He didn't confess to anything. We don't have a case."

"Ms. Nance accused him, and he was silent. That silence was an admission," Vatch said.

"Wrong. I'm not taking that to trial. It's not enough. You still have nothing. When the banks give us records, *then* we might have something. But this recording is not enough to indict him." Gadd looked at the clock. "I've got to catch a flight back to New York in an hour. As of this moment, Agent Vatch, you are on leave. Do not come into the office until our internal investigation is completed. Good day, gentlemen."

CHAPTER FIFTY FIVE

The elevator door slid open. Michael stepped out into the marble hallway in a suit and tie. He was always amazed at the costumes people wore and how it altered the perceptions of others. Just four hours ago, a woman called 911 and told dispatch that he was a homeless person. Now he was a lawyer. All he did was change his costume.

The return trip to Miami gave Michael time to clean himself up. Michael had showered, shaved, and gotten dressed on the yacht. His suit was a little wrinkled, but not too bad.

He looked up at the ornate gold clock on the wall. The little hand ticked to 9:25. He was late, but that was the least of his worries.

The doors to the courtroom were about 15 yards away. The heels on his wingtips clicked and echoed as he walked down the hall. He wasn't sure what was going to be on the other side of those doors.

Maybe he would be placed under immediate arrest. Maybe Judge Delaney would find him in contempt for being late. Maybe nothing would happen; the trial would simply proceed.

Michael thought about it, but he was ready for the future, whatever the future may be. Something had happened to him. Something had changed. He had resolve.

He wasn't going to be stupid, but he wasn't going to be afraid either. He could only control himself. If they wanted to arrest him, then they would arrest him. If Judge Delaney was going to scream, then let him scream. For the first time in a long time, Michael felt a tiny sense of peace. It was surrounded by nervousness and anxiousness, but at its core, there was still a fragment of peace that he could draw upon.

He just had to take care of himself.

That wasn't easy. Michael's whole body was tied in knots. But it was that fragment of peace that propelled him forward.

He pushed open the courtroom doors. Everyone stopped, turned, and looked.

The courtroom was packed. They had been waiting. He didn't recognize most of them, but he saw a few familiar faces. Justin Kent sat next to Agent Frank Vatch. Michael ignored Vatch, but locked eyes with Kent. Michael felt his jaw tighten as he glared, and then Kent finally looked away.

Elana Estrada sat at the plaintiff's table. She had been alone, waiting, just as Michael had imagined. Michael felt bad that he had almost forgotten about her. He had almost abandoned her without giving it a second thought. He was so self-absorbed that he was forgetting the people that mattered in his life. He was forgetting the faith that people had placed in him.

She stood as Michael crossed the bar separating the gallery and the plaintiff and defendant's tables. He walked over to her. Michael put his briefcase down on the table, and he gave her a hug.

She relaxed in his arms. He felt her relief.

"I couldn't leave you. We have to finish," Michael whispered in her ear.

Michael knew that he was a lot of things, some good and some bad. He had lied. He had dropped out. He had run away.

Because of that, some people might think he was a quitter. But he wasn't a quitter, at least not this time. He wasn't going to quit. He was going to win this case for Tommy Estrada and his family. Then the future would present itself. Michael couldn't control the future.

The side door that led from the courtroom to Judge Delaney's chambers opened. A bailiff began to instruct the people in the courtroom to rise, but Judge Delaney waved the bailiff off.

Judge Delaney wasn't in his robe. He looked casual, wearing dress pants and a white dress shirt. He didn't have on a tie or his suit jacket.

Instead of walking up the three steps to the bench, he came down to the same level as the attorneys.

He stood a few feet in front of the attorneys' tables, near the podium where Jane had questioned Dylan McNaughten less than 24 hours before.

Judge Delaney looked out at the people in the gallery.

"My understanding is that we have a number of federal agents and law enforcement officials here. This is a free country. This is a public place, and you have every right to watch these proceedings. But I'd like to talk to whoever is in charge if I'm going to continue this morning. Let my law clerk know who that is, and we'll meet in a few moments. I'm going to speak with the attorneys first."

Then, Judge Delaney looked at Harrison Grant, and then Michael.

"Both of you," he said. "Let's go."

###

"First I apologize that I was late this morning. I should have––"

Judge Delaney raised his hand, cutting Michael off.

"Let's move on to more important things." He leaned back in his large leather chair, thinking.

"We have a situation," he finally said, "and I have some thoughts."

Harrison Grant opened his mouth, but Judge Delaney shot him a glare before Grant could say anything.

"First, we have an attorney who was hurt badly last night." Judge Delaney looked at Michael, and Michael could tell that the judge knew everything. "Ms. Nance is a wonderful attorney. As you all know, she's in critical condition, but stable."

Michael nodded. He was relieved. His feelings toward Jane were complicated, but he didn't hate her. He didn't want her hurt, and he appreciated what Judge Delaney was doing. Judge Delaney was passing information along to him.

"So here we are." Judge Delaney folded his hands together and placed them on the top of his desk. "We are in the midst of a trial. I have jurors who have no idea what is going on, but obviously they will notice if Ms. Nance is not present at counsel's table."

Judge Delaney leaned in and lowered his voice.

"So here is what I propose." He paused, making sure that he would not be interrupted. "We will continue this trial. I will tell the jurors that there has been a medical emergency and that Ms. Nance would like to be here, but that she is unable to do so."

Judge Delaney turned to Michael.

"Then, Mr. Collins, I believe that you were going to recall several witnesses to testify about Deputy Maus and rest, correct?"

Michael nodded.

"Correct."

Then Judge Delaney turned to Harrison Grant.

"And then it's your turn, Mr. Grant. Correct?"

Grant started to nod, but stopped himself.

"Your Honor, while I respect the court's effort to continue, I don't have much choice but to again ask for a mistrial."

Judge Delaney half-smiled and leaned back in his chair.

"On what grounds?"

"The absence of Ms. Nance – in light of the other testimony – it may suggest that my client was somehow responsible for her absence. It could also create sympathy for the plaintiff."

Judge Delaney shook his head.

"I'll listen to those arguments on the record and keep an open mind, but I don't think so. I'm not interested in starting this trial over in the future. The facts are the facts, and they aren't going to change three months or six months or a year from now."

Judge Delaney turned to Michael.

"Any objection from you related to my plan?"

Michael shook his head.

"No, Your Honor. I'd like to finish this case, and my client wants to go back home."

Judge Delaney smiled. He liked that answer.

"Very well."

The attorneys stood. They started out the door, but Judge Delaney stopped them.

"Mr. Collins, I'd like to talk with you for a moment." Judge Delaney looked at Harrison Grant. "Any objection to me speaking with Mr. Collins *ex parte* related to matters beyond the scope of this trial?"

Michael could tell that Harrison Grant wanted to object. Grant wanted to tell the judge that his conduct would be highly irregular and improper, but Grant also knew that it wasn't worth the fight. It was clear that Judge Delaney had turned on him and his client, and Grant didn't want to make matters worse.

"No, Your Honor, that's fine," Grant said. "Provided that it isn't about this case."

"Of course not," Judge Delaney said. "And Mr. Grant, please close the door on your way out."

Michael returned to his seat as Grant left the room. The door closed behind them, leaving Michael and Judge Delaney alone.

"Mr. Collins," Judge Delaney tilted his head to the side. His crystal blue eyes softened. "Are you okay?"

The question took Michael by surprise. Judges weren't known to be sympathetic to attorneys or their feelings, but Judge Delaney was different. While the rest of the judiciary slouched into a political gutter, Judge Delaney was a judge's judge. He wasn't there to root for one side or the other. He wasn't trying to get appointed to a higher court or advance his career. He simply wanted to do a good job, a refreshing concept and increasingly rare.

"Frankly," Michael said. "I have no idea." Michael thought for a moment about the tangle of emotions inside of him. Then he returned to that small fragment of peace to drive him forward. "I just want to finish. I want to finish what we started here."

Judge Delaney took a deep breath. He stood and walked over to his large window.

"I want you to finish as well," he said. "A case is not a bottle of wine. It doesn't get better with time. Whether you win or lose …" Judge Delaney's voice trailed off, and then he shrugged. "I think Ms. Nance would want you to finish."

"I think you're right," Michael said.

"Sounds like you've got a lot of other things going on out there." Judge Delaney didn't look at Michael or elaborate. Instead, he turned from Michael. He looked down and watched the cars and people below. He was thinking.

"I'm going to see if I can persuade them to hold off on whatever they're doing until we're done. I've got no power to do so, but I'll try."

Judge Delaney turned away from the window, and then he looked right at Michael. His eyes cut Michael down, and Michael could see them evaluating him. Judge Delaney was figuring out whether he could trust Michael.

"I need you to promise me that you will not make me look bad. I need your word that you will not run. I need your word that you'll see this trial all the way through. Do you promise?"

Michael didn't shrug or laugh or joke or dodge. He didn't blink.

Judge Delaney had asked him a question. It was a fair question. It was a question he had asked himself and already answered back on the yacht. He wasn't going to be stupid. He wasn't going to confess or plead with Agent Vatch for mercy. But he wasn't going to run, either. He was going to finish what he had started.

Michael held out his hand.

"I promise," he said. "You have my word."Judge Delaney walked over to Michael, took Michael's hand, and they shook.

CHAPTER FIFTY SIX

The trial continued for three more days. Michael re-called each of the workers that had previously testified, including Miggy. This time, however, they were allowed to tell their full stories. They were comfortable and confident. They talked about Deputy Maus and the brutal and grueling life of the farm workers in Jesser.

Finally, Michael called Elana Estrada to the stand as the plaintiff's last witness.

The gallery of seats in the back of the courtroom had mostly returned to its prior status. Occasionally a law clerk or a student would come to watch the trial, but the army of federal agents and law enforcement officials that had greeted Michael on the morning after Jane's accident were gone. They were all gone, that is, except one. Agent Frank Vatch sat by himself in the back of the courtroom in his wheelchair.

His lips were tight. His eyes glared at Michael. He had hunted Michael for years, only to see him leave New York and have his supervisors order him to back off the case. It was obvious that it took everything in his power to remain quiet, but he did. And each day, Michael ignored him. Michael continued to find that small reservoir of peace and drew upon it. He walked past

297

Agent Vatch a dozen times a day. Michael never met Vatch's eye, and neither man spoke a word.

When Michael finished questioning Elana Estrada, he allowed her time to wipe away her tears. Then he waited as she slowly walked down off of the witness stand. She came back to the table and sat down.

Michael had been at the podium. He followed behind her, but remained standing. He put his hand on her shoulder. He looked at Harrison Grant. He looked at the jurors, and then Michael looked at Judge Delaney.

"At this time, Your Honor," he said, "the plaintiff rests."

Judge Delaney nodded, and then looked at Harrison Grant and Brian McNaughten. "Counsel?"

Harrison Grant rose. His chin held high, defiant. Even after days of damaging testimony, Grant still managed to exude confidence.

"Your Honor," he said, and then paused. "The defense also rests."

Judge Delaney couldn't hide his surprise. He had heard the same comments that Michael had heard before and during the trial. Grant continually dismissed and minimized Jolly Boy's conduct. He had alluded to witnesses that would testify and undermine the case against his client. But in the end, Grant had nothing. A case that he had offered to settle for only a few thousand dollars was now going to cost his client far more.

Judge Delaney looked at Michael, and then back at Harrison Grant.

"Very well."

He nodded and turned to the tired jurors.

"We will take a recess until after lunch so that I may talk with the attorneys. We'll return, listen to closing arguments, and then you will begin your deliberations."

Judge Delaney gaveled the proceedings to recess, and everyone in the courtroom stood as the jurors walked out the side door to the jury room in a single file line.

Once the jurors were gone, Judge Delaney gathered up his papers.

"Be here at one so that we can finalize the jury instructions. You can make whatever motions you'd like to make at that time."

He walked down the steps behind the bench and through the door to his chambers, leaving the attorneys.

Soon after the judge had left, Harrison Grant and Brian McNaughten left as well. Michael stayed seated at the plaintiff's table with his client.

Michael turned to Elana Estrada.

"One more step," he said. "Just one more step."

Elana nodded. She was reserved, unsure. She looked back at Pace. Pace had been seated in the front row behind them the whole time. He sat in the same seat every day, while his aunt took care of his sisters back in Mexico.

Elana turned to Michael, seeking another confirmation.

"Then it's done?"

"Yes." Michael put his hand on her hand, gave it a gentle squeeze, and then he picked up his worn and battered briefcase. "After closing arguments, it's done."

Michael turned, and saw Agent Vatch waiting for him.

Agent Vatch had rolled his wheelchair into the center of the aisle. He was one of the few who remained. There was no way Michael could avoid him. There was no way that Vatch would let himself be ignored any longer.

Michael walked toward Vatch, and Agent Vatch glared at him. Neither said anything until Michael was just a few feet away.

Michael stopped. He looked down at him.

"Francis," he said, knowing that Agent Frank Vatch hated the name Francis. "It's been a while."

Agent Vatch nodded. His narrow tongue flicked out each side of his mouth.

"It has," Vatch said. "You miss me?"

"Not really," Michael said. "I did, however, enjoy breaking your nose back in New York. Now, if you'd excuse me, I need to go prepare for my closing argument."

Michael took a step to the side and started to walk around Agent Vatch and his wheelchair, but Vatch reached out and grabbed Michael. Vatch's hand was a vise, pinching Michael's wrist.

"Hold on," Vatch said.

Michael struggled, and then, after a few pulls, he was able to break free. He put a little distance between himself and Vatch, and then Michael stopped and straightened his tie.

"Are you placing me under arrest?"

Vatch didn't answer.

Michael smiled.

"I didn't think so," he said. Michael had thought a lot about what had happened on the night of Jane's accident. She was wearing a wire, but he had never said anything. There was no confession.

"You've got no case," Michael said. "You forced a good attorney and a friend to turn on me, but it didn't work and it nearly killed her. You're an embarrassment."

Michael turned and began walking toward the door.

"Mr. Collins," Vatch said. "You know I'm never going to stop."

Michael opened the door and walked out into the hallway. He pretended that he hadn't heard a thing.

CHAPTER FIFTY SEVEN

Closing arguments were an art form, but they had unwritten rules. Michel had learned them as a young associate at Wabash, Kramer and Moore. His mentor and senior partner, Lowell Moore, may have been a horrible person, but he had been a great attorney.

Three months after starting at the firm, Lowell had taken Michael to watch the closing argument of a civil medical malpractice trial in downtown Manhattan.

They had sat in the back of an otherwise empty gallery and had watched an elderly man with white hair, two hearing aids, and a bow tie stand in front of a jury.

He had been making his closing argument on behalf of a woman who had fallen off an operating table during brain surgery. Her head had been cut open. The doctors had been in the process of removing a small tumor from behind her ear, but the nurse hadn't properly restrained her on the table. She fell when they had attempted to adjust her position. The patient had hit her head on the floor, landing on the open incision.

She had suffered a permanent brain injury, and the old plaintiff's attorney had sought punitive damages on behalf of the family.

Lowell Moore had leaned into Michael, just before the argument had been about to start. He whispered, "Listen and learn these rules: Keep it simple, don't be afraid to show emotion, and always ask for a specific amount of money."

Michael repeated those rules to himself as he walked toward the podium. He put his papers down, and then he continued to the area directly in front of the jury box. Judge Delaney had just spent the past 15 minutes instructing the jurors and reciting the elements that must be proven in the case. Now it was Michael's turn.

He kept repeating Lowell Moore's rules, silently in his head.

He was going to do this. He was going to ask for more money than anyone on that jury had ever earned or had even thought about earning in their lives. He wasn't going to blink. He wasn't going to be ashamed. He was going to pretend that he did this every day. He was going to make his case.

Michael made eye contact with the first juror in the front row.

"Cold," he said, and then he slowly made eye contact with the remaining jurors.

"Callous," he said, "and calculating."

Michael took a breath, and then he just let the words come out. He channeled everything he had seen since coming to Jesser. The harsh working conditions, the trailers, the hot fields under a low chemical haze, and the dead body parts of Tommy Estrada spread out on a metal cart.

"We eat every day," he said. "Most of our kids think that vegetables are grown in the grocery store. Most of us live in cities. We don't go out to the farms. We don't grow our own food. We don't know and don't really care where this food comes from. We just look in the newspaper every week. We read the ads, find a coupon, and then go and buy what we need. The grocery business is cutthroat. The profit margins are thin, and we all want the cheapest possible food we can get. ... And that's where Jolly Boy comes in."

Michael took a step back. He looked over at Harrison Grant and Brian McNaughten sitting at the defense table. Michael shook his head in disgust, and then he looked back at the jury.

"So we have a company that cuts corners. But you heard that they don't just bend the rules. They don't just skirt regulations. ... No, they have killed people. To Jolly Boy, my client Tommy Estrada wasn't a person. He was a machine made out of human flesh, designed and built to pick our fruit and vegetables for a few dollars a day. But we're not here to render a verdict on how we grow and purchase our food. We're here to decide whether Jolly Boy was so reckless that its actions killed my client. To that end, the evidence is overwhelming."

Michael recounted the testimony of Miggy and the former Jolly Boy employees, and then he spent 10 minutes reciting the testimony of Dylan McNaughten.

"My client isn't here. He died and left a family behind. The defendant took a job farther away from his wife and children. Nobody knows what Tommy Estrada's future would be, but we do know that Jolly Boy profits every day by mistreating and abusing its workers. We know that it has grown into the second largest agribusiness in Florida. It had $750 million in profits last year, after Brian and Dylan McNaughten were paid millions in stock options and performance bonuses."

Michael paused.

"$750 million," he repeated. "$750 million a year in profits, which works out to be just over $2 million a day or $14 million per week."

Michael scanned the jurors again. He wanted to make sure they were listening.

"One week." He nodded. "One week. That seems about right." Michael pointed at Brian McNaughten. "One week to force them to give Tommy Estrada and his family some justice. As punishment for taking Tommy Estrada's life, as punishment for mistreating its workers, as punishment for being cold, callous, and calculating, I think it's appropriate to dock Jolly Boy one week's pay."

Michael paused. He caught his breath.

"I ask you to award Tommy Estrada and his family one week of Jolly Boy's profit as punishment for its conduct. When you fill out the verdict form, there is a blank space for you to write the amount of the punitive damages award. I'm asking you to write down $14 million in that space. That's just one week's profit." He paused. "One week."

Michael turned away from the jury, concluding. He looked at Harrison Grant and Brian McNaughten. He did not shout. He did not point. He just lowered his voice to an audible whisper, and closed.

"Show them that, as jurors in this case, you now know where your food comes from. Tell them to respect the people who bring that food to market. The people like Tommy Estrada."

Michael closed his eyes, nodded, and then slowly walked back to his seat.

His hands were sweaty. His heart pounded, and he sat down in a daze. Michael was sure that he had blown it. He immediately started to second-guess himself. He started to think he had sounded preachy. He had sounded too much like a radical. He should have focused more on Jolly Boy's conduct.

Michael picked up his pen and started to write on his pad of paper, just to do something. Although he wasn't taking notes, he wrote nonsense as a way to channel the adrenaline.

Then, Elana Estrada's hand reached out and covered his. She calmed him.

Michael's hand stopped shaking, and he accepted that the decision was now out of his control. All he could do was listen to Harrison Grant, and then wait.

CHAPTER FIFTY EIGHT

Harrison Grant wasn't going down without a fight. His closing argument focused on the numbers. He didn't really address the liability, because he didn't have anything to say. His client hadn't told him the truth, and so Grant had been blindsided. So he didn't argue that Jolly Boy had nothing to do with Tommy Estrada's death, nor did he argue that Jolly Boy treated their workers in accordance with the law. Instead, Grant focused on the money. He wanted to limit damages.

"In polite society," he said, winding his way to summation, "we don't talk about money. Discussing the value of a life is crass and inappropriate. I agree, but unfortunately, that is the task that you all have been assigned."

Harrison Grant turned to Michael, and then back again. "He asked you for over ..." Grant pretended he didn't remember the amount. "What? Fourteen million dollars?" Grant shook his head. "This isn't a lottery. This is a court of law. And while I grieve for Mrs. Estrada and her loss, we have to be realistic."

Harrison Grant put his hand on his heart. He played the role of the sage advisor, a sharp contrast to Michael's passionate closing argument.

"I do not believe that the plaintiff proved causation. We have the testimony of a man accused of murder, Dylan McNaughten, who is inherently not credible. We also have the stories of men who were flown here from Mexico, put up in a fancy hotel, and allowed to tell their tales."

Ignoring the recorded jail conversations between Dylan and Brian McNaughten, Grant then shaded the truth. "None of these stories were corroborated or backed up with hard evidence."

Harrison Grant stepped closer to the jury box. He lowered his voice.

"But, if you do find liability, let us be reasonable. Tommy Estrada was dying of cancer. The plaintiff's own doctor testified that he was not going to live more than a year. The plaintiff's own doctor admitted that he could not conclusively pinpoint how or what caused Mr. Estrada's cancer. So, how much did Tommy Estrada make per year? The answer is about $10,000 per year, which assumes he continued to work for Jolly Boy. If Tommy Estrada had stayed in Mexico – and had not come here illegally – then his yearly wage in Mexico would be about $4,000."

Grant continued with his math lesson.

"That means that Mr. Estrada's lost wages would be about $10,000 on the high side. And if you ignore the cancer, and think that Mr. Estrada would live a full life, say another 20 years, then, adding up those lost yearly wages, the damages would be $40,000. Such a verdict would still be a windfall for Mrs. Estrada, but we would avoid the unseemly act of transforming our legal system into the Florida State Lottery."

Michael watched the jurors as Harrison Grant concluded. He noticed a few of the men nod their heads, and it concerned him. Juror Number 5, the engineer, actually looked at Michael and laughed.

"That's all I ask. Respect the system." Harrison Grant turned and walked away from the jury box and back to the defense table.

Judge Delaney waited for Grant to sit down, and then Delaney looked at the jurors.

"All right," he said. "Now that the closing arguments are completed, I will give you some final instructions."

Judge Delaney continued, reminding the jurors of their obligations and the standards that they should apply in evaluating the evidence and testimony that had been presented. Michael's mind drifted while the judge spoke, wondering if he had made a mistake by asking for $14 million. He wondered if the jurors now viewed him and his client as too greedy.

Michael looked over at Elana Estrada. Her eyes were squinted as she tried to understand all of the words being spoken, and then Michael looked behind him. The gallery had more people in it, but it wasn't full. Of course, there was still Agent Vatch sitting in the back, staring at him. There were also a few reporters, and various law clerks, students, and courthouse gadflies who had come to watch the show.

Michael looked at the jurors one last time before they were released to begin deliberations. They were all focused on Judge Delaney, listening attentively. If anybody had won the case, it was Judge Delaney. All of the jurors loved him, and they would do whatever he said. But Judge Delaney kept his remarks level and objective. He had probably given the same speech hundreds of times, but he still managed to make it sound fresh.

"Ladies and gentleman, in considering this case, remember that you are not partisans or advocates, but that you are judges of the facts. The final test of the quality of your service will lie in the verdict that you return to the Court, and not in the opinions any of you may have as you retire from this case. Have it in mind that you will make a definite contribution to efficient judicial administration if you arrive at a just and proper verdict." Judge Delaney paused, and then finished. "This concludes my final instruction. You are now in deliberations."

Judge Delaney motioned for the bailiff, and the bailiff led the jurors silently out of the room.

Once the jurors were gone, Judge Delaney looked at Michael and Harrison Grant.

"Anything further that either of you would like to put on the record?"

Harrison Grant stood.

"No, Your Honor."

Grant sat down, and then Michael stood.

"No, Your Honor."

"Very well," Judge Delaney said. "Then this court stands in recess. Please make sure that you are both available via cell phone in case the jury has a question that requires your presence or the jury has reached a final verdict." Judge Delaney rapped the gavel.

"The court is adjourned."

After the judge left, Michael and Elana Estrada stood. She gave Michael a hug. "What should I do?" she asked.

"Go to the hotel," Michael said. "Order room service – whatever you want. I'm paying for it. And then wait. I'll call if you need to come back."

"Thank you," she nodded.

Michael watched her walk out of the courtroom. Near the door, Pace joined her. Pace put his arm around his mother, and then they both walked the rest of the way down the aisle and into the hallway together.

As they left, Kermit entered the courtroom. He wore Bermuda shorts and a loud Hawaiian-print shirt.

"I got some cold ones waiting for us on the boat, *mi amigo*." Kermit's voice filled the room, and Michael saw Agent Vatch's face turn sour.

Michael picked up his battered briefcase.

"Sounds great. I'm exhausted."

CHAPTER FIFTY NINE

The suit and tie came off within a few minutes of stepping on board the yacht. Michael changed into his swimsuit, rubbed a little sun block on his nose, and then settled into the plush leather chair on the back deck.

By the time Michael sat down, Kermit was already a half-mile from shore and far out into Miami's Biscayne Bay. Michael checked his cell phone. He had three bars on the top of his display. He called information. When a robot recording prompted him to say what he was looking for, Michael hung up. The phone was working and he was available. All he had to do was try to relax while waiting for the phone call from the judge's law clerk.

Michael located the old sunglasses and put them back on.

"Drop anchor here." He called back to Kermit. "I don't want to get out of cell phone range."

Kermit said that he would, and, a few seconds later, Kermit cut the engine and dropped the anchor.

Michael sat in the back of the yacht. His feet were up. His eyes were closed, and he listened to the waves pulse against the side of the boat.

Bobbing in the water, Michael rocked to sleep.

###

The phone woke him. Michael opened his eyes, orienting himself. He picked up the cell phone on the fifth ring, pressed a button, and answered.

It was Judge Delaney's law clerk. She told Michael that the jurors were going home for the day. They would continue deliberating in the morning.

Michael thanked her, hung up the phone, and sat up in his chair.

There was a slight chill in the air as the sun set. An orange light bathed the distant Miami skyline, and the water leading to the shore alternated between ripples of deep blue and black.

"Kermit, are you up?" Michael heard some pots clang below him. He got up out of the chair and walked down the steps to the yacht's galley.

Kermit was in the kitchen. He looked up when Michael entered the dining area.

"Hey, boss." Kermit held up a stock pot. "I found some pasta, a jar of sauce, and two bottles of *vino*. What do you think?"

"Sounds perfect." Michael sat down at the narrow counter that separated the kitchen and dining areas. He watched Kermit fill the pot with water and put it on the stove. "Got a call from the judge's clerk. Looks like we're free for the night. The jurors went home."

Kermit smiled.

"Then we got no excuse. We gotta open up these bottles of wine." Kermit put a lid on the pot, and then opened a cabinet by the refrigerator. He found two wine glasses, and then he put them on the counter in front of Michael.

He used a corkscrew to open a bottle of Pinot and poured some in each of the glasses.

"You done good, *mi amigo*, no matter what happens." Kermit raised his glass.

Michael picked up his glass, and the two clinked.

"I don't know. I think I may have overplayed my hand. I think I sounded shrill. My voice was too high. I had too much emotion."

Kermit took a sip of wine, shook his head, and then set the glass down on the counter.

"Bull crappy," he said. "You were you. I was there, man. The jurors paid attention. They understood where you're coming from. You had heart."

"Maybe." Michael swirled the wine in his glass, replaying his closing argument in his head.

"Well, you ain't gonna be zeroed out, man," Kermit said. "I can guarantee that, and anything is going to be more money than Elana and Pace have ever seen in their life. Don't forget that. If it wasn't for you and Jane –" Kermit caught himself when he said her name. He ticked his head to the side.

"Well you know what I mean. There weren't exactly hundreds of esquires beating down Elana's door to take the case."

Kermit turned to the stove and started looking for a sauce pan.

"You can say her name, you know."

Kermit nodded.

"I know, I just figured I'd avoid it."

He crouched down on the floor, and rummaged through the cooking utensils and pots.

Michael took a big sip of wine, and reached for the bottle to refill his glass.

"You think I should go see her? Go see Jane?"

Kermit stood up. He was holding a small saucepan that he had found. He set the empty pan on the stove, and he put his hands on his hips. His gray dreadlocks dangled as he thought.

"Depends," he said. "Is she your friend or enemy?"

Michael shrugged.

"Don't know."

CHAPTER SIXTY

Michael slept hard. The only place that he had slept better in the past five years was Hut No. 7, and hopefully, he'd be back at the Sunset within a week.

Michael swung his legs over the edge of the bed and put his feet on the yacht's polished oak floor. He found a pair of pants, stepped into them, and then walked out of the cabin.

Michael heard Kermit walking around above him, and so he went up the steps to the top deck. Earlier in the morning, Kermit had lifted anchor and brought the boat back to the marina.

The yacht was tied to a large wooden dock that jutted into the bay.

"Morning," Michael said.

Kermit looked over at Michael. He was sitting on a built-in bench at the front of the yacht.

"Figured spaghetti wouldn't be good for breakfast, so I brought us ashore." Kermit smiled. "Hope you don't mind."

Michael shook his head.

"Not at all."

"Any word from the court?"

Michael looked down at his cell phone.

"No calls and no messages."

"How long do you think the jury will take?"

Michael shrugged.

"No idea. Supposedly, if they take longer it's better for the defendant, but I don't know if that's just a tall tale told by old lawyers or if that's true."

"Do you want to go grab a bite, get some groceries and go back out for the day?"

Michael thought for a moment.

"Sounds good," he said. "But I need to change into my suit, just in case the court calls and wants us to come in."

"Oh-ka-lee-doke-a-lee." Kermit got up. He started picking up some of the extra ropes and moving them to better secure the yacht while they were gone.

"Kermit," Michael said. "One more thing."

Kermit looked up after finishing a complex knot.

"What is it?"

"I want to stop by the hospital while we're out," Michael said.

Jane was at the Ryder Trauma Center at Jackson Memorial Hospital. Michael got her room number from a young girl at the front reception desk. He took the elevator to the fifth floor, and then started down the hall toward room 520.

He didn't know what to expect, and he didn't ever come up with an answer to Kermit's question. He didn't know whether Jane was a friend or an enemy. Michael just knew that she was hurt. He wanted to see her. He wanted to tell her about the trial, and he also wanted to say goodbye.

When he found it, the door to Jane's room was open.

He knocked a few times on the door frame, and then he walked in

Jane laid in bed. She was conscious, but her head had a thick gauze bandage wrapped around it. Her eyes were bruised black and blue, but they were open. She was watching CNN on the television mounted in the corner of the room.

"Hey." Michael put his hands in his pockets and walked toward her.

Jane thought he was a nurse at first, and then, when she turned away from the television screen, she realized who it was. Jane looked at Michael, and then averted her eyes, ashamed and guilty.

"Thought you might want an update," Michael said.

Jane finally looked at him, and she nodded her head. She reached down. She found the cord with the remote attached to it. Jane pressed a button, and the television turned off.

"I'd like that," she said. "Justin has been stopping by, telling me what's happening, but I'd rather hear it from you."

Michael took off his suit jacket. He laid it on a table, and then pulled a chair next to Jane's bed. He reached out his hand. Jane hesitated at first, but, eventually, she took it.

"I want to hear every detail," Jane said.

Michael nodded, and then told Jane about recalling their witnesses, Harrison Grant's decision not to call anybody from Jolly Boy, and then their closing arguments.

"Is she happy?" Jane asked.

"Elana?" Michael thought about it. "I think so," he said. "I don't know how much she understands, but I think she's glad it's over."

Jane took a breath. She closed her eyes, resting, and then opened them, again. She was tired and sad.

"I'm sorry," she said. "I don't know what I was –"

Michael cut her off.

"Forget about it." He was about to continue when his cell phone rang.

He took the cell phone out of his pocket, and then Michael pressed the button to answer. He listened, and then turned off the phone after a quick conversation.

"The jury has a verdict." Michael stood. "I've got to go."

Jane nodded her head and watched him as Michael picked up his suit jacket. He slipped the jacket on, and then started walking out the door.

After a little struggle, Jane managed to sit up in her bed.

"Will I see you again?"

Michael stopped, and he turned back. He looked at Jane, and then shook his head.

"Probably not."

CHAPTER SIXTY ONE

W hat happened at the courthouse was surreal. The beginning was clear. It began like any other hearing, but then
it dissolved into something different.

The people in the courtroom rose as the jury entered. The jury walked in a single file line behind the bailiff, and then they
took their seats. They were the same seats where they had sat
the entire trial.

Judge Delaney instructed the people in the courtroom to sit,
and everyone sat.

He turned to look at the jury.

"Members of the jury, have you selected a foreperson?"

A mousy woman at the end of the row raised her hand, and
Judge Delaney nodded at her.

"And have you reached a verdict?"

The mousy woman nodded her head again.

"Yes, Your Honor."

"Then please hand it to the bailiff." Judge Delaney directed
the bailiff toward the mousy woman, and she handed the verdict
form to the bailiff.

The bailiff walked the verdict form to the judge. Judge
Delaney looked down at the form. He read it silently, and then
he handed it back to the bailiff.

The final dance continued as the bailiff walked the form to the court clerk, and the court clerk read the verdict aloud.

"In the matter of Thomas Estrada versus Jolly Boy Foods, Inc., we the members of the jury find in favor of the plaintiff, Thomas Estrada. We find the defendant, Jolly Boy Foods, liable in Count One of the Complaint: Wrongful Death ..."

For Michael, it was at this moment that the lines and figures in the courtroom dissolved into splotches of color. The voices melded into waves of sound.

Michael felt a hand on his shoulder, a pat on the back. He looked at Elana, and she bowed her head and started whispering a prayer.

More noise and blurred movement of color occurred.

Michael looked over at the jurors, and they began to stand. The entire courtroom was standing, and so Michael stood without knowing why. He watched the jurors file out of the room. The sound around him grew and then faded, and then came back again, but none of the words made sense.

Moments later, Harrison Grant stood in front of him. His hand was out, and Michael shook it.

Harrison Grant spoke, but Michael didn't understand anything except the word congratulations.

As Harrison Grant walked away, Michael took a step. He was unsteady at first, and then he regained his footing. Michael picked up his battered briefcase and walked down the aisle toward the back. His head and his thoughts became clearer with every step.

Had he heard correctly? The jury had disagreed with his proposal. Michael had asked them to take away one week of Jolly Boy's profits. Instead, the jury had awarded Elana Estrada and her family *two* weeks of Jolly Boy's profits: $28 million.

Michael saw Agent Vatch sitting by the door. He kept walking toward Vatch. His confidence came back.

Michael walked up to Vatch, and then crouched down so that they were eye to eye.

"Francis," he said. "I'm going home."

Michael waited for a response, but Vatch didn't say anything. The look in Vatch's eyes told Michael everything he needed to know.

"There's no warrant, is there? There's nothing you can legally do to stop me."

When Vatch stayed silent, Michael nodded his head.

"I didn't think so."

CHAPTER SIXTY TWO

The day after the verdict, the sun peeked up over the horizon at 6:14. It was time to start working the fields. Some of the fields needed to be weeded where the machines couldn't reach. Other fields had crops that were ready to be picked.

The Jolly Boy van arrived at the trailer park just outside Jesser. Usually there were 15 men standing at the side of the road, waiting for the van to arrive.

The driver stopped the van. He looked out the window at the trailers. The trailers were silent. There was no movement. The driver checked his watch to see if he was early, but he wasn't early. He was right on time.

He honked the horn once, and then waited.

Then he honked the horn again, but nobody came.

This made him nervous, but he didn't know what to do. So he continued to drive to the next set of trailers, but it was the same thing.

No workers were waiting. Nobody came when he honked his horn.

He took out his cell phone and he called his supervisor. He was instructed to go to the Home Depot. There were usually 50 Mexicans waiting to be picked up to do gardening, roofing, and other odd jobs in the area.

The driver started the engine and drove away. He got onto the highway, and then drove to the Home Depot as instructed.

When he arrived, the driver was relieved to see that there were still about two dozen men waiting there for work.

He pulled into the parking lot and stopped near the group of men. A few of them stepped forward. They started to get into the back of the van, when one of them stopped and asked where they were going and what they were going to do.

The driver told them that they were going to weed and pick.

"For who?" one of the men asked. The driver told him that they were going to work for Jolly Boy.

The men shook their heads, and then they all walked away.

The driver yelled, "What's going on?"

One of the older workers looked at him with a hard stare.

"Nobody's going to work for Jolly Boy today."

CHAPTER SIXTY THREE

The party started in the afternoon, but it was clear that the odd collection of characters that resided at or near the Sunset Resort were going to stay at the bar all night.

Michael watched as Pace and the other kids on his soccer team took turns whacking a piñata. Then after the piñata cracked and candy spilled all over the floor, Michael walked over to Elana and he put his arm around her.

Kermit shouted, "Speech! Speech!" And the room grew quiet.

Michael raised his glass.

"I just want to say that I missed you all while I was gone, and I'm glad to see that our little slice of paradise is as weird and as unprofitable as ever."

Cheers erupted from the crowd that had gathered.

"We left to fight for Tommy Estrada and his family. We filed a lawsuit to get justice." Michael looked at Elana, and she smiled back at him.

"We won. Elana and her family are going to have a better life, and I couldn't be prouder to have played a little role in that. So cheers."

Glasses throughout the bar raised in congratulations, and then the music was turned back on. Michael gave Elana another hug, and as he let her go, Michael saw a familiar face standing in the back corner. It had been well over a year.

His heart started to pound. He wasn't prepared. He wanted to pretend that he hadn't seen her and leave, but, they had made direct eye contact. He couldn't ignore her.

Michael walked over to Andie Larone.

He looked down at his feet like a school boy with a crush.

"Hey," he said. It was all that he could manage.

"Hey," she said.

Michael looked up. She was still as beautiful as ever.

"It's been awhile."

Andie nodded.

"I know."

"You here for a few days or. ..." Michael's voice trailed.

"I don't know," Andie said. "Depends a lot on you."

Thank you for reading "No Time To Die"
Don't wait to read the next book in the series...
"No Time To Hide"

Printed in Great Britain
by Amazon.co.uk, Ltd.,
Marston Gate.